Logical Love

Pacific Coast Romance, Book 1

Kate Pelczar

Logical Love (Pacific Coast Romance, Book 1)

Copyright © 2024 by Kate Pelczar

Published by Pelczar Publications, LLC

Edited by Grace Johnson

Cover Designed by Shey Kolee

ISBN 9798989966202

To Mike,
from four a.m. alarms that interrupted your slumber so I could
write before work,
to helping me fix plot holes while pacing around our kitchen as
you cooked,
may this be the beginning of our future.

Content Warning

Logical Love *contains themes of explicit sex, physical assault, sexual assault (historical, off-page), and mental health (PTSD, depression).*

To anyone who knows me in the real world. I adore you, thank you for reading this labor of love; we will not be discussing any of those scenes.

Contents

I'm Done Dating

"No, I've MADE UP my mind, I'm done dating." I declare into the phone.

"What happened this time?" Tipp's concerned voice asks down the line.

My fingers fidget with the gear shift to my right. I don't want to admit to her that I got screwed over yet again, but our friendship has always been based on honesty, so I have to. I take a breath to steady myself and then sheepishly admit. "He was fine I guess. We went to lunch and everything seemed normal. The regular getting to know you shit in dating."

"So where did it go wrong?" Tipp asks.

I move the visor down to shield my eyes from the blinding Southern California afternoon sun. I twist the steering wheel cover of my Beetle anxiously as I gear up to tell her about yet another failed experience in the San Diego dating pool. "So we went to see that new action movie, you know the one with Leonardo DiCaprio?"

I hear her scoff down the line. "No, but I doubt that's a detail that I need to understand the story."

I roll my eyes at her sass, no matter the situation Tipp always has something to say. I don't know if I'm ready to deal with her opinions just yet. My apprehensive fingers move from fidgeting with the steering wheel to messing with the zipper on my backpack in the passenger seat. They can't seem to settle on just one thing. I repeatedly pull the zipper open and closed in a one inch gap. The repetitive motion soothes me better than the pieces of my car did.

"Bitch spit it out!" Tipp yells at me this time.

I sigh and crane my neck back. I stare at the ceiling of my car as I admit. "In the middle of the movie he asked me to give him a blow job."

"What!" Tipp screeches down the line. I pull the phone away from my ear and rub it gingerly. This woman regularly reaches pitches I wish only dogs could hear.

I switch hands holding the phone and deepen the plot. I bait her with, "It gets worse."

"No." Tipp makes the two-letter word last long enough you'd think it has three syllables.

"I thought he was joking around, I mean it was a first fucking date. So, I shook my head and just went back to watching the movie. He leaned over and whispered in my ear, 'Come on, my ex got me off in the theater all the time.'"

I hear rustling on Tipp's end of the phone. A door closes in the background as she asks, "As if he thought *that* would convince you?"

"I know right?" I fling my hand in the air for emphasis even though I know Tipp can't see it. "Like what? Date one and I'm already in a competition with your ex? Guess you better go back to her, buddy."

"Did you stay for the whole movie?"

I check the time, class is going to start soon. I need to end this humiliating phone call. "Gods no. I walked out on him mid-movie without even a goodbye. I'm at the gym now. Time to work through yet another horrible date."

The other end of the phone is silent for a moment. "Well," Tipp begins with uncharacteristic timidity, "There's always next time."

I flat out laugh at her idea. "No. I'm officially done dating."

Tipp, my best friend, scoffs, "Sure, Veronica Welch is done dating."

"I mean it this time," I retort, "With only 18 months left in school I want to enjoy my time with friends and family instead of wasting it on any more dreadful first dates. Besides, if I find anyone now it will be too late. I have enough self awareness to know that I don't do long distance." At least, not since I got burned while living only ten minutes away from my ex. If he couldn't respect me without distance being an issue, there's no way another guy will be able to handle a thousand miles between us.

"You say that now Nikki, but once classes start up again, you never know what could happen." She sing songs through the phone.

I know she means well, but I've heard it all before, "Tipp, enough. I'll see you tomorrow okay? I'm gonna go work out now."

"Okay babe, love ya!" she cheerfully responds.

"Bye, bye, love ya too!" I reply. I don't move to get out though. Instead, I sit resigned in my Beetle and stare blankly into the crowded parking lot ahead of me.

It's not like I am over love or anything, but with the amount of crummy dates I've been on in the last year, I am done being letdown. Who wants to keep putting themselves out there over and over again, just to get the same result every time. Isn't that the definition of insanity or something?

I'm tired of trying. Being so close to San Diego means there are a lot of military guys on the dating apps. I figured if I tried one with a small monthly cost there would be men looking for more than just hook ups. I almost found a good one here or there but when you mix them in with with the rest, it's not worth it. First, there was the one who lived in his mother's basement. Then, the one who lied about his height, and apparently I'm shallow enough to care if I'm taller than him or not. I sigh as I remember that super hot Navy Seal who happened to always be on some secret assignment. He was carved into existence but I didn't do well with his unpredictable availability. My eyes roll on reflex as I think of the guy who dumped me for being too *"mean spirited"* —no kidding, those were his exact words. After all those dismal courting encounters, I am maxed out. Besides, it was all going to end a few months down the road anyway. Relationships only ever end.

The dark storm cloud that always seems to be hovering a few feet over my shoulder threatens to move nearer. I push back thoughts of the boy from my past, contained within that brooding storm, as I get out of my Satellite Blue VW Beetle. I square back my shoulders. It's the last night of summer break and time to make the most of it. I'm feeling fired up and passionate about this semester. A year and a half of community college left, and then off to Oregon. First, I need to kick Zumba's ass. I grab my bag from the back seat, lock up the car, and prepare to sweat out these pent up frustrations around dating.

When I enter All Hours Fitness I see a way too cheerful receptionist. No one should be that happy greeting a bunch of strangers that are in the building for the sole purpose of sweating. *Maybe she's a masochist and enjoys watching people suffer?* I guess that's what brings me here, physical suffering for mental gain. Tonight my favorite instructor, Bliss, is in charge of Zumba. She's a petite, black haired woman with contagious energy. I've been coming here consistently enough that she knows me by name.

"Nikki!" Bliss calls out, "Ready to work up a sweat tonight?"

I grin. She may have the same cheesy greeting every class, but it's her thing, "You know it!" I call back. I go to the back section of the room, get out my risers and set up for a satisfying workout. One uninterrupted hour of loud music, dancing, and forgetting about stupid boy drama. Yes please.

I look around and grin at a few familiar faces that are here to get their asses handed to them as well, and class begins. I lose myself to the rhythm and the hour flies by. There's nothing a good workout can't fix.

After class I quickly rinse off in the shower and get dressed for dinner with Nana. She's wanting to celebrate the beginning of a new semester. It's been fun living with her and getting to know her better during community college. We're going to meet up at one of her favorite Mexican restaurants in La Mesa.

When I arrive she's already seated in a corner booth. Nana looks up from her menu and smiles at me with that familiar twinkle in her eye. It's reserved specifically for her grandchildren. I bend over and give her a quick hug and catch a waft of her Amber Musk perfume.

As I sit Nana asks, "So, how was working out? Which class did you attend today?"

I smile at her genuine interest in something so mundane as I fill her in on the details of my evening. She listens intently as if everything I say has value.

We chat about small things that bring us joy for a while and then she breaks into the heavy content. "Your classes begin tomorrow right?"

I nod as I respond, "I have a front loaded week this semester. Mondays and Wednesdays I have French II, English, and Math. Actually, Math is a weird class this time; it's for two hours only on Mondays. I don't know how much I'll like that but it's all that would work with my schedule."

Nana's decades of teaching shine through as a preset to her personality. She always has something nice and supportive to contribute, "I'm sure you'll adapt just fine, you've always been a good student."

I continue on, "Tuesdays and Thursdays will hopefully be more fun. I have P.E. for Elementary Educators and then I'll have a pretty long homework break and the nights will end with Astronomy."

"Sounds like a well balanced workload. Good variety without being overwhelming." Nana replies as she dips a chip into some salsa. Then she inquires, "Which classes are you taking with Tipp this term?"

Nana's always a stickler for manners and talking with a full mouth would not be received well. Only once I've finished chewing my bite do I inform her, "We have French II with Madame Krasse again. I don't know if we'll have more overlap than that. She's been cagey about her schedule. You know how Tipp can be with details."

She nods her head in agreement. "I do, she's not the best at communication, but she's also your best friend. You need to invite her over for dinner soon so we can all catch up."

"Okay Nana, I'll ask when she's available." Nana's always enjoyed Tipp's infectious personality. It's hard not to, people are naturally drawn to her, even though she thinks she's a scary bitch.

We eat our meal enjoying one another's company and talking about the day to day happenings of life. When the check is delivered Nana pays as she always does, telling me to put what I would have spent on our dinner together into my savings for a rainy day. I love her and the time we get to spend together. She heads off to one of her retired life extracurriculars. Her schedule is so jam packed I can never keep straight if she's going to choir, a retired teacher organization, or another group I can't manage to remember the name of. I hope that fifty years from now I'll manage to lead such a fulfilled life.

As I drive home to go to bed and prepare for my first day of classes tomorrow, I'm excited. I excel at school. I know how to study and manage my time. I have a feeling this is going to be a wonderful fall semester.

Two

Lucky Number 13

THE ALARM CLOCK BLARES into the dim morning light as I reluctantly open my eyes. That noise— its relentless beeping interrupted a very pleasant dream. I was the sole focus of the Winter Soldier and a D-1 college hockey player. I've never experienced an Eiffel Tower in real life, but in my dreams, I was about to. I groan as I recall that Bucky Barnes was going to be in front and Dean DiLaurentis was in the back. According to my enthusiasm in that dream, I'd be a fucking champ. Tipp's devious mind would be proud that's where my unconsciousness wandered to this morning.

I get ready for the day while rocking out to the newest country music the radio can find. A killer song that you feel in your soul: that's the right way to start off every morning. I choose to wear my signature "smokey eye" that's actually an ombre blend of beige and brown. I tried teaching myself how to do a traditional smokey eye in high school and this was the outcome. I've been rocking it ever since.

My hair is its usual wavy self. We're not on the coast but I swear my hair still feels the salt in the air. I choose a sundress to round out my outfit. It's a complimentary mixture of browns, yellows, and reds in a repeating floral pattern. I look cute, I feel pumped, and I'm ready to get this semester started off right!

I hear Nana rinsing off her breakfast dishes as I emerge from my room. "Dressing up for your first day?" she asks as she observes my outfit with a soft grin.

I smirk internally at her observation but offer her a kind smile outwardly. "Just felt like looking as good as I feel."

She smiles at my response. "Have a good first day of honey. Are you home for dinner tonight?"

"Not tonight, I'll have to fend for myself on campus. Thanks for thinking of me though." She's so sweet always making sure I have my needs met in whatever way she can.

With a quick hug, she exits the kitchen and is off to live her busy life.

It's still early and my first class doesn't start for another three hours. Guess that's a side effect of waking up at three a.m. for work over the last year. I shrug at the extra time I've created this morning and settle on bringing my current read to campus with me. I'm not sure where all my classes are located at school though. If I leave now I'll have enough time to walk around, find all the buildings, read a little, and make it to class early enough to choose the best seats for Tipp and myself.

"I'm sorry. You dreamed of an Eiffel Tower with my man? Girl, what the fuck were you thinking? Sebastian Stan is *mine*. Especially when he is portrayed as the Winter Soldier." Tipp squeals a little too loudly behind me as we wait for French II to begin.

I can feel my ears turn crimson with embarrassment as I scold her. "Keep your voice down! I don't need the entire class to know about my unconscious sexual exploits."

She pulls out her supplies for class as she sneers, "No one cares."

I do the same and remind her with an unabashed grin, "Maybe if you didn't send me constant photos of *"your man"* I wouldn't have had his face in my mind as I was falling asleep. So, technically him being one third of my Eiffel Tower is your fault." My nose scrunches up at the end of my teasing. I love using math in arguments with Tipp —it's her least favorite subject.

She points her finger at me with a glare, "Oh don't you use logic or math to try and work your way out of this. You know he's mine, and your subconscious needs to back off. Find your own man to drool over."

"You know I don't like drooling over fictional—"

"Sebastian Stan is not fictional!" She yells at me with affronted eyes. Our volume is definitely drawing attention from our classmates but Tipp doesn't care. She loves being the center of anyone's attention.

"Oh come off it! You know you'll never get to be with him in a million years. Besides, Bucky Barnes is fictional." Tipp glares at me but I continue over what I'm sure was about to be a smart ass retort. "I know you have a million and one book boyfriends, but they can't exactly come through the pages and satisfy me the way corporeal men do. Or at least try to... You know, one where I could actually have all the sex I wanted instead of waking up from a dream and reminding me how long it's been since I got laid."

She laughs at my misery, "You have Belladix, that should be helping at least a little."

I roll my eyes, a smile still plastered to my face. "You're such a bitch. You have a real life boy toy, and you claim all the fictional men too. How does Lucas feel about not being your favorite?"

She looks offended. "You know perfectly well that my fictional men benefit the level of action my regular booty call gets. Don't be petty and try to switch the narrative, you need some dick and I'm just better at finding a solution for my libido than you are."

I fold my arms preparing a retort for her comments about my sex life as Madame Krasse begins our lesson. She jumps straight into the deep end, pretending we aren't rusty from summer break. I may look the dutiful and studious student, sitting near the front of the room with my supplies ready for learning but my brain wanders. Tipp has her safe sex, regular partner, but not in a committed relationship, relationship. That's just not for me. There's not enough time for dating, not to mention I don't have the emotional energy to expend on a guy right now. I guess I'll just be spending more quiet nights with Belladix. It could be worse, I could live somewhere where dildos are against the law. That really would be unfortunate.

Now that I've remembered perspective and that my life is really rather wonderful, I refocus on Madame Krasse. The past participle is something I've been working with since high school, but that doesn't mean I'm skilled at conjugations by any means. This is going to be a long two hours of the passé composé...

When class wraps up I declare to Tipp, "J'ai fini de sortir." *I'm done dating.*

She stares blankly at me. At first I think she doesn't comprehend and I've fucked up my translation somehow. Then she rolls her eyes, "Do you have something to say I don't already know? Or are you hoping if you repeat it enough you'll actually believe it?"

I hate how she's this honest all the time, but I also love it. "I don't know," I whine as we exit the classroom. "I just want it to be over with. Can I skip the awkward *nice to meet you's* and go straight to the connection and trust and fun stuff? I don't care how they look, just a good fit would be nice. Can't the universe do me this solid?"

Tipp stops walking, turns, and stares directly at me. "Alright, honest, brutal, bestie moment. Ready?"

I grimace, preparing for whatever she thinks I need to hear. My voice comes out as more of a question than a statement, "Ready?"

"You're getting annoying and really whiny about this. So you've been on fucked up dates, who hasn't? Either get over them or shut up. Stop repeating the same thing using different excuses or I'm putting my headphones in and sending you to voicemail until this pity party is over. The world is your oyster or some shit like that."

My mouth pops open and my eyebrows pucker together in surprise, "Damn, you weren't kidding about it being brutal were you?"

"Love ya babe, that's why you keep me around. Besides, we both know you'll be *done dating* until the next suitable smile looks your way."

I scoff at her with eyebrows retreating into my hairline in surprise. Once the shock of her statement subsides I realize a horrible fact, she's not wrong. *Not that I'd ever tell Tipp that.*

"I gotta get to class, but want to grab dinner together on Friday? I got the day off."

That reminds me, "Oh let me check with Nana, she wants to catch up too." Tipp turns and struts off to her next class. She calls over her shoulder, "Okay, let me know!" and disappears into the horde of students milling about campus.

I still have no idea what her schedule is, but that's why we always make sure to get a minimum of one class together.

Tipp's words were brutal, but I needed to hear them.

I spend the rest of my Monday classes in a bit of a daze. Of course Tipp was right, she frequently is.

English is boring, which I expected because I had Mr. Jedidiah last semester. He is a bit pretentious, but I know what to expect from his course load. I'm comfortable with how he grades his assignments so I stuck with him instead of learning a new professor's style. I don't want to have to go through the effort of learning another professors preferences and rules when I already know Mr. Jedidiah's.

Math takes forever. Nothing interesting there, just another new teacher to adjust to for the semester.

I go home, do my nightly stretches and pass out rather quickly from a long first day back.

When I wake up to my three-thirty a.m. alarm, disappointingly I wasn't in the middle of any spicy dreams. I get dressed quickly in my smelly uniform. It's a burgundy shirt that never smells as if it's actually been washed. As my neck pops through it I get a waft of the sandwiches I'm about to be surrounded by for endless hours. One benefit of working at the sub shop is that I get to wear sweatpants. The downside is that they're always paired with a clunky pair of non-slip sneakers. Would it kill the design department of some company somewhere to produce decent looking non-slip shoes? My hair is pulled up into a high pony and my visor takes care of the rest. It's a horrible outfit, but working gets me money to go have fun with... and to pay my tuition with.

Work passes in its monotonous way: slice the veggies, smile and greet customers, use my high pitched customer service voice, and make the sandwiches. It isn't challenging in any way. Lucky for my half awake self, it only requires enough brain power to not slice my fingers off while prepping the vegetables.

Once my shift wraps up I take my lunch sandwich to go. It's a simple variety and made to perfection for my taste buds. I arrive at campus with just enough time to scarf down my sandwich before P.E. for Elementary Educators begins.

Our professor, Coach Walker, is the movie stereotype of every physical education teacher ever filmed. He is older, has a beer belly, wears gym shorts and calf high white socks with his sneakers. His whistle is around his neck, he wears some sort of sports team t-shirt, and is comically happy to be here.

Smiling, he calls out, "Hey everybody, pick a number and take a seat! This is going to be just like when you were in elementary school P.E. We're all friends here, and most importantly, we're going to have fun!"

Is this guy serious? I look at an acquaintance, our familiarity with one another is limited to a few classes throughout the last three semesters at community college. We both shrug, take a seat on the gym floor, and wait for class to begin.

Coach Walker, isn't lying. P.E. for Elementary Educators is exactly like first-grade gym all over again. He is a silly man who immensely loves his job. He tells us all about the playlists he'll be making for our classes every week and that every time we attend we will be entered into a drawing to win that class's CD. He seems so cheesy, but it is infectious. I have a great time goofing around like I'm six again and my cheeks end up hurting from smiling so much before the class is over. I'm so glad this is on my roster for the fall semester.

After P.E. I trek across campus and scope out the science building for a study spot. It's my favorite location to hide away and get work done on campus. The courtyard is naturally shaded by the building; the center of the area has a beautiful smattering of nature with various shrubs, flowers, and trees. It's such a contrast to the beige desert of Southern California that I can't get enough of the greenery. Lining the walkway on either side are abundant outdoor tables and chairs for students to use. The building creates a quiet sense of calm seriousness. People rarely talk too loudly, and it fosters the ideal work environment for me. I settle at a small table on the side of the courtyard and pull off my backpack. I sip on my reusable water bottle and dive into some passé composé homework for French. Time ticks slowly by as I wait for my last first class to begin: Astronomy 112.

As our class time nears the room empties out from the previous session. I wait for students to leave before entering and finding my sweet spot. The classroom extends out from the doorway with four rows of heavy duty science lab tables with outlets built into them. Hard plastic rolling chairs stand ready to make sure we stay awake. The professor has an additional row of tables to the left and whiteboards beyond them on the wall.

I am a Hermione Granger: I want to sit in the front row, but slightly off to the right hand side so that I can sit sideways in my chair and still be able to write comfortably. I choose the perfect spot and doodle in the edges of my notebook while I wait for class to begin.

With less than five minutes to go, some pretentious kid saunters into the classroom like he owns the place. From his arrogant smirk to his impeccably styled short blond hair, his entire persona radiates privilege. He isn't wearing designer clothes, but he struts around like everyone should want to be his friend. I size him up and quickly decide that I'm not interested in getting to know him in the least. I get distracted as another meathead enters my field of vision and look away from Mr. Privilege. The second guy that enters is wearing white sunglasses that went out of style what was it, fifteen years ago? He has a heavy chain attached to his jeans and what I assume is a wallet hiding in his pocket. His hair is spiked like a nineties boy band and much to my chagrin, he sits down right next to me.

"Hey, I'm Brock," he greets as he sticks his hand out for a shake.

I stare at him for a moment longer than necessary and then shake, "Nikki." I remove my hand quickly and don't offer any more details. I hope my flat demeanor accurately communicates my lack of interest.

Apparently, it doesn't. He makes another attempt at idle small talk. "So, you have Mr. Fitzgibbons before?"

"Yes."

He keeps trying, "Do you like him as a professor?"

"Obviously." *Can fuck off be written any plainer across my face?* Tipp said to get over my bad dates. I can tell one with this guy would just add to that list of repressed memories. His jeans are a little too crisp making me think his mother ironed them for him, and he places his car keys down on the table in a manner calculated to draw attention. I get it honey, you like your car, but that's not going to draw me in. He reminds me of the douchebags I went to high school with. Attractive nerd is more my type, thank you very much.

My attitude must not be enough of a hint because he doesn't give up. He drapes an arm over the back of the chair next to him and asks, "I uh, I haven't seen you around here before, you new to campus?"

He must be kidding right? There are thousands of students enrolled here. I see new faces every single day. I'm about to respond in a much bitchier way than warranted when Mr. Fitzgibbons silences me by beginning our class.

"Good evening everybody. It's great to see some familiar faces from last semester. Who's ready to get started?" Professors who love the subject they teach are much more fun to learn from than those who just go to work for the paycheck. Mr. Fitzgibbons is one of the former. He's a balding man with a few dark freckles across his nose and cheeks. His forehead glistens in the fluorescent lighting of the classroom. He always wears a polo with slacks.

I'd never tell him this, but I think Professor Fitzbiggons is my favorite professor on campus. His rules make sense, he's not ostentatious, and he absolutely adores outer space. "Now that you're in Astronomy 112, I'd like to change things up a bit. You may have made friends, and could be seated next to them currently, but they will not be your lab partners this semester."

"Thank gods," I mutter under my breath. Douchebag Brock doesn't react so I'm guessing he didn't hear.

He moves around the table he's standing behind and carries a tray in each of his hands. "The first two rows of the class will pick a random number from this tray," he places the one in his right hand in the middle of the first row of tables. "And the last two rows of students will pick a number from this tray," he nods to the tray he's putting down on the last row of tables in the room. When he's done depositing them at either half of the classroom he continues, "Whoever has the matching number to you will be your lab partner for this semester." Mr. Fitzgibbons walks back to the front of the room, perches himself on the edge of his teaching area, and watches the chaos unfold.

While I'm happy to get away from Brock, I have little reassurance about who my mystery lab partner will be. I mean, whoever I'm stuck with will have the power to make or break my entire grade this semester. Please don't let my companion be a moocher. I hate carrying academic dead weight. I approach the tray and pick a small piece of paper that's folded in half. I open it and see the number 13. I call out, "13," and wait for a reply. There isn't one so I go back to my seat and wait.

A few minutes later I hear someone behind me say, "Are you number 13?"

I look up and realize there could possibly be a worse lab partner than douchebag Brock. It's the pompous kid I was making a snap decision about right before class started.

He waits for my reply and when there isn't one he offers, "My stuff is back there," and motions to three rows behind me. His belongings are piled on a table nestled in the back, furthest away from our professor's eyes. "Shall we?" he motions to help me move my backpack.

"No thanks, I prefer to sit in the front. You're welcome to come join me up here," I quip back.

He gives me a cute one-sided smile that I try really hard not to notice. He offers a compromise, "I don't do front row, but how about we meet in the middle and sit here," pointing to the desk directly behind my current one.

I weigh my options and quickly conclude this is probably the best I'm going to get with my new mystery lab partner. Why couldn't Mr. Fitzgibbons stick to last semester's setup? I chose him again because I thought I knew what to expect. I begrudgingly move my supplies to the table behind me and wait for the rest of the class to find their spots so we can begin learning.

My new lab partner joins me and sticks out his hand. What is with all the handshaking in this room? "Stefan," he introduces himself.

"Nikki."

"Not one for small talk then I take it?" He asks.

"Clearly, I'm here to learn, not make friends." I look down at my notebook again and take up my doodles. The chatter of the classroom is dying down, but Mr. Fitzgibbons hasn't started class yet and I can't fathom why.

"And you're doing a great job at that." He replies, sounding annoyed, before giving up. That stings a little bit, but it is what I asked for.

Professor Fitzgibbons finally launches into a review from last semester about the different phases of the moon. We're tasked with
identifying the moon phases from 16 different slides he has on shuffle.
I identify the first two, a Waxing Crescent and a First Quarter before
hearing anything out of Stefan.

He questions, "Are you sure about your First Quarter decision?"

I look up from my paper and reply, "Yes, but apparently you
aren't?"

He seems to enjoy my attitude because that smug half grin appears
again. This time I can't drag my eyes away from it as he suggests, "Well
if you look a little closer when the deck cycles through again I think
you might change your mind." He leaves his opinion as cryptic as that.

I feel a faint flutter in my chest as I wait for the slides to shuffle
through and inspect number two closer. When the slides start over
again, I notice what Stefan's pointing out. He's right. *Dammit.* Mr.
Fitzgibbons was trying to confuse us with his image of what I thought
was a First Quarter moon, it's barely a Waxing Gibbous. I bite my
bottom lip. I'm impressed by Stefan not only catching my mistake
but also being brave enough to tell me. I erase my answer and update
it thanks to his attention to detail. Maybe this privileged, furthest
away from the teacher, stupid cute smile, lab partner of mine, isn't
completely useless after all.

Three

The Goods

"Hey, did you get The Goods?" Tipp whispers conspiratorially to me as she finds her seat.

I love when we do this, two straight-laced students who really don't do anything wrong in life, talking as if we're about to do a drug deal. Or at least that's how we think we sound. "Shhh, don't let people around you overhear," I murmur back to her.

No one around us listens in, or even cares. This is community college, we're all too self absorbed to notice much about strangers and their idle conversations. Still, pretending to be rule breakers makes life more entertaining. I pull out a bag of Skittles from my backpack and pass them to her discreetly. It's our Wednesday tradition. Tipp opens the bag and pours some out onto a paper on her desk and then hands them back to me. We enjoy the treats and catch up about our first week back.

Tipp informs me, "Classes are pretty good. Work's good, basically it's all good. What about you, girl?" She's always nondescript, unless it's a sexploit. Then I will hear *way* too many details.

"Pretty good, I guess." I shrug as I pick out a red and purple Skittle. They're the best flavor combination. I pop them in my mouth before continuing, "I got partnered up with some guy that I'd really rather not be working with long term. At least getting him as my lab partner kept me away from a douchebag that's set his sights on me."

She smirks, "Catching people's eyes already, huh? Not surprising."

I love the confidence she has in me. "Not trying to, I heard what you said and I'll stop repeating myself, but I'm not looking for anything. There's just no point."

"Do you *have* to leave in a year and a half? There's nothing stopping you from moving in with me," she offers.

I sigh. *This* is a conversation Tipp's willing to have a hundred times. "Just because I *can* move in with you doesn't mean I should. You know how uptight I can get by having to share my space."

"Yeah, but with me it could be different," Tipp objects.

"I tried locker buddies in high school, but every year those friendships didn't last." I shake my head at her as I continue, "I started paying for a solo locker so that I could have my own space. It's a boundary that, apparently, I need to adhere to."

I need my space. I need my rules and cleanliness standards understood and respected. Most importantly, I value Tipp's friendship more than any other I've had and I don't want to fuck up and lose it because I can't afford to live here on my own.

"Okay, fine. But there are other options out there. Just because Nana needs to downsize once you're done with your Associates doesn't mean you have to run vertically across the country."

"Oregon is only one state away," I counter.

She knows this argument too well, "It is one thousand and ninety one miles from here to Portland. One state distance doesn't mean shit when that state is California!"

I've pissed her off now. Hesitantly, I hand her The Goods, "Which is why you should follow me up there."

Tipp scoffs and takes what's left of the candies.

I turn around, having nothing left to say on the subject, and get ready for class. I can tell that I'm irritated. My shoulders feel tense and when I look down at the hand gripping my pencil I see that my knuckles are white. I drop it and flex my fingers, roll my shoulders back, and try to loosen up. Tipp's coming from a caring place, but I don't see how I'll be able to afford living on my own in Southern California. Unless you make six figures a year, it would be a constant struggle. I'd rather be somewhere different, able to enjoy things in life, not just over working to barely make ends meet. In Oregon things could be different. Things will be better than this bleak San Diego alternative.

Madame Krasse enters the room and begins the lesson before she even makes it to her podium at the front of class. She instructs us to switch homework with a peer for grading and I find myself centered and focused on the task at hand: trying to learn more French.

Four

The Monotony Continues

DINNER WITH NANA AND Tipp is a great time for the three of us to catch up. It's still too cold to eat outside so Tipp and I sit at Nana's kitchen island and keep her company as she whips something together for the three of us. I enjoy our easy banter and genuine joy of one another's company. We both take turns updating Nana about syllabus week. Somehow, Tipp manages to provide sufficient information to appease Nana, but not enough for me to learn her schedule for the semester. The best part about hanging out with Nana is that she is authentically curious about what is going on in your life. If you tell her you're interested in buying a truck the next time you two chat she'll have done research about various brands in order to have a more meaningful conversation with you. No matter what's going on in your life, she wants to know about it and support you however she can. I think that's why Tipp loves her so much too; it's easy to love wonderful people.

The days quickly bleed into the weekend and before I know it we're in the third week of term.

When Mr. Fitzgibbons wraps up our lesson on Tuesday, he announces our first quiz of the quarter will be the following week. I am feeling pretty strong about my knowledge of the moon phases but the different planets and their characteristics aren't connecting as well.

Stefan and I have found a rocky truce. We've moved into the acceptance stage of our lab partner relationship and I am even nice enough to say, "Hi," to him and engage in minuscule amounts of small talk. My eyes may search for his appealing smile every now and then, but my brain can't control that. I can't help comparing him to a Border Collie at times: a little too energetic, thinks everyone likes him, but not quite as likable as a Golden Retriever. Still, Border Collies are rather cute dogs. I guess in an objective observation one could argue Stefan fits that description too. Really though, does this guy ever stop smiling or chatting up the people in his vicinity?

"So Nikki," Stefan begins, "I was wondering if we could exchange numbers in case we need to ask one another a question while studying. Promise, no small talk," he holds up his hands in innocence and smiles at his own joke. Why is that so stupidly charming of him?

I weigh my options. I could always block him if he's too annoying. "Sure?" I draw out, as if it's a question.

Once our numbers are exchanged, I edit his contact information and add a dog emoji to his name. A small grin pulls at the right side of my mouth.

"So, getting my number makes you smile huh? If I'd known that I could have handed it out our first week of class," Stefan comments smugly.

"Ugh no," I blush nervously as I scroll over to Tipp and my text chain. "My best friend just texted me. You just wish you had that strong an effect on anyone of the opposite sex, don't you?"

"Damn girl, I'm just kidding."

I look up from my phone and notice he looks a little embarrassed.

"Well, then I suggest you learn how to take a joke in response to your own," I say before picking up my backpack and walking out of the classroom. Once I reach the top of the stairs of the science complex, I take a breath. What the hell was that? I mean, shit, I was harsh. Why do I care though? Why is having Stefan as my lab partner turning me into a salty, sensitive, bitch?

I walk to my car and drive home. I try not to picture Stefan's self-righteous grin as he called me out on my smile. It *wasn't* because I got his number. Right? I'm feeling a little angsty and put on Avril Lavigne's *The Best Damn Thing* album for my drive. Once I hit shuffle of course "Girlfriend" blares into my stereo system. My brain immediately thinks of his half smirk that just does something to me. Concerning? Yes. Do I rock out the whole drive home? Also, yes.

Nana is sequestered in her room doing whatever it is Nanas do at nine-thirty in the evening on a Tuesday. I'm still feeling pumped up from my steering wheel rock session, so I decide to do a light at home workout routine with my favorite yoga flow before showering the day away.

When I'm almost finished my phone dings. While moving to pick it up, I assume it's a message from Tipp about her most recent sexcapade. I am surprised when Stefan's name appears on the screen.

> What are you up to?

I roll my eyes. I told him no small talk. As I go to leave him on read, another message dings through.

> It doesn't count as small talk if I actually want to know what the answer is.

I'm smiling. *Why the fuck am I smiling at his message?* My fingers fly across the screen with my reply:

> Working out.

I sit down on the carpet and fling my phone to the side. On the floor I transition my workout into a cool down round of stretches. As I'm working on a toe touch another ding chimes through my bedroom.

> Why are you working out at 10? Isn't that more of a morning thing?

I scoff at his judgement as I type out:

> There's no rule about when someone can and can't workout.

I remind myself to pull my chest to my shins as I deepen the stretch as I switch legs. A few seconds later another chime sounds.

> Let's try this again, why do YOU choose to workout at 10 at night?

My cold dead heart wants to thaw at his interest in my choices. I only allow that spark of warmth to ignite for a second before I douse it with my sass.

> Because I still had energy from the day so I'm working it out before I shower and go to bed. Satisfied?

He's seriously interrupting my cool down at this rate. I switch to a Z-sit and focus on my hip mobility, trying not to visualize Stefan's signature smirk. My phone goes off again but I make him wait on my reply as I evenly stretch both hips.

Definitely. I didn't think you'd respond.

I slide into a left leg split as I think through the best way to wrap up this exchange. I settle on brutal honesty.

I'm about to stop.

I only have one stretch left before I want to shower, but Stefan doesn't need to know my reasoning.

Before you go, do you know the answer to number 22 on the review sheet?

Haven't opened it up yet. Can I hit you back tomorrow once I've checked it out?

I switch to my right leg split, that doesn't quite make it to the floor. I balance, and take some weight off my legs, with my hands braced at my sides. This stretch always tells me how tight my hamstrings are with painful clarity but this time, for some unknown reason, I'm smiling through my suffering. My phone chimes from another message and I collapse onto the carpet. My hands grab for my phone a little more eagerly than they should.

Sure.

Well, that's that. I put my phone down on my bed and head to the en suite shower. I love how Nana's house was designed with a granny flat on the opposite end of the house than the master suite. I have my own large bedroom, a huge closet, and a private bathroom. This is probably why I'm succeeding at sharing my space with her. The built in, innate respect that's required because she's the world's best Nana, might also be a factor in keeping my attitude in check.

Once my shower is over and I've blow dried my bangs, moisturized my face, and brushed my teeth, I'm finally feeling ready for bed.

I pick up my phone to check that my alarms are set for work in the morning. A three-thirty wake up is going to come around way too fast. When the screen lights up I see another text from Stefan. It reads, *"Sweet dreams, Nikki."*

I sit there staring at it for a few seconds before I snap out of it. Why would he text me that? I definitely can't reply and make him think that we're text, "Goodnight," and, "Good Morning," type friends. Tipp and I aren't even that codependent.

My alarms are set and I go to sleep without a reply.

I was hoping to respond to Stefan's question efficiently today, but between my opening shift and back to back classes immediately after, it's been over twenty hours since he asked. I've finally made it home for the day and am beat. I really want to crawl in bed. Five hours of sleep is not enough for me to function, but I know Stefan is waiting on my input for number twenty two.

My backpack is sitting on my desk and I know one problem won't take that much effort to solve. I pull out our study sheet and read the problem: *How many years does it take for Neptune to fully orbit the sun?*

Is he serious? This question is so easily Googled!

I was starting to feel slightly, microscopically bad, but that feeling has passed. I sit down at my desk and look over the long driveway and all of the native trees and bushes Nana's spent thirty years planting and cultivating in her front yard. Time to draw out his suffering for asking me for help with a question fit for *Are You Smarter Than a Fifth Grader?*

> I will never forgive whoever decided that Pluto isn't a planet.

It doesn't take him long to respond.

> I know *eye roll emoji* how could they?

I purse my lips in confusion to his weird message.

> Why are you saying the emoji instead of just using it?

I smile knowing he agrees about Pluto's change in solar system status. I swear bringing up that topic at a party could start a fight between generations.

> There will always be 9 planets, they can't demote Pluto like that.

I watch the trees down the drive sway in a light breeze as I wait for Stefan to respond.

> Crack in my screen, can't click over to the emojis anymore... *hysterically crying emoji*

> Agreed. Any success with number 22?

I laugh as I realize that he is just the kind of guy that would type out the emoji he wishes he could insert instead of not using them altogether. He seems to be just a little bit extra in an entertaining way. I laugh softly as I type out a message to tease him.

> Impatient much?

I pull out my computer and open Google to find the answer for my needy lab partner.

> It's been almost 24 hours.

I bite my lip. Why do I like that he knows how long it's been since we chatted last?

> Maybe I should actually make it 24 hours before I put you out of your misery.

I click onto a website about Neptune and search for my answer among the lines of script.

> Harsh *wink emoji*

I just need to bait him a little longer while I find the answer to number twenty two.

> Unless you wink in real life, which I know you don't, you shouldn't be allowed to use that emoji.

He must be completely engaged with our thread right now because his message comes through almost instantaneously.

> How would you know whether I wink or not?

I shake my head in response to his absurdity.

> I've been forced to sit next to you for 3 weeks and you've never winked once.

> Maybe I just don't wink at you.

My brain wants to be snarky back, but the thoughts don't come fast enough. Nana's cat, Otis, hops up onto my desk and starts demanding pets. As I scoop his adorable grey tabby self into my arms, my phone dings a second time. I settle Otis on my lap and pick up my phone again.

> You're going to make me wait the full 24 hours aren't you?

I found the answer in less than five minutes of work, and half of that was spent on waiting for the computer to load. This is a ridiculous question for him to ask for help with.

> You have to answer a question for me first.

> Shoot.

I clear my throat and type the question that will force Stefan to say it how it is.

> Why did you waste time asking me a question that you could have easily Googled?

I pet Otis as I wait patiently. Nana is cooking dinner for us and I can smell the tuna melts wafting through the house. Otis must notice it too because he promptly jumps off my lap to get his reward for existing: canned tuna juice. My phone dings as I'm about to get up and help Nana in the kitchen.

> I didn't think you'd agree to meet up with me next week before our exam if you didn't first think I was a slight idiot.

That annoying feeling is back. My heart feels like it's beating faster. Ah crap, there's a smile on my face too... That is somehow exactly what I wanted to hear. Wouldn't you know it, Nana also walks in at that exact moment to let me know that dinner is ready. I guess I'll have to let Stefan sweat it out. I send him one final text.

165 years.

I don't text Stefan again before our next class. First, because I want to make him squirm. (I'm a self admitted bitch like that.) Secondly, if he was going to ask me out, he needs to be brave enough to do it face to face, not hiding behind his phone screen.

I arrive at Astronomy early as always. Once my supplies are out and ready for our lesson to begin, Stefan appears beyond the doorway. He's talking to someone and I have to remind myself to look away so I don't seem too eager to see him again. His early arrival is strange, because he usually strolls in a matter of seconds before the class is about to begin. Today, he's five minutes early.

I pull out my study guide to try and memorize some obtuse facts about space.

36. The Sun makes up 99.8% of our solar system's mass.

37. Hydrogen and Helium are the most abundant elements in the Sun.

My eyes read these facts but my brain is focused on how Stefan is walking in calmly. He's not greeting every person he passes by like normal. He even pulls out his spiral notebook and pencil before Mr. Fitzgibbons begins. Is he okay?

Stefan gently nudges my arm with his elbow. I take a few seconds to pretend I'm reading our study guide before looking up, "Yes?"

He scratches the back of his neck, "You didn't text me back yesterday."

It's a statement, not a question. I pull out my phone and show him no unread messages. Then I open our chat thread and point to my last response.

His brows draw together slightly and he swallows before nervously saying, "You know that's not what I meant."

"Do I?" I grin as I taunt him.

Stefan sighs, "Nikki, do you want to meet up with me before class on Tuesday so we can quiz each other for our exam?"

"Sure," I easily answer. "What time?"

He visibly relaxes, his brow quickly evening out. "My class ends at three forty-five, so closer to four?"

"I'll meet you in the Griffin Center so we can eat something too."

"Perfect." Stefan gives me a blinding grin. How did this cocky outgoing guy go timid and shy so quickly? It's not even a date, it's a study session. Right?

As I go back to studying my quiz guide and trying not to overthink what just happened, Mr. Fitzgibbons asks us to flip to page thirty two to get class started. There will be plenty of time for over analyzing later.

On my drive home, I call Tipp. I update her about my upcoming class and my not-quite-date study-date-invitation.

Once I'm through the recap she's quiet.

"What?" I ask impatient to hear her thoughts.

"I told you so." I can hear the smile in her voice as she taunts me.

I roll my eyes in irritation even though she can't see it. "Yes, fine. You were right. Happy?"

Tipp finally starts talking about things that matter. "Definitely. So, do you want it to be a date?"

I throw my hands in the air and cry, "I don't know. He's not my typical type, and he really can be annoying."

"So go! Study. And that's that. You don't have to do any more than study with him, plus you'll be in the middle of the Griffin Center for fuck's sake! Not like you'll be getting hot and heavy when you're surrounded by the food court."

She's got a point. "So why do my emotions turn idiotic around him, oh Wise One?"

I hear her chuckle. "Because, you haven't gotten any in too long and your vag wants some action other than Belladix!"

I pretend to slam my head into the steering wheel in agony. "I never should have told you her name!" I exclaim.

Tipp questions, "I still don't understand why your dildo has a feminine name. It's a substitution for a dick..."

"You don't have to understand. Besides, *they* could have been feeling more like *she* when the name was assigned."

There's silence from her end for a few heartbeats. "Huh?"

"It's my sex toy. Its name is Belladix. You don't need to understand anything beyond that." I lightheartedly scold.

"Okay bitch, you do you. Almost home?"

"Yeah, only two more exits. I'm good if you need to go," I reply.

Tipp lets out a long breath, "My break is almost over, I'll talk to you later."

"Bye, love." I chime out of habit.

"Bye, babe! Don't think of Stefan too much when you're using Belladix this weekend!" she mocks right before I hear the line click.

How am I supposed to get the last word when she hangs up? I'm going to be spending a lot of energy this weekend proving her wrong and not thinking about Stefan at all.

Five

Lunch Date?

UNFORTUNATELY, TIPP WAS RIGHT. I thought about Stefan all weekend long. I may have also gotten my money's worth from Belladix. I will not shame myself for this, because it's better than getting an STI from a random hookup. Nonetheless, my morning alarm arrives too quickly. The blood in my veins chills as I realize it's Tuesday, my study date day with Stefan. I rush to get ready for work while trying to remember that I want to look somewhat cute. I put a little effort into my bangs and clip them back in a pump. My ponytail may have a little more height to it than usual, we'll chalk that up to a physical representation of my high hopes for this afternoon. I grab my makeup bag so I can apply a bit in the car after work and head off to the sub shop.

My shift and early afternoon classes pass by in rapid succession. It's suddenly only an hour before Stefan and I are scheduled to meet up. I've already been sitting in the Griffin Court for an hour being unproductive with my French homework strewn in front of me. The problem is, every time I go to read the problem, the same problem I've been trying all afternoon, a visual of Stefan's smirk hovers over the words and I get stuck in a daydream about him. I keep wondering about how studying with Stefan will go. Is it a date? He never called it a date, but he acted like it was a harder conversation to have than two friends eating a meal and quizzing one another before an exam. Why must dating, or not dating, be so fucking complicated?

I see Stefan approaching from across the building. He's got this natural draw that makes people want to be around him. Stefan strolls toward me with an easy going smile on his face. His Converse paired with black shorts and crisp graphic t-shirt add to his slightly pretentious appearance. His hair is tousled so perfectly it can't be by accident, but it manages to seem like he spent no time on it. He waves and smiles at a few people as he passes by. Gross. No one is actually that nice, it's just a facade people are stupid enough to believe. I put my head down and pretend to be focused on my work, not one of his adoring fans.

"Hey, Nikki," he calls out before reaching the table.

I look up, "Hey, Stefan."

"How's it going?" he asks.

I roll my eyes. "Small talk?"

"Oh right, straight to business." He gives me a smirk and asks, "Which planet has the strongest winds out of any in our solar system?" He keeps quizzing me while setting his bag down and taking the seat to my right. He's in quite close proximity to me, which seems unusual if this isn't a date.

I feel more at ease with my mind being preoccupied with science instead of his ridiculously good looks.

"Neptune. Give me a harder one."

"Well, for a harder one, I'll have to get out my flash cards." He then pulls them from his pocket. "What chemical are Neptune's storm clouds mostly composed of, and at what speed do said storm clouds travel?"

Now that's what I'm talking about. "Bringing out the big guns, thank you. But that's a two-part question so technically, cheating. In answer, Neptune's clouds are composed of methane and the storms can travel at speeds up to 1,200 miles an hour."

"Damn Nik! Did you memorize the study sheet verbatim?" He looks impressed.

"I did, and did you just give me a nickname?" I raise an eyebrow as I ask.

Stefan shrugs, "We're friends now, that's what friends do, isn't it?"

It's my turn to shrug. "I guess I don't completely hate it."

"Good, cause it's sticking around. Let's get some food before you show me you know the entire study guide by heart. Can I cheat off of you during the exam? Also, what food are you in the mood for?" He hops from question to question at a rapid fire as my brain struggles to catch up.

"Slow down, Energizer Bunny, one question at a time!" I chuckle at him.

"No, you can't cheat off of me. I'll never be hungry for a sub, so I'm thinking either the taco shop or a burger." Just then I inhale deeply and pick up slight notes of fresh tortillas, spices, and meat sizzling away in the distance.

"No, I definitely want taco shop."

He looks defeated. "I thought you'd be my ticket to an A. Dang Nik, cutting me deep this early into our friendship hurts."

I glare in response to his teasing.

"Okay, you go get your Mexican food." He says, "I'm feeling rebellious and want a sub now that you've said it's the last thing you'll want."

I can't tell if he's joking or not. "I will sit at a different table if you get a sub. I already have to smell that for seven hours a day. The smell is stuck in my hair right now, and I will not be subjected to it any further." I snap at him.

Stefan's eyes widen, "Oh, I uh, I thought you were joking."

"I don't say please often, so mark this. Please, don't get a sub."

His lips barter against giving me his signature smirk, "On one condition."

"What?" I deadpan.

"Let me smell your hair."

"What!" I shout a little too loudly.

He grins mischievously at me. "Let me smell your hair. If it actually smells like subs, then I won't eat one. Deal?"

I can't believe this guy! He wants to smell my hair. Although, it could be worse, and I really don't want him to eat a sub. The odor infects everything it goes near. I literally have a separate bag that I put my dirty work clothes into so they don't stink up my car when I'm in class.

"I can't believe I'm agreeing to this." I lean over and put my head into his personal space without encroaching too much.

I sit there frozen, staring at his knees, waiting. Then it happens. I feel his body shift toward me. His nose rests gently on the top of my head and he takes a deep inhale. It feels more intimate than I thought it would. My cheeks flush a little at that thought as I wait for him to get his fill.

The first thing I hear is a startled cough. "I didn't need to inhale that deeply," he mutters between stifled coughing fits.

I lean back and cross my arms smugly, "So, let's go get some taco shop."

Once we have our meals we head back to the table that no one sat in while we were up. I got rolled tacos with guacamole, sour cream, shredded cheese, and a side of rice and beans. Stefan got cheese enchiladas with rice and beans. We dive into our respective meals and I reluctantly engage in small talk.

"So, you live with family?" Stefan asks me between bites.

I grin, immediately thinking about Nana. "Yeah, I moved in with my Nana straight out of high school. It's just the two of us and her cat, but it's kinda perfect." My smile is instinctual when she's mentioned.

He nods and continues, "Why did you choose to move in with her?"

I could get deeper with my reasoning, but this early in a relationship, whatever kind of relationship this is, Stefan only gets my superficial answer. "I wanted to get to know her better. I've always enjoyed when we got to hang out at family gatherings or when my mom would take us to her house for the weekend or whatever. I thought it would be a good launching point to figure out how to be an adult."

"Like a safety net?" He asks, cutting his enchilada.

I take a bite and think through my answer before responding. "In a way. I mean I know I won't become homeless, but I also get to figure out how to balance a job with school and a social life. Also, she's a wonderful cook and probably the nicest person you'll ever meet. Even if she has something negative to say, she approaches it so diplomatically you can't even argue against her logic."

Stefan's eyes crinkle at the corners as his smile widens. "Sounds like you two have a wonderful relationship. You're lucky."

I agree with him and our talking switches to his backstory.

During a lull in conversation, my mind focuses on the chatter of the Griffin Court surrounding us. It's a crowded and lively environment, perfect for people watching. I observe couples sitting close together and having quiet conversations. Friends are joking around and showing one another various things on their smartphones. I'm drawn to the "loners" who are content being alone with their headphones in and ignoring the world around them. Up until this meal, I was one of them and happy about it. Now, I'm sitting next to the guy who greets every person he walks past.

Stefan interrupts my people watching by saying, "So, my girlfriend, Mia, is away at boot camp in Oklahoma right now."

I nearly choke on the bite I'm trying to swallow. His what? Not a date then. Definitely not a date. What a motherfucker! Flirting and shit, when his girlfriend is thousands of miles away!

Well, he didn't actually do anything to be considered cheating did he? Technically, he's just a disloyal flirting piece of shit. *Oh great, I made it all up in my mind, didn't I?*

I play it cool and try not to act surprised. "Girlfriend, huh? How long have you two been together?"

"Almost a year now," Stefan replies. "She's going to be in town for break in a couple weeks and I'm planning a get together for her. I think you should come." He has a constant smile pulling at his lips the whole time he talks about her. Not that smirk he gets when he's talking to me, but a full-blown, cheek-to-cheek smile.

"Wouldn't that be weird? A girl she's never met coming over for a party for her?" I inquire.

He thinks on it. "Well, as I'm sure you've witnessed by now, I'm a rather outgoing guy. Besides, I have a secondary angle," he says lifting an eyebrow.

My eyebrows lift suspiciously and my voice lilts with a questioning intonation. "Yes?"

"You see, I think you'd be the perfect match for my best friend," Stefan suggests.

I'm surprised at this change in conversation. "Okay? Continue?"

"Well, he looks almost like my twin."

I purse my lips, "I can work with that, what else?"

His cocky smirk returns accompanied by one eyebrow lifting. "Well, now that I know you think I'm hot."

"What, no!" My eyes go wide in realization that I just complimented him accidentally. "Oh my gods, that's not what I meant!" I stammer.

"Too late to take that one back sweetheart, but he really does look practically identical to me. We get asked if we're brothers all the time," he taunts me. "He's a mechanic at a fun park near here, but he's also going to school," He explains.

At least this new guy Stefan is bringing up checks off my bare minimum requirements in dating someone: a job, and in school. I'm not miffed by the idea. Yet. "So, why do you think we would work together?"

The grin never leaves his face, "I think he'd like your permanent sour attitude."

I narrow my eyes at Stefan. "I am not permanently sour. Take it back."

"Irregardless—"

"It's regardless," I cut him off.

Stefan sighs. He does that a lot. "As I was saying, I think your opposites would compliment each other nicely. I can't sell you on the guy just by talking about him. How about I arrange a blind double date?"

"But you just told me you have a girlfriend?" I remind him.

"Yeah, I don't want a date, so tell whoever you bring along they're there for fun, not to get in my pants," Stefan chides.

How is this man so arrogant? *I really hope Tipp will go along with this.* "When are you thinking?"

His answer comes quickly, "How about next Friday? That'll give you enough time to figure out someone to bring along." Stefan must have been thinking this through for a while to have anticipated all these hurdles.

I narrow my eyes at him, "Does your mysterious friend have a name?"

He seems surprised I asked this. "Why do you always look suspicious when you're talking to me?"

"Because we're here to study for the exam we have in less than an hour and you're throwing this giant curveball at me! I have no idea what will come out of your mouth next!" I grab my study papers and start shoving them into my backpack. "You know what, nevermind. I don't want to go on this blind double date. I've got enough on my plate already and entertaining you with my dating life isn't on my agenda." I zip up my backpack and sling it across my shoulder. He doesn't get to fuck with my brain before our first exam of the semester.

Stefan puts his hand on my forearm.

"Remove your hand from my body. Now. I won't ask twice," I threaten, my voice dripping with menace. I'm done with his joking around.

Stefan immediately takes his hand off of me, "Hey, I'm sorry," he begins. "I just thought you might be a good fit for my best friend. His name is Will, he's six foot three, enjoys surfing in his spare time, rents a room at his sister's condo, likes dogs, and is trying to figure out what career path suits him best. Honest, I wasn't tyring to mess with you. Sorry I dropped this at an imperfect time."

I stop packing up mid-description of Will. What the fuck? I don't need a man, but he seems kinda great... "I'll go on the date with one condition." I finally reply.

"What's that?" Stefan asks.

"You pass our exam, I'll go. You fail, I'm off the hook. This way, it's entirely your fault if your best friend doesn't get to meet the woman of his dreams," I finish by pointing at myself.

Stefan puts out his hand, waiting for a shake. "Deal."

That exam was way too easy. Stefan would have to be a complete imbecile to fail it, which means I'm stuck going on a date next Friday. Tipp better be ready to be my wing woman or I'm going to coincidentally come down with food poisoning.

I call Tipp on my drive home, yet again.

"Hey babe! Tuesday nights going to turn into a regular chat for us?" Is her opener to our call.

"Apparently, Stefan doesn't know how to exist without creating a plot twist in my life," I respond.

"What happened this time?" She's always ready for whatever life throws at her, and it's one of the reasons I love her.

"I need you to be my wing woman on a blind double date next Friday," I sputter out way too fast to be coherent.

"Sure, I'll see if someone will switch me shifts," she agrees immediately.

I'm shocked. "No questions asked?"

Tipp chuckles down the line. "Nah babe, ride or die remember? I told you you weren't done dating. Now tell me all the details."

Six

Double Blind Date

"I NEVER SHOULD HAVE agreed to this," I complain to Tipp as we drive to meet up with the guys. "Last week this seemed so far in the future, now it's here. We still have time to get the plague or something, we're not there yet."

Tipp chuckles, "If it wouldn't involve wrecking my car I'd reach out and slap your senses back into you. We're doing this. You're not bitching out. You are fabulous, and we are here." She's right, we just pulled into the parking lot. "Too late now, so let's go show the boys exactly who Veronica Welch is."

I swallow the growing lump in my throat. I'm stuck. This is happening. Either I can look like a complete fool, drop out of community college, move to another state, and restart my life. Or I can woman up and be my dazzling self. Why does the latter seem so much harder to accomplish? "Okay," I relent on an exhale.

Tipp parks in front of To Die For, Frozen Yogurt. It's a newer place that we haven't tried out yet, located near campus. A neutral meeting area, according to Stefan. As Tipp and I get out of the car, I see Stefan standing next to someone who actually could be his twin. He's tall, blond, and definitely works with his body for a living. Somehow there's an edge of nerdiness to him as well. I immediately like the combination.

Tipp whispers to me, "Stop objectifying him."

How does she know? "Fuck off," I spit at her.

Once we're in earshot Stefan begins the introductions. He quickly engrosses Tipp in conversation so that Will and I are awkwardly stuck talking to one another.

We all walk into the yogurt shop and while Stefan and Tipp banter as if they've known each other for years, Will and I hang back a bit. The new shop has ample chairs and tables which are modern with a slight retro nod. The sample cups are to the left of the entrance and the entire back wall is lined with probably twenty different fro-yo flavors. To the right is the toppings bar and a cashier that looks like life is being sucked out of them with each dreadful customer interaction. The storefront is entirely made out of windows and the sun is setting behind the mountains of El Cajon. Rather perfect setting for a romantic first date. It's a good thing we're here getting to know some strangers and not trying for that insta-love you see in Hallmark movies.

Will and I move to the samples section so that we can determine the best fro-yo for such a serious outing.

Will asks, "What's your favorite flavor?" He seems a little shyer than Stefan, which isn't hard to believe. Stefan could become friends with a tree.

I give him a small grin. "I love Cookies n' Cream, but I'm lactose intolerant so I have to deny my deepest desires and settle for a dairy free sorbet."

"Man that sucks," Will replies compassionately.

I think he might genuinely mean it, too. "Cruel twist of fate I guess. I didn't know I was intolerant until about a year ago. Though I think if that's the worst dietary constraint I have, I'll be okay."

"I'll just have to enjoy all the dairy for you." His grin transforms into a full on smile. "I'll be sure to inform you of all the delicious flavors you're missing out on."

"You wouldn't!" I exclaim, swatting his bicep with my free hand. "That's so cruel."

He maintains eye contact with me. "I get the feeling you'd lose interest if I was entirely sweet." Will winks and turns to sample the Dulce de Leche behind him.

My jaw is slightly dropped. Tipp makes eye contact with me and I shake myself to snap out of it. Will's got game, but two can play at this.

We make our yogurt choices and I have to settle for a Raspberry Sorbetto. I do cheat and put a little bit of the Cookies n' Cream on the side. My toppings are always the same though, one gummy bear dropped all the way to the bottom of the bowl, mochi on top, and some fresh fruit. I wish I could do something more fun like ground up Butterfinger, but it doesn't combine well with Raspberry. Will goes with the Dulce de Leche and keeps his toppings simple with chocolate sauce and some gummy worms. He pays for my fro-yo as well as his, and Stefan pays for Tipp's. Then we all find a table to socialize at.

Stefan immediately asks, "So what kind of name is Tipp?"

Tipp's lips pull to a sly smile. "It's a nickname. Have you not heard of those before?"

I don't think Stefan realized that Tipp would be such a formidable opponent for his snark. "You know what I mean," Is the only retort he musters up.

"Tipp, be nice," I encourage her.

She rolls her eyes at me. "Only for you, babe." Then she looks at Stefan and Will, "My full name is Tristain Powell, when you combine those you get Trip. That's not a nickname I'm willing to go by, so Tipp it is."

I've heard this all before and chime in, "Once you get to know her better you'll see why Tristain doesn't do her justice."

Stefan nods. "I'll take your word for it."

Will changes the direction of our conversation. "So Nikki, what do you do for work?"

"Ah, the dreaded work question," I reply.

He tilts his head to the side and asks, "Why is it dreaded?"

After I finish my bite of fro-yo I say, "Well, currently I'm a sandwich artist at a sub shop, but that's not my goal in life. I want to graduate, transfer to a university and get my Bachelor's in education so I can be an elementary school teacher. It's a dreaded question because where I am isn't where I want to be." Once I finish, I realize that may have been too honest, too quickly. *Shit.*

Will smiles at me though. "I get it. I'm a mechanic at the moment but I don't plan on that for my entire life."

"Where do you want to end up?" I ask, intrigued.

He licks his spoon clean and my mind wanders to inappropriate thoughts related to his tongue and whether or not it's skilled.

Naughty! Too naughty for a first date, Nikki! I internally lecture.

Will interrupts my self barrage. "I'm not entirely sure yet. I'm getting my Associates in Mathematics, but I don't know where that will end up taking me. I guess I'm keeping my eyes and ears open for the time being."

Stefan speaks up. I forgot he was here. "So Nikki, what's the weirdest encounter you've had with a customer lately?"

"That's a hard one, only because we get so many," I laugh.

Tipp reminds me, "What about the salt lady from last week?"

I grimace. "Oh gods, the salt lady!"

Will and Stefan both look intrigued. "Do share," Will encourages.

"Okay, it was an opening weekend shift and I was in the store with one other sandwich artist. This lady came up to order a six-inch sub. She tells me the kind of bread and then asks what kind of salt is in the turkey breast."

"What kind of salt?" Stefan confirms.

"Yes, so I ask her what she means." I'm getting into the story at this point so I put down my spoon and start embellishing my story with various gesticulations, "The lady leans up on the glass display case, which you should never do, those suck to clean, and looks me in the eyes. Not in a respectful way, but in an are you an idiot kind of way and repeats, 'What kind of salt is in your turkey?'" They're all intently listening now. "I don't know what to do at this point so I say, 'Sodium chloride?' You know, the chemical makeup of salt?"

This draws a chuckle from Will.

I shake my head and continue. "Well, she's still not satisfied. She demands that I go read the box the turkey comes in. She needs to know if it's table salt or ocean salt that's in the turkey."

"What the hell?" Tipp asks, even though she's heard this story before.

I smile and raise my eyebrows conspiratorially knowing what comes next. "So I go to the back and my coworker asks me what's up with this order. I update him and pretend that I was in the back reading the box. I go back to the front end of the store and tell the lady it only says salt, not where the salt is derived from. She's still not accepting this. Now she demands that I bring the box our turkey comes in up to the front so that she can read it herself."

"Wow," Will responds with a shocked look.

I hold my hands out showing my defeat at this point. "I bring the box to the front for her to read. She sees with her own eyes that the box simply says that the turkey has salt in it, no indications as to where the salt was gathered. When she saw that, she decided she no longer wanted to get a sandwich and left ranting and raving about how it matters where salt comes from."

They all stare at me. I admit, it wasn't the most exciting story, but definitely one of the more interesting characters I've encountered working my early morning shifts.

Stefan breaks the stunned silence. "On that note, anyone know where the sugar in this fro-yo comes from?"

It was perfect timing, we all break into laughter at his comedic relief. Once we wrap up our yogurt, Will suggests that we take things back to his sister's place, informing us it's nearby.

As we walk out to our cars Stefan puts his arm around Tipp's shoulder and her reaction is comical. Her face scrunches up, her side eye could kill, and her body language clearly states, *"What the fuck do you think you're doing?"* while simultaneously mimicking Kuzko's *"No Touchy,"* expression.

As Tipp dodges Stefan's attempted physical contact she bluntly informs him, "Ha! No fucking touching, honey, you can't afford this ride."

Stefan takes a step back, realizing that he misunderstood their tentative friendship. I cut in and inform him, "We'll follow in our car."

Once we're back in Tipp's car and out of earshot she asks, "How do you like Will?"

A smile spreads across my face. It feels so natural like it could have been there all night. "He doesn't give serial killer vibes, so that's a plus."

"That matters for sure. Anything more than that?" Tipp prompts, putting her car in reverse and pulling out of the parking lot.

"Ugh, fine Mom," I tease her. "I think I like him, but this is just the getting to know you phase so don't start wedding planning yet."

"I see what you mean about Stefan being a bit of a pompous asshole," Tipp says redirecting the conversation.

I roll my eyes as I tick off the options of how she arrived at that conclusion on my fingers. "Oh yeah, which part? Him trying to put his arm around your shoulder or his general arrogant mannerisms?"

"I would say where he immediately cut us apart in the fro-yo shop. You seemed okay with Will so I didn't make a scene of it, but he is *not* my type. Thank fuck he's not the one you're interested in dating." I laugh at her assessment of my lab partner, and I realize that I agree.

Will's sister's place proves to indeed be incredibly close to the yogurt shop. We all arrive within ten minutes. He pulls a u-turn and parks on the curb. Tipp follows suit and I hope she's parking where he wants us to. The boys get out of Will's beige Toyota Camry and we meet them on the sidewalk.

"Welcome to my sister's condo," Will motions to the building behind him. "She'll probably come out at some point to spy on us. Her name's Meghan, and she's nosy, but in a loving kind of way," he warns me.

I grin at his explanation. "Thanks for the heads up. Lead the way."

We all walk past the single-story condos that lines the street and head up a flight of stairs to a second story condo. Inside it is clean and smells of fresh washed linen. There's a dark blue couch facing the front door and a TV off to the right. When we walk further in, there's a small galley kitchen and three bar stools to the left of the living area. A circular wooden dining table lies to the right of the kitchen. All in all, it's a cute, simply decorated, clean living space. Meghan is in the kitchen, it appears that she's just finished pouring herself a glass of red wine.

"Oh, hi guys!" She calls cheerfully, seeing Will and Stefan enter. Once her eyes land on Tipp and me she adds with a smile, "And gals."

Tipp and I wave hello and Will politely introduces us to his sister.

"Well, I just finished baking a batch of cookies, so if you want any they're on the counter." she finishes by pointing to a glass jar filled with delicious looking cookies.

"Those look wonderful," I comment.

Stefan smiles, "Will's sister is a pastry chef at one of the nearby casinos. It's guaranteed that her desserts will always be delicious."

Meghan beams at the compliment. "You guys have fun, and let me know if you need anything." She heads down the hall to where I can only assume her bedroom is located.

Will opens the cookie jar and offers one to all of us. I take a small bite and immediately realize Stefan was right, these are absolutely delicious. She made a simple lemon cookie but the flavors are anything but. The texture is heavenly, the lemon is the perfect mixture of tart and sweet. My taste buds have never experienced a cookie this divine. My body betrays me and I moan at this decadence. My eyes go wide and I feel my cheeks flush. Did I just moan due to the flavor of a cookie? *Please tell me Will didn't notice.* I peek up from my cookie and see him grinning at me like the Cheshire Cat. Great, I can die now. I've just thoroughly humiliated myself on night one of knowing this guy.

Tipp jumps to my aid. "These are absolutely incredible!" She directs her comment at Will.

It's to no avail, as his eyes remain glued to me. With nothing left to do but own it, I explain, "The way to my heart is through my stomach."

Will nods his head and replies with a devious smile, "Noted."

Stefan clears his throat, cutting our tension, "Who's up for some *Epic Spell Battles: Battle Wizards*?" He suggests and holds up a game I've never seen before.

Tipp and I make eye contact. She shrugs in an "up to you way," and we both head over to the table to sit down to learn about the game.

The guys quickly go over the rules but I'm lost after the second sentence.

"Maybe we should do a practice round?" Will suggests as he takes in the confusion plastered across my face.

"Let's do it." Stefan agrees drawing his cards.

We all put our cards down with an open hand. Will leans over and I get a quick waft of citrus and woods emanating from him. "Try these three out together," he recommends tapping on my cards. "They'll deal the most damage to Stefan, and he's going to be the hardest to kill."

I nod at his directions and close my deck from Stefan and Tipp's eyes. I lean a little closer to Will hoping to catch a little more of his aroma before whispering, "I bet he's telling Tipp the same thing about you right now."

His face pulls into a competitive smile that brings a glint to his eyes. "You can count on that."

We wait for Tipp and Stefan to wrap up their plotting before the game begins. When their decks disappear from open play Stefan declares, "Remember, you have to read your spell out loud to everybody. No matter what."

"You have to do what?" Tipp practically yells at Stefan's directions.

He repeats, "You're required to read the spell aloud for the rest of us to hear."

"Yeah, that's the part I don't like," Tipp interjects.

"It's what's required for the game," Stefan challenges her, leaning back in a cocky pose, and crossing his arms.

I meet Will's eyes and we exchange a smile. Watching them go head to head sporadically throughout the evening has been more entertaining than my imagination could have fabricated. Turns out, Stefan and Tipp are incredibly similar human beings. They both need things to go their way, they both enjoy pushing people to the edges of their comfort zones, and they're both stubborn fools. Apparently, Will and I are the sidekicks to their particular brand of crazy.

"King Tentakillz, Menstruating, Finger Banger." Tipp grumbles with a scowl.

Stefan howls with laughter. When he catches his breath he taunts, "No wonder you didn't want to read that aloud. Priceless! I only wish I'd recorded that!"

Will and I snicker behind Tipp's back, trying not to become the focus of her temporary rage.

"Alright Tipp, destroy Stefan with your spell!" I cheer her on.

In one move she manages to destroy his character's Life's Blood and Stefan's jovial mood sobers quickly. He transitions to attack mode and they go back and forth while Will and I can quietly talk between hands and try to fly under the attack dogs' radar.

"What do you prefer to do in your downtime?" Will inquires.

That's always been a hard question for me to answer. I think about it for a little too long and he must get nervous. "I know it's small talk," Will stammers, "but I do want to know."

I smile reassuringly at him. "It's not that it's small talk, I just don't have a lot of downtime. If I'm not working, I'm at school. If I'm not doing either of those things I'm probably reading or working out. I don't think I've really had downtime since summer break."

He ponders for a moment. "Guess I'll just have to come up with a second date idea on my own then."

"Oh, you think you're getting a second date? Don't you think a first is required before a second?" I inquire.

He seems puzzled, "Doesn't this count as a first date?"

I laugh in response. "Something that your best friend did all the work for? Thanks for the yogurt and all, but this isn't a first date. We've had them," I point at Stefan and Tipp, "as a buffer the entire time." They're still arguing about a component of the game, paying no attention to us.

Will says, "Fine, but in order to set up a first date I need to get your number." He pulls out his phone.

I have to admit that was a nice setup, so I don't challenge him any further. "Smooth, real smooth. Give me your phone." I ask as I hold my hand out for it.

Will reveals a flip phone that's contained entirely within his large fist. *A fucking flip phone! Is he from the '90s?* I stare at him in disbelief.

"It makes phone calls doesn't it?" Will asks.

"But what about texting? Don't you get charged per message on a phone that old?" I tease.

"I don't text."

"You don't text?" I repeat, shocked.

He shakes his head at me. "It's ten cents per text message. If you want to talk with me, you'll have to call me."

He seems a little stuck up about this topic, but there are bigger red flags out there, so I'll let this one slide for now.

Tipp cheers loudly at my side. "Take that bitch! No health left for you!"

I forgot we were playing a game... or rather I was losing a game, clearly more focused on chatting with Will. Stefan throws down his spell and picks up a Dead Wizard Card signaling his demise.

The game quickly wraps up after that. It's late, so Tipp and I decide to head home for the evening. The boys are sweet and walk us out to the car. This time Stefan doesn't try to overstep and put his arm around Tipp. They wave us off from the sidewalk and Tipp immediately interrogates me.

"Okay, I know I was sitting right there, but I got a little wrapped up in kicking Stefan's ass! How did chatting with Will go?"

I tell her everything we talked about, most importantly how he doesn't text. She thinks it's weird, but not too major. Tipp drops me off at my house and I'm showered and ready for bed quickly. I lay in my soft sheets fantasizing about what a first date with Will could entail.

As the sweet embrace of sleep beckons me closer, my eyes pop open. I ask my ceiling, "What happened to me being over dating?"

Seven

Thirty Cent Conversations

My alarm blares too early, as is always the case with an opening shift, but that's the price I pay in order to fit all my classes into my schedule. Our breakfast sandwiches are such a draw that some mornings we bring in more revenue than the lunch rush does. I guess I could also go to sleep at a reasonable hour for waking up at three-thirty a.m., but where's the fun in that?

Luckily, for work I don't bother with much makeup or a cute hairdo. Also, because today is Saturday, I can go directly home and take a nap before attempting anything else with my life. I keep that in mind while the soothing rhythm of slicing bell peppers threatens to lull me to sleep later in my shift.

Opening goes as monotonous as ever, slice, sandwich, hydrate, repeat, until my shift ends. During my lunch break, which, happens at six-thirty in the morning, I see an unexpected message from Will on my phone.

Good Morning beautiful.

I thought Will didn't text... he did say that last night, didn't he? Something about it costing ten cents a message goes through my mind.

> Well good morning to you too, I thought you didn't text?

I dive into my sub while I wait for a reply. It comes quickly.

> I don't normally, can I call you?

I beat him to the punch and hit dial.

"Hey," comes his sleepy morning voice down the line.

"You just woke up, didn't you?" I ask in my chipper, been up for three hours already, voice.

"You sound so awake. Why are you so awake this early on the weekend?" He groans down the line.

"Wow, you really aren't a morning person, are you?" I tease. "I work openings so I'm always lively in the morning."

"I'm going to have to keep that in mind the next time I try to call you before one of my shifts."

It clicks for me now. "Oh, that's why you sacrificed ten cents on texting me this early?"

"Actually it was twenty cents because I texted you twice." I can hear his grin as he replies.

"How much does it cost when I message you back?" I ask.

"Ten more cents," he answers.

"Better get up man, you're down thirty cents before seven a.m." I taunt him.

"It will be worth it if I can convince you to go on a first date with me," Will declares.

It's been less than twelve hours, but I've been hoping for this... just a little bit. "What did you have in mind?" I ask. I'm seated in the back of the shop at my manager's desk. She won't be in for a few hours yet, so she won't mind that I'm sitting in her chair. It's the most comfortable spot in the entire shop.

I hear him exhale and sheets rustle in the background. "Well, what does your schedule look like for the next week?"

I grin at the blank computer screen in front of me. "It might be easier if I let you know the times that I'd be free for a date, than all the other commitments I have in my life." I pull out my planner. "Looks like this upcoming week I'm free on Friday and Saturday after one p.m. Do either of those work for you?"

It takes him a few seconds to respond, "No, dang, I switched shifts with someone on Friday and on Saturday my sister is throwing a party I need to be present for."

"Well, that is a bummer," I reply genuinely. "I guess you'll have to put in some effort by calling me over the week before we find a connecting time then."

"Challenge accepted, Nikki. I get the feeling you're someone worth putting effort into." That makes me smile. "But I gotta go get ready for work, enjoy the rest of your shift." Then the line goes dead.

"Will?" I ask into my phone. There's no response.

He hung up the phone, no goodbye, nothing. We're definitely going to have to work on that during our next call. I surprise myself that I'm already thinking of a next call with him.

An annoying grin plasters itself to my face for the duration of my shift, which goes quickly, thanks to the conversation with Will. Once I'm home, the nap that I enjoy is a blissful one. Part of me was hoping to hear from Will again before the day ended, but I also admit to myself that I've known the guy for one day, it's a good sign he's not being that clingy after our first thing in the morning phone call.

The weekend wraps up without another call from Will, which starts to bug me a tiny bit by Sunday night. However, not enough for me to call him. In French on Monday I update Tipp.

"He hasn't called you since first thing Saturday?" She interrogates.

"Yupp." I make the p's pop when I say it.

Her face shifts. One of her eyebrows is raised, and I see her index finger preparing to point at me before she speaks. "So, why haven't you womanned up yet and called him?" That index finger is pointed directly at my chest now.

"But—, I—" I stammer. "Because," I sigh.

"Give me your phone," she demands.

"No." It's barely an audible word.

"Veronica Welch, give me your phone!" She has her palm opened up waiting for me to place it in her hand.

That bitch just full named me.

"Fuck no." I sound like a chirping bird at this point.

"So you're going to sit here upset he hasn't called you, and wait around for him to telepathically know he needs to pick up his damn phone. Didn't he text you first?" She's entered lawyer mode.

I'm in trouble now. "Yes..." I trail off sheepishly.

"Either you call him, since now it's your turn, or stop being upset about it."

I glare at her. "Why do you always make sense?"

"Because babe, I'm removed from the situation. I can think clearly about it, unlike you," she laughs at me.

Madame Krasse enters the room and immediately starts speaking in French, no English thrown in to help us out. My brain can't spare any energy to think about Will now. I have to completely focus on our lesson, and barely manage to keep up. When I glance over my shoulder at Tipp it comforts me to see she's a little bit lost too. I guess French II does up the difficulty level after all.

Later that night I woman up, as Tipp says, and press on Will's number in my phone. It rings once, I'm calm. As it rings a second time, I pace around my room. It rings a third time and the self doubt kicks in. After the fourth ring he picks up.

"Hey!" Will sounds excited.

"Hi," I greet nervously.

"How's it going?" he asks, still sounding happy.

My body relaxes a little, "Good, finally found a moment to call you back from Saturday." I cringe at myself in the mirror. *Why did I get so specific? Why did I mention the last time we talked?*

"Yeah, I wanted to call again this weekend but ended up getting asked to work a double and then I had no idea how late I could call without interrupting your beauty sleep," he explains.

Now I'm full on smiling. "Couldn't risk spending another thirty cents to figure out if I was awake or not?"

He's quick. "That would be sixty cents on a girl I haven't even had a first date with yet. You think I'm made of money?"

I giggle. "Yeah, I'm bummed about our schedules not working out. Are you on campus tomorrow?"

"Yes, I'm off on Tuesdays. I have classes back to back from nine a.m. until a little after four. You?"

My grin grows larger. "That's perfect, I have a gap in my schedule from two until six. Want to meet up and grab an early dinner on campus?" Once the words are out of my mouth I realize that's exactly what Stefan did to me. "Not like a date, just two people getting to know each other while eating a meal."

"That's the definition of a date." Will tells me.

"Well apparently things don't count as a date if your best friend plans it all, or if we're on campus during it." I clarify for Will. *I don't know why he's confused, it's not like I made up these rules five seconds ago.*

"Nikki, I'll see you tomorrow in the Griffin Center for our *not* date."

The tell tale disconnected note chimes telling me he's hung up again. I really need to remember to talk to him about that.

I pull the phone from my ear and stare at myself in the floor to ceiling closet mirrors. A smile slowly breaks across my face as I inform my bedroom, "I've got a *not* date tomorrow!"

I look up from my French homework and see Will and Stefan walking toward me.

Will greets, "I thought including Stefan in our 'not date' would officially make it not a date for you." He air quotes 'not date' while he says it.

I'm not sure if he thinks he's being cute or funny. I'm definitely sure it's neither. "Well go get yourself some food then. I'll save this table."

Will seems confused by my cold tone. He asks cautiously, "You hungry, Nikki?"

"No, I'm feeling a bit hangry." I bite out as a cover. I should have known that Stefan would end up joining us, he has this time free too. I sigh, wishing I'd had the forethought to realize this instead of being unpleasantly surprised by his presence right now.

Will directs us. "Okay Stefan, you save our table. Nikki, let's go get some food."

I don't overthink it and follow Will to the food court. "I want the taco shop."

He readjusts our course and takes me over to the taco shop. We order and he insists he pays. "Thirty cents for texting is too much but you'll feed me?" I ask.

"Absolutely," he smiles while picking up our food from the counter when it's called out, "First off, I get to hang out with you while we're eating, and second, you already told me the way to your heart is through your stomach."

Shit, I did admit that already. "Well, withholding food in front of a starving animal is a way to get your hand bitten off."

He gives me the bag with both our meals and follows me to our table. Once we're seated, Stefan gets up to get his own food. Will hands me some napkins and says nothing while I eat my first rolled taco. After one taco and a few bites of rice and beans, I feel more like a human than a rabid beast. I look up to see Will watching me.

He hasn't touched his food yet, though he's removed it from the bag. I see he ordered carne asada fries and a side of spicy carrots. They look delicious. Will notices me eyeing his food and starts eating it. He still hasn't said anything.

"So those are carne asada fries?" I ask.

He nods while chewing. At least he isn't speaking with his mouth full.

"I've never had carne asada fries before, they look good," I hint.

"Are you trying to suggest something Nikki?" Will asks, and takes another bite.

I scrunch my nose and scratch a nonexistent itch on my temple before admitting, "Maybe?"

He finishes chewing again. "Then you'll have to ask nicely. I will stab you with my fork if you try to sneak one off my plate."

Did he threaten violence? I feel warmth pool between my legs. *Why do I like that? Focus!* "Will, may I please try one of your carne asada fries?" I ask with a submissive tone in my voice and a saccharine smile on my face.

He smirks at me and then focuses on his plate. Will chooses one of the best looking fries he has, with the perfect proportions of morsels to fry. He offers me his fork and I take it, eating the fry without any hesitation.

I hand back the utensil as Will says, "Damn, my fork knows what your mouth feels like before I do."

"Who knows if you ever will?" I tease him back.

"How's it going, hmmmm?" Stefan's voice slices through any tension that was gathering between Will and me.

We both look at him, shocked at his startling return. "Really man, mimicking Mr. Webber? Don't you have any new material yet?"

"I'm confused," I chime in.

Will looks at me, "Mr. Webber is our World History professor. We have his class right before this." Then he sighs, "Stefan has been obsessed with copying his 'Hmmmm?' since week one. I've also been annoyed by it since week one."

Stefan has already opened up his sandwich and is halfway through it in only two bites. He shows no remorse as he takes another bite.

"Dude, first the mimicking, now you're eating that in front of me?" I chide.

Stefan swallows. I don't think he even chewed his bite. "I'm almost done Nikki, you can't permanently ban us from eating subs in your presence. They're one of the best foods around," he whines.

Will ponders, "You have a problem with subs?"

Now it's my turn to sigh. "Imagine if every time you clocked off you were still continuously surrounded by whatever it was you were working on that day. The smell, the taste —it never left your presence. You'd be annoyed too."

"I'll take your word for it." I don't think Will necessarily understands, but he doesn't argue my opinion either. He looks at Stefan, "No talking until it's done and you've thrown the trash away." Then he looks at me. "That will give us about two more minutes of peace and quiet, and then he'll never shut up."

I grin. I can tell they've been friends for a while by how directly Will can talk to Stefan. That makes me curious. "How did you two meet? I guess it will have to be Will's side of the story, since you're banned from talking," I leer at Stefan.

Will dives in while I polish off my meal. "It's a rather short story actually. I sat behind him in sophomore math in high school. He decided we needed to be friends, and that was that. We did Swim and Dive together for the next three years, and we try to have at least one class together here. He's outgoing and annoying, and like a brother to me." Then he claps Stefan on the shoulder. "An exasperating brother, but family."

I smile. It reminds me of how I feel about Tipp. Stefan opens his mouth to add on, but he still has a bit of the sandwich left and snaps it shut. I decide to change the subject to irritate him further. "Alright Will, what do you do for fun in all your free time?"

Our dinner break continues in lively chatter until it's time for Stefan and I to head off to class. I'm shocked that it feels like we have only been talking for five minutes as opposed to the two hours it has actually been.

After waving goodbye to Will, Stefan and I head across campus to the science complex. Once we round the bend of the library and there's no way Will can see us anymore Stefan elbows me in the ribs.

"Oi! What was that for?" I demand.

"I was right." He grins.

"About what?" I'm rubbing my ribs. *Why are his elbows so pointy?*

"You two are a good fit together." He states it, no question in his tone.

I deny it, "Too soon to tell. We haven't even been on a date yet."

"Yeah, because your schedule sucks."

I do a double take. "How do you know that?"

"He's like my brother, remember? We both know you and Tipp chat about what's going on, or not going on, because your schedule is stupid."

Stefan's wrong though. "It's his schedule that's being the problem this week," I remind him.

We're at the science complex now and Stefan beats me down the stairs. He turns around from the bottom and challenges, "So, work with him to figure out a better time."

I shuffle down the stairs careful to not trip over my own feet as I ask him, "When? How?"

Once I'm down the stairs we walk to our classroom.

He looks at me with his signature smirk. "That's not for me to figure out, but based on the tension I saw at dinner, you should put some effort into it. I think you two really are perfect together. I've known the guy for five years. He's never spent thirty cents on texting me."

Eight

The Most Important Meal of the Day

I DIDN'T REALIZE THAT Will spending thirty cents on texting me was that big a deal until Stefan said something. *Annoying little match-maker Stefan. Thinks he knows what we both need, ugh! His comments totally didn't convince me to call Will and set up our first date.* At least, that's what I tell myself as I pull out my phone to call Will after class. With some fine tooth combing, we settle on breakfast. We both have busy schedules, so bright and early will have to work.

We decide to drive separately because we are barely fitting this date in as it is, and I've only known Will for a week. He doesn't get to know where I live yet. He chose a diner in Santee, halfway between campus and my work. It's in a corner spot of an outdoor shopping center. Due to the early hour, and it being a weekday, there is ample parking and I snag a spot to the left of the entrance. There are bear carvings all over the exterior of the building, with two large black bear pillars guarding the front door. I wait in my Beetle until I see Will get out of his car and head to the entrance. As I hop out of my car he spots me. An ear splitting smile spreads across his cheeks as he approaches me and wraps me in a tight hug. It's quick and over too soon for my liking.

His arms drop to his sides and he offers, "Shall we?" as we walk in together.

Inside the diner there are even more bear decorations, and an entire gift shop with various black bear covered items. While scanning the gift shop I'm reminded of a pair of sleep shorts I had in high school. Maybe they were bought at a similar restaurant. I'm brought back to reality when I hear Will's sultry deep voice tell the hostess we need a table for two. They take us to a secluded booth in the back. As we meander through the empty tables, there are even more bear decorations adorning the walls, curtains, and even the light fixtures.

Our booth has fake leather seats and the menus have a slight stickiness to them where you can tell someone went through the routine of their job without checking if anything needed a more thorough cleaning. For a small diner in Santee at seven in the morning, it is exactly as I expected.

Will puts his menu down and asks, "What do you plan on getting?"

While unwrapping my silverware from the napkin wrapper and placing them on the table I reply, "An orange juice, glass of water, and the eggs and sausage breakfast. What about you?"

"I always enjoy a breakfast burrito, so basically the same as you but wrapped in a tortilla. With hot sauce, of course," he answers, doing the same with his silverware.

I force a grin, but why is this feeling more awkward than when we chatted previously? Maybe a better subject will help get us in the groove we had when Stefan and Tipp were around. "So, how did your sister's party go?"

My question makes him stiffen slightly. "It was fine, what I'd expect of a party hosted by Meghan."

A cagey response, I can tell he doesn't want me to push. As I'm trying to think of something else to talk about, our waitress comes over to take our orders.

When she's done I change subjects yet again, "So you and Stefan were on Dive together in high school? Wasn't being up on those diving boards scary?"

Will grins, "Yeah at first, but once you realize it's water below you, and that you don't have to jump until you're ready, it's not so bad."

"I don't think I could do that," I admit.

"Well, we didn't take it too seriously. Stefan actually invented a dive that's now banned in competitions."

"Really now?" I ask him, my curiosity rising.

"Yeah, basically you jump as high and as hard as you can, then while in the air you're supposed to lay horizontally on your side with your arm bent like you're propping your head on your hand, almost as if you're lounging on the couch." He's still grinning. "That's all it was at first, then Stefan decided to make it even funnier by angling his body to be looking at the judges. The best part is when he would give them a wink before changing position and getting ready to dive into the water."

"He didn't!" I guffaw.

"Oh, he did. I think at the first meet the judges were surprised. He met all the technical requirements for a dive, but it was seen as disrespectful."

I push some loose hair back over my shoulder and comment, "It doesn't sound like it would be too hard to pull off."

His face turns slightly more serious. "Maybe from the outside looking in, but it takes skill to be able to perform that dive. You have to lay perfectly horizontal in the air. If you mess that up, the entire dive is thrown off and there's no recovery from there."

I didn't know one could take Dive so seriously. I avert my eyes, feeling bad for offending Will. "Oh, sorry, I didn't know."

His face softens, "Well, how could you? Unless you've been on the Dive team before it's hard to know all the rules."

I appreciate his passion about this, and how he is understanding that I know nothing about the subject. Our food arrives quickly and I dig in. I didn't realize how hungry I was until I smelled the perfectly cooked eggs and sausage. Add a side of sourdough toast and I'm in heaven.

After we each enjoy a few bites of our breakfasts Will asks, "So, Nikki, do you have any siblings?"

I give a genuine smile and feel my heart warm a little. I love my little brother dearly, "One little brother, his name is Jamie."

"How much younger than you is he?" Will follows up.

"Five and a half years, but we usually round it to six."

Will quickly calculates. "So he's fifteen right now?"

"Yeah, he's a bit of a butthead, but what else can you expect from a little brother?"

Then I hear it, a laugh that should never be repeated. I have to hide my abject horror as a loud, "Her, her, her, her, her, her," comes from Will. His laugh sounds like Santa Clause and Woody the Woodpecker had a baby that was tone deaf.

Will takes a bite.

I internally shake my head hoping I'd just hallucinated that sound.

He raises an eyebrow signifying his curiosity about my brother so I indulge him. "A few years ago, I got home from golf practice: he and my parents were all sitting in the living room when I walked through the door. Jamie looks at me, full blown eye contact and says, no hesitation, 'Nikki, you're a cock.'"

Will's eyes pop as he laughs again. My previous description was too kind. The second round of suffering sounds more like a chainsaw being taken off of life support. When he's finished assaulting my ears he asks, "What?"

I try not to show my visible discomfort at the noise he keeps making in place of a laugh. I muster the strength and continue, "I know! My parents sat there and didn't do anything. They laughed at the comment!" I hope my disdain for his laugh is appearing as indignation for the story about Jamie.

"Why were they okay with that?" Will inquires.

Thank the gods he didn't laugh again. "Well, apparently they were talking about the Chinese New Year before I'd gotten home. Jamie had looked up all our animals. He and my parents are all tigers, and I'm a rooster," I explain.

Will only smiles and connects the dots. "And another word for rooster is cock?"

"Yupp," my p's pop as they always do with that word. "My parents knew my response would be funny, so they let Jamie go with it to see what would happen. They were correct, my shocked reaction was rightfully scorned, and now it's a funny story that we all enjoy reliving from time to time."

Will takes a drink. "I see."

"That's my family in a nutshell I guess. My brother is six years younger, my parents have been together since I was five, and we enjoy good natured humor. What about your family?" It's only fair that since I just shared it's his turn now. I have to hope that he's not as entertained by his own family as much as he was by the story about mine. I've never heard a laugh that makes me that physically uncomfortable before in my life.

"Not much different honestly, my sister Meghan is eight years older than me. My other sister, Kasey, is a year and a half younger than me, and we bicker like two siblings that are a little too close in age for anyone to expect to get along." Will smirks and adds on, "I'm always right, she just hates admitting it." Then, much to my chagrin, his her-her laugh accosts my ears again. This time it's quieter and comes off more lame than cringy.

Luckily, there are only a few bites of our meals left, and our schedules won't allow us to dally around afterward. I can endure this. What Will's saying about his sisters makes sense, everyone has some sort of sibling animosity, right? I ask follow up details for the sake of the meal. "What about your parents?"

"They're the greatest." Will's eyes twinkle talking about them. Holy shit, I don't know how I didn't notice them before. They're the most beautiful shade of sea blue I've ever seen. Talking about his parents truly brings them to life. "My Dad met my Mom at a bar, his pick up line was, 'Pull my finger,' and the rest is history."

My jaw would drop, but my mouth is full. Once my bite is consumed I ask, "He didn't?"

In a breathy, annoying, chortle he laughs again. How I manage not to physically cringe away is beyond me. "He did. Worse yet, my mother ended up marrying him. They're cute, married for over twenty years and definitely still in love. I hope I can have a marriage as happy as theirs someday." Okay, that's adorable. We're absolutely not there yet, but he has long term goals. Too many guys around here don't think past what they'll eat for their next meal.

That laugh though. I like joy, humor, and jokes in my life. I can't end up with someone who has a laugh I find to be physically repulsive. Why did it transition from the nice chuckle he emitted whenever we hung out before to this monstrous noise he's doing today?

I finish my meal and we get out of our booth to pay at the entrance to the diner. Will is a gentleman and pays for my meal, something I appreciate but did not expect. A woman needs to always be willing to pay for her meal, feminism and all, but having a man be chivalrous is appreciated.

We walk toward our cars and the awkward how do we say goodbye dance ensues. I don't know if I want to give him a handshake, (that seems too formal especially with how he embraced me before the meal), but a kiss is way too personal. I settle on a hug as safe, neutral territory.

"Well, I hope your day goes smoothly," Will offers as a beginning to our goodbye.

I take a step closer. "Thanks."

"I guess I'll talk to you later?" Will asks.

I really don't want to commit to that. I need to process this new uneasy feeling that's suddenly developed around him. "I'm not sure, Tipp might have a weird break in her schedule before Astronomy tonight so I think I'm going to hang out with her." I hope he doesn't sense my dismissal.

He reaches an arm out. "That's good, I hope you have fun with her," and gives me a solid hug.

He's tall, and decently built. As I wrap my arms around his waist I feel like I'm the perfect size in comparison. My head reaches his shoulder, my arms are so comfortable around him, but my mind wanders back to that milk curdling laugh.

I withdraw first. "Thanks for breakfast Will, I'll see you around." With that I turn and get in my car.

Whether Tipp is available or not, we need to talk. He's sweet and his hugs are divine, but the two of us at breakfast didn't feel right or natural. I was having to force conversation. If a relationship doesn't start off right, what's to keep the guy from getting mad at me for being myself in the future? There's no way we'd make it moving to Oregon together, I couldn't even get through breakfast. Perhaps, most importantly, I can't be with a guy whose laugh makes me want to shove his face into a pillow in hopes of smothering the sound. *What the hell am I going to do?*

Nine

I Need Infectious Laughter

As the day wears on I begin wondering how smart it was to have a date with Will on a day when I wouldn't get to process with Tipp. My heart flutters as I realize not only that, but tonight I'll be forced to spend over an hour with Stefan in Astronomy.

For the duration of P.E. I go through the movements but have no idea what we're actually learning. It has something to do with jump rope, one of my least favorite games as a child.

As an adult, I have an even better reason not to enjoy rope jumping. Two reasons actually. Boobs. Breasts. Ta-tas. The only people at the gym you see jumping rope as adults are men in compression shorts, or women who are less endowed. These D cups? They aren't meant to be flung around and smacking side to side to the beat of the mix tape Coach Walker made for today. Is this P.E. for Elementary Educators, or a scene from Baywatch?

I don't have a lot of experience with children yet, but I'll let their future P.E. instructors teach them how to jump in without getting hurt. I'll instruct everything else. For the rest of class I stick to simple light impact, walking jump roping, just hoping the torture will end soon.

When it seems like my back is a river of sweat, the class finally ends. For the first time this semester I wish there was a way to shower before my next class. I don't know how some girls sweat pretty. At the gym I see women all the time with their hair done in cute French braids, and a full face of makeup, making it look like working out is as relaxing as reading a book. Then I look in the mirror and get reminded that I am not that kind of pretty. When I work out, there is sweat, a lot of it. My face is red: bright, shiny, sweaty red. There's no way I want to run into Stefan or Will having just done more jump roping today than I've done in the last ten years combined.

With a four hour break between classes I could manage making it home to shower and getting back to campus with plenty of time before Astronomy, but that would be such a waste of gas money. I weigh my options: sweat or gas money?

As I walk to the parking garage across campus a feeling of resignation consumes me. I know I'm avoiding seeing the guys, however I don't know why this morning was so horrible. I sigh as I check the time and know that Tipp isn't going to pick up if I try to call her now. I decide going home would solve my sweat problem as well as create a way to avoid Will and Stefan this afternoon.

Once at my car in the parking garage I see my gym bag thrown in the back seat. *That's it!* I can take a quick trip to the sister gym of my main membership down the street and wash off. It gets me off campus to avoid the boys, and I'll be able to clean up! Thank you past tense me for not being responsible enough to take the bag inside after my last workout. Sure, the towel might be a bit musty, but that's better than me being downright gross.

The side quest to the gym for a quick shower and new deodorant application is efficient. A small miracle happens and I find a spare shirt in the bottom of my bag that has me feeling better. Now, I am ready to tackle the challenge of running into Stefan while trekking across campus. I choose to avoid the Griffin Center where he and Will will most likely be eating and head straight to the science complex.

There's a perfect spot nestled into the courtyard of the building where I can avoid being noticed. The table glistens in the soft natural light that's shining through the tree leaves, and a slight breeze is flowing as well.

I'm enraptured with correctly conjugating some French verbs when there's a tap on my left shoulder. I finish writing *vous ricanez, ils/elles ricanent*, and look up to find none other than Douchebag Brock from the first day of Astronomy. Shit, I assumed it was Stefan interrupting me.

"Hey," he greets with a cocky grin.

This is so not what I want to endure before seeing Stefan. "Hello," I reply and immediately look back to my paper. Trying to show him that I'm not interested in socializing I work on the next verb I need to correctly conjugate.

Brock doesn't walk away... apparently fuck off wasn't written clearly enough across my face. "Mind if I sit?" He asks.

"I do mind actually. I'm trying to get some work done, thanks." Maybe that will be clear enough?

"Oh, I won't disturb you," Brock says as he pulls out the chair opposite me. "I've got work to do too."

"Doubtful," I object.

He tilts his head. "Which part?"

"Where you said you wouldn't disturb me, you already are. Oh and look," I throw my hands up. "You're interrupting my homework as well. Way to immediately fail a task."

Brock blinks at me and then pulls out his own work without another word. He hasn't left, but at least he's shut up for now. Our classroom should open up in a few minutes, so I guess getting any more homework done will no longer be possible.

As I pretend to read part of my text book I hear a voice call out, "Hey Nikki!" Then a hand lands on my shoulder.

Why does everyone want to talk with me all the sudden? "Hey, Stefan," I reply flatly.

He makes a face. "You good, Nik?"

Brock interjects, "Since when do you go by Nik?"

"I don't," I quip at him. Then I turn to face Stefan. "Not really. Let's just get ready for class." I gesture with my hand at the kids pouring out of our room.

"Sure, let's go." Stefan waits for me to get up. He looks to Brock. "Later man," and we head to our Astronomy classroom.

"Okay Nik, now that Chad is gone, what's going on?" He asks as we reach our table.

I don't want to meet his eyes. I don't want to lie to him, and I don't want to tell him the truth. "I don't wanna talk about it," I say as I get out my things for our lesson. "And his name is Brock."

"I know what his name is, what I don't know is why you're brushing me off, and why you didn't eat lunner with Will and me today. Nik, look at me."

I reluctantly look up.

"Thank you! Now, what's going on?" Stefan pushes.

I double down, "First, I don't want to talk about it. Second, P.E. was extra sweaty today so I ran to the gym to shower off. Third, if you know his name, then why did you call him Chad?"

He smirks. He's always fucking smirking. "That was out of order, but I called him Chad because anyone with a brain can tell you detest him and I thought it might, just a tiny bit, make you smile. Apparently I was wrong on that."

"Apparently," I agree.

"So if you don't want to talk about whatever is making you a crusty witch, what can we talk about?"

I purse my lips as I mull it over. "I honestly don't feel like chatting today. Can you get those social needs of yours met elsewhere?"

"I could, but instead I'll just be here. Let me know if what you need changes," he says closing the conversation and leaving me to my thoughts.

I appreciate Stefan respecting my wishes about socializing tonight. We suffer through Mr. Fitzgibbons lesson and I'm barely a useful lab partner. Stefan definitely carries my weight; I'll have to remember to thank him when I feel like being nice. When class wraps up, I don't linger for idle chit chat. Instead I give him a wave and am one of the first people out of the classroom. I decide I can't wait to talk to Tipp in person tomorrow and dial her as I walk to my car.

It rings through to voicemail. I hear her chipper, "You know who I am, you know what to do," message.

I leave a message after the beep, "Bitch, call me. Please." No emotion, no explanation.

I don't know why I'm so worked up about this. Will was nice. We had fun on the double date. We had a decent breakfast. That laugh. Somehow it sounded worse than nails on a chalkboard. We're not even together. So why do I care so much that I never want us to be defined as *"together?"*

I drive home repeating that question to myself a million times. Luckily Nana is at choir practice, or retired teacher group, or whatever group she's president of this year. I should ask her for a schedule just so I can know when I'll be seeing her around. I'm spuddling around the kitchen, seeing the options of what I could eat for dinner if I had an appetite, when I hear Tipp's assigned ringtone go off from my bedroom.

I sprint across the kitchen, skid around the corner, and dive from the hallway onto my bed, scrambling to pick it up by the fourth ring. "Tipp!"

"Bitch, what the fuck?" She shouts into my ear.

I flinch. "Whoa, what?"

"You leave me a four word voicemail and that's it? You sounded so defeated, your tone alone had me worried about you!" She scolds me.

"I'm sorry, that's not what I meant to do. "I take a breath. "It's about my date with Will this morning." There, I've said it. Tipp will force me to talk about it.

Her tone immediately softens. "Aww babe, what's up?" She asks it as if I'm made of glass.

"No! You don't get to go all nice now! You need to be your regular badass self and smack some sense back into me."

"What did you do?"

"Nothing, yet," I mumble as I dramatically fall across the bed and cover my eyes with my arm.

"So what are you *going* to do?" Tipp inquires.

"I think you need to tell me what to do." *She can tell me how to live my life right?*

"Well first you gotta tell me what the hell happened," Tipp reminds me.

It was worth a shot. I fill her in on all the details about Will and my breakfast date. The Cliff Notes version tumbles out like word vomit until I come to a sudden halt.

"That's it?" Tipp asks.

My voice elevates an octave. "What do you mean that's it?" I swallow. "Did you hear the part about his laugh?"

"Yeah." I hear her judgment. "It's a laugh! You're really going to call things off with Will because of his laugh?"

I shake my head as I pace the length of my bedroom. "You don't understand. It's the worst laugh you've ever heard in your entire life, multiplied by infinity."

"Babe, that's not possible. There's no way you picked some guy that happens to have the worst laugh on the planet."

"No, I didn't! Stefan did it," I accuse. "He set me up on the date, this is his fault."

"You're deflecting. So what do you need me for? My break was up like three exaggerated sentences ago." She sighs waiting for me to screw my head on right.

I scoff, "Don't you call me out like that, I'm in crisis. You just need to tell me how to live my life."

"Nope, that's not what I'm here for. Guidance, of course." I can visualize exactly how her hands are talking in the air as she says this. "Emotional support, always." That one had a head nod for sure. "The best person you know with the filthiest mouth, you bet." She would be pointing at me with that one. "Telling you how to live your life... that's all you. Break up with him or don't. You have to choose." If we were in person Tipp would have ended that as if she were serving your last meal, fancy, open palmed, and ending with a flourish.

I let out an exaggerated sigh. "Yes, Mom."

"Fuck you, you know I'm Daddy," Tipp bites into the phone.

"I'm never calling you that," but now I'm grinning.

"I can hear your smile," she teases.

I roll my eyes.

"And I saw that!"

Damn Tipp's good. "Okay love, thanks for the limited words of advice, I guess."

"Nikki, you've gotta choose for yourself, if you say it was that bad I believe you. If you break it off oh well, at least you got a free breakfast out of it. I will tell you one thing, I don't think his laugh is why you aren't interested in him. Logically speaking, there's probably something else bugging you. Is it at all possible that maybe you're just afraid of getting hurt again?"

I freeze, contemplating her words.

Before I get a chance to reply she says. "Okay babe, gotta go, hopefully my manager hasn't noticed!" She immediately hangs up the phone and I'm left to my thoughts again.

Am I afraid of being hurt again? Yeah, Will's laugh was atrocious. Was is that bad though? Why did I think Tipp would be any help? She says one damn thing and I'm just spiraling down a rabbit hole of confusion.

I don't have enough of an appetite to attempt dinner. After a scalding shower I really didn't need, I crawl into bed and debate my options. I manage to drift into a restless sleep while hoping that the morning will provide clarity.

"Her, her, her, her, her," rings in my ears as I startle awake. Okay, that's it. That's my answer. If I am having nightmares about this man's laugh, I'm done. There is no second chance. He is literally haunting my dreams. There's no way that Tipp is right and my subconscious is telling me we'd be perfect together by haunting me with his chortle.

I need to rip off the bandaid, but not at three twenty-five in the morning. If today is Wednesday, I think Will works all day, which leaves tonight. I will not be allowing myself to have any more haunted dreams from him. I guess once I make it through English tonight I'll have to give him a call. Which gives me approximately twelve hours to overanalyze exactly what I plan to say.

Every time I try to go about my daily tasks my brain interrupts with different ways for me to end things with Will.

"You'd like a turkey sub?" How about a side of, *"It's not you, it's me, with that?"*

"That will be five dollars for your almost twelve-inch sub." And would you also like to know, *"I'm focusing on school right now."*

"Bye guys, have a great rest of your day!" It's pretty obvious, *"We're both looking for different things."*

"If only we had met a few years from now," rings through my mind as I flip my signal on the freeway.

Tipp looks up from her desk as I enter French and I blurt at her, "You're going to make someone really happy someday, I'm sure of it, it's just not going to be me." *Shit, that one actually left my mouth.*

"What the fuck did you say?" Tipp asks me looking puzzled.

"Ummm, I may have been practicing how to dump Will all morning at work..."

Her eyes bug out. "You haven't?"

I stare intently at the ceiling. "Maybe..."

"Babe!" She exclaims way too loudly slamming her hand down on her desk. "You haven't even been officially dating him, it was one date, why are you stressing so much?"

I rotate toward her slowly with a grimace on my face. "It's a really bad reason to break up with someone though."

She breaks into a fit of laughter.

"Don't make fun of me," I beg her.

As Tipp recovers she requests, "Do it, do the laugh."

I hold up my hands. "I can't, it's impossible to replicate."

She doesn't yield. "Try your best."

I give a guttural, "Ho, ho, ho, ho, ho, ho. No that's not right, that's too close to Santa." Then I try an amused, "He, he, he, he, he, he. That's definitely not it, way too nasally."

Tipp is looking shocked. "Those were worse than Will's right?"

I shake my head. "Nope."

"Girl," she sighs as her whole body bends in question.

"Let me try one more." I engage my core muscles, access the deepest region of my throat and for some reason my nose flexes as I groan out, "Her, her, her, her, her, her." I look at Tipp's horrified face and grimly confirm, "That's the one. The male version of Janice from *Friends*."

I think Tipp is stunned into silence. She's staring at me, but she's not saying anything. I don't think I've ever heard her speechless before. I take a minute and sit here enjoying the silence. Maybe now she finally understands what I've been going through. As I turn in my seat to face the front of the room while Tipp processes, I notice other people from our class staring at me, faces stricken in variations from entertained to worried about the noises I had been making.

"Nikki, are you okay?" Our classmate LeAndre asks.

"Um, yeah," I answer him, feeling my ears and cheeks pink from embarrassment. "But that last laugh was absolutely horrible, right?"

LeAndre looks around the room as random people nod at my question.

"Thanks!" I say chipperly. "Just needed support, that was a horrible laugh." As I reach down to my backpack on the floor I hear a suppressed giggle escape from Tipp.

"You bitch, you knew people were listening," I whisper shout at her. I glance over my shoulder to see her trying to hide a grin behind her hand and pretend to focus on my books while the prattle of my classmates begins to pick up to its usual volume.

She breaks our silence after a moment of letting me stew. "I did. So it seems like Will isn't the right guy for you then? What ever happened to my bestie who was done dating?" She asks me sarcastically.

I purse my lips searching for a response. "I guess I figured that if he was the right guy for me, that would also mean moving next year would be a good fit."

Tipp surveys my entire being before responding. "I don't buy it. I know you Nikki. You don't get this way over meaningless guys."

"What does that mean?"

She shrugs at me. "I can't tell you the answer to all your problems. Take a minute and really think about why you want to end things with Will. Is it his laugh, or is it something deeper?"

Our conversation is forced to end as Madame Krasse begins class.

After French, Tipp rushes off to make it to her shift on time and I'm left with my thoughts once more.

I choose a table in the Griffin Center and pull out a chair as my brain resumes the break up line montage, *"I'm not ready for a serious relationship."*

I wave my greeting to a classmate in English and go through the monotony of class, dreading its end. I know I need to call Will and get it over with, but I don't want to do it where others can overhear me. I haven't even figured out what I'm going to say, for Satan's sake.

I owe him a better break up than a bra-held speaker phone call on my drive. So I decide to wait until I'm home. Hopefully, Nana will be at another practice tonight.

As I pull into the driveway, my hopes are indeed answered. Time to walk in, call Will, and get this over with. Out of habit, I put my backpack in my bedroom and then walk to the kitchen. I haven't eaten much in the last 24 hours and I think my body is trying to tell me that's not a good thing. I still have no appetite though.

As I stand over the silverware drawer I pull out my phone and call Will.

Please don't answer, please don't answer, I mentally plead as I hear ringing.

"Hey," Will's voice cheerfully greets after two more rings.

I groan internally. "Hey Will," I reply timidly.

"You okay?" His voice raises in question.

I start pacing across the smooth linoleum. "I mean, technically yes, but can we talk?"

"Uh oh, I know what those words mean."

I rub the back of my neck. "Yeah, I'm sorry, it's just." My voice trails off... "Look Will, you're a great guy, and any logical girl would choose you, but for some reason, I'm not."

"Okay? That's fine. Good luck with everything Nikki," he replies, even kilter, as if he saw this coming.

"Thanks Will, you too." I pull the phone from my ear, end the call, and steady myself by gripping the edge of the counter. I focus my brain on the white subway tile and trace the grout between a few pieces while I recenter my emotions. Then I turn around and cross the kitchen to the fridge. My appetite hasn't returned, but my stomach needs something in it. Comfort toast it is. I get two pieces of bread and put them in the toaster.

I stare through the kitchen window and get lost in thought. I broke up with him because that laugh was so horrid it woke me from a sound sleep. There's no way, not one iota, that Tipp was onto something with her comment earlier. It has nothing to do with what my ex did to me. I'm not a commitment phobe. I just need to refocus. Keep my head down, get good grades, and move to Oregon. I can find the perfect partner once those goals are met.

The toaster dings and startles me from my dazed state. I butter my toast and eat it over the kitchen sink, sans plate. As I'm looking out into the moonlit backyard, I see Nana's cat, Otis. He slinks through the shadowed perimeter that is covered overhead by large trees. He is small and on a mission. I chew and enjoy his hunting while reflecting on how much I was unnecessarily stressing over ending things with Will. He was so calm and understanding... did I make the right choice in ending things with him? I've never heard a guy be so respectful while getting dumped; he didn't argue or put up a fight.

My eyes bulge out as I realize I just broke up with Will by saying, "Any logical girl would choose you, but for some reason I'm not?" *Who the fuck says something like that?*

Ten

Filling the Void

THE NEXT DAY I sit in Astronomy waiting for Stefan to show up. I chew on my bottom lip with worry as the minutes tick by. I'm concerned that when I see Stefan again he might be upset with me for cutting things off with Will.

As he saunters into our crowded classroom, swagger in place as always, I feel my stomach drop. I know he thought that Will and I would be perfect together, but he was clearly mistaken.

Stefan approaches our table and takes a seat calmly. "Hey Nik, how's it going?"

I'm surprised by the nonchalant direction of his statement but I go with the flow. "Pretty good, ready to make up for my abysmal contribution to our grades on Tuesday."

He waves me off. "That, don't worry about it, we all have off days, especially when we're planning the stupidest way to break up with someone."

My jaw drops. "What— I— You?"

He gives me a knowing smile. "Oh yeah, I heard about how logical a thinker you are," he says giving me a wink.

A fucking wink? "You asshole, I can't believe he told you about that!"

"Really? You can't believe that my best friend told me about how you broke up with him in one of the stupidest ways I've ever heard of?"

I cross my arms and face the whiteboard.

"Oh come off it Nik, you know I'm just messing with you," Stefan pushes.

I give him a slow and exaggerated side eye.

Professor Fitzgibbons walks in and tries starting the class. As he plugs in his laptop to project our lesson, nothing happens. He may be a little older than us, but he should still be part of the generation that has at least a loose grasp of basic technology functions.

Stefan uses this extended beginning of class to his advantage. "Well, why did you dump him?"

"It's hard to dump someone you only went on one date with," I counter.

"I agree, yet you managed to do it."

Hex him, and his future children. "I just, didn't get the right connection from him?" I try to explain while uncrossing my arms and fidgeting with my pen. I really should have thought through a legitimate answer before seeing Stefan tonight.

"That sounded like a question, not an answer."

"Ugh, I don't know. It just wasn't right." How can I get him to believe this when I'm not sure I believe it myself?

He nudges my arm to get me to look at him. "You sure it wasn't his horrible awkward laugh?"

My eyes bug out in surprise from Stefan guessing it correctly.

"Thought that might be it." He gives me a cocky grin, like he thinks he's solved some huge puzzle.

"How do you know about that?" I question.

Stefan folds his arms now. "You think I don't know about my best friend and his horrible awkward laugh? It's one of the worst things I've ever heard. I begged him not to do it."

"I don't think a horrible laugh is something you can control." *Wait, why am I defending Will?*

"True, but you still dumped him because of it," Stefan might not have said he's mad, but the way his words cut me was definitely meant to be personal.

I did dump his best friend for a stupid reason, I knew it, but what am I supposed to do now? There's no way I'm letting him know that I think I might have made a mistake.

Mr. Fitzgibbons announces to the class, "Does anyone know how to work this? I'm not getting anywhere closer to a solution."

Stefan immediately gets up to help.

As I sit there chewing my cheek, I know there's no way I want Stefan to know I'm doubting my choice. I made a decision, and it may have been impulsive, but Will's laugh literally gave me nightmares. I made the right decision for me, and Stefan doesn't need to know any more than that.

After a few minutes of Stefan and another student clicking buttons and turning things off and on again, the screen lights up with Mr. Fitzgibbons' lesson for the evening. Stefan rejoins me at our table and we settle in for a lesson centered about evidence that the Earth is, indeed, round.

After class I take my time packing up my supplies. Stefan, being a minimalist with only a pencil and notebook, is cleaned up quickly and leaves the building without so much as a goodbye. Guess he's a little more upset with me than I initially thought. He'll have to get over that.

"Nikki?" I hear from behind me.

I turn and see many of our classmates have already dispersed but Brock is still standing there. "Yes, Brock?"

"I was wondering if you'd like to get something to eat with me tomorrow night?" He boldly asks.

I mull my choices over. I tried a date with Will, someone who seemed so sweet and kind. Maybe I should try a date with Brock... he could end up not being such a douchebag, right? Maybe it's a front? "Like a date?" I ask.

"Exactly like a date," he says while picking up his backpack.

I do the same and we both head to the classroom door. "That depends, what do you have in mind?" I've got to make him at least put in some effort.

"That's up to you," he tries.

"Nope, I'm not planning a date you're asking me out on," I say flatly.

Brock tries again, "Do you like Mediterranean food?"

"Actually yes, it's one of my favorite types of food." I wasn't expecting him to enjoy cuisine that focuses on delicious combinations of vegetables and fish. His persona gave me more of a BBQ vibe, but maybe I had misjudged him. In my defense, steel toed boots, Famous Stars and Straps t-shirts, and the chain connecting his wallet to his jeans didn't scream conscious eating.

Then he grins, and while it really is a pretty grin, it's still attached to his douchebag face. "Okay, meet me tomorrow at seven p.m., Grossmont Center. I'll drive us to the restaurant from there."

"You think I'm getting in your car alone?" I ask.

"Here's the deal," he explains, "You can meet me in a public place, and send someone a picture of my I.D. and truck so they know exactly how to find me if you mysteriously go missing." He motions for us to go up the stairs toward the parking structure. "You won't be going mysteriously missing, but I thought you might want some assurances in order to agree to a date," he says sarcastically.

I'm surprised he thought this hard about it. "You have everything figured out don't you? Anything else I need to do for this date?" I respond to his sarcasm with my own.

"Nah, I'll see you tomorrow at seven. Meet me in the bookstore." With that he turns and walks off. I'm still getting douchebag vibes from him. Apparently that doesn't matter enough because now I'm going on a date with him tomorrow night. Tipp's going to lose her shit over my genius execution of intelligence.

As I drive to Grossmont Center Friday night I reflect on my lack of critical thinking skills this week. I managed to break up with a sweet guy after one date, because of a laugh. Then I decided to go on a date with a guy I know is a douchebag. I thought I was done dating. Did breaking things off with Will affect me so badly that I literally had a temporary lapse of sanity? Maybe I have a brain tumor, those can effect your judgement, right? Nice guys can be hiding jerks on the inside, but when does a jerk on the outside ever turn out to be a sweetheart on the inside? Never, that's when! I've agreed to go on a date with a wolf who walks around wearing his wolf clothing, too. Worse yet, I actually thought this was a smart decision twenty-four hours ago. The only bright side to this scenario is that I'll be getting some free dinner tonight.

I pull into the parking lot and decide to scope out the Fantasy section of the bookstore. Maybe they finally got their heads out of their asses and have started carrying the Twisted Sisters' books. I just finished reading about the Elysian Mate Bond in *Zodiac Academy: Cursed Fates*. I've got to know what happens next.

As I enter the bookstore it feels like I'm coming home. I can smell the books mixed with aromas coming from the coffee shop next door. I wander the familiar aisles until I get to the best section, Fantasy. I don't see what I'm looking for on the tables of new releases so I change the direction of my hunt and head to the P section. I fervently skim the shelves hoping that my eyes are mistaken. Sadly, yet again, my favorite series is nowhere to be found. I hope this isn't a bad omen for how the entire evening will work out.

I continue wandering the aisles waiting for Brock to show up. It's a shame that big brand stores don't realize the level of magic that independent authors can create. The Twisted Sisters are proof of how impactful one, or two, persons' stories can be to thousands of others. Feral is probably the best word to describe me when I get one of their newly published books in my hands. I forget about schoolwork, and I barely remember to make it to work when I'm devouring those pages.

I browse the shelves looking for my next read. I know you're not supposed to, but I judge books by their covers. If the author chose artwork that doesn't hit right, it's a warning that the content between the covers won't be what I'm looking for. As I take random books off the shelves and read their jackets, the hairs on my neck go up and I feel as if someone is watching me. I put the book I'm holding back slowly and turn around to find Brock leaning on a shelf down the way, staring directly at me.

He licks his lips, "I had you pegged as a romance reader."

I take my hand off the shelf. "What made you think that?"

He pushes off the shelf and stands straight as he strolls toward me. "Don't all pretty girls want a guy to come sweep them off their feet?"

Did this motherfucker just say that? "No, we don't. Most of the time we prefer the morally grey character to murder the assuming and pretentious first love interest. After that, the best books have a heroine who learns to kick ass and never again wants a man to defend her."

"Well baby, my morals are all sorts of grey." He states as if that's something to brag over and slings his arm over my shoulder guiding me toward the front of the store.

I duck and twist out of his arm and scold him, "I'm not your baby, and this isn't a fantasy novel. In real life either your morals are on point, or your dick won't be attached to your body by the end of the evening."

Brock tucks his hands into his pocket and leads the way through the parking lot. "I like this version of you Nikki. Feisty. It's a lot more fun than the demure student facade you try to get others to believe in class."

I use my best mocking voice in reply, "I'm surprised you knew how to use those words correctly in a sentence."

This only serves to rile him up more. *Fuck, I'm gonna have to check my attitude. It appears it's feeding his douchebaggery.* He clicks his key fob and opens the door to his truck for me. I climb up and wait for him to walk around. I've got to keep my cool. This night has only begun and I have a feeling I've only seen snippets of the prick that Brock truly is on the inside.

He drives out to Coronado Island for dinner. It's only a twenty-minute journey and Brock puts on some decent music for its duration. Unfortunately, he is stuck in his middle school locker room phase, because his truck reeks of excessively applied body spray. My nose is overwhelmed by the scent inside the cab of his truck, but I can't turn back. As I sit there in silence, wondering why I let him drive me to the restaurant, I manage to find a bright side. From what I can tell, he didn't cut anyone off on the freeway. That's how much I lowered the bar of my expectations for this evening. He is getting points for basic driving etiquette.

Brock pulls up to a restaurant named Steaks and Chops. I guess the owners weren't feeling particularly creative with their naming that day. The name isn't the worst part of this situation though, it's that I don't like steak.

We get out of the car and walk to the entrance. As soon as the doors open I'm assaulted with the odor of red meat and beer. The walls are adorned with taxidermied wildlife. There are chandeliers made out of antlers above the tables. The wait staff are all wearing jeans, plaid, and cowboy boots.

Did I die on the drive over and wake up in Hell? This place is the closest I've been to fiery pits of torture outside of my dreams. Brock doesn't notice my abject horror and walks up to the hostess, letting her know we need a table for two.

My shoes stick to the ground as we're taken to the back of the restaurant. Brock sits in the booth with his back to a wall, leaving me seated opposite with an open restaurant to my back. I'm used to sitting where I don't want coming from a family of 4, but it would have been nice for my date to have considered my preference.

The hostess tries to give us our menus but Brock cuts her off, "We won't be needing those."

"Oh, okay Sir. I'll let your waitress know you're ready to order." She hastily replies and walks away swiftly.

I'm tired of this macho bullshit. I cross my arms and my tone follows suit, "I thought we were going to Mediterranean food?"

"Changed my mind," is the only answer I'm given.

"Thanks for the heads up," I deadpan. "Why don't I get a menu?"

Brock leans back arrogantly in the booth. "Because baby, I know all the good options on the menu already."

"What if I'd wanted to make that decision for myself?" I demand.

His shoulders move upward a fraction of an inch. "When you're out with me, you don't need to. I'll take care of you."

Does he think he's being chivalrous? "So, you must already know I don't eat red meat then?"

Brock looks genuinely surprised, but recovers his facial expressions quickly. "Don't tell me you're one of those hippy chicks that only eats vegetables like a rabbit."

I chuckle, "No, I'm not a vegetarian, but I still don't eat red meat. Rather, I don't eat steak."

"Ohhhh," he utters like he suddenly understands something. "You just haven't had this steak yet. Don't worry, it's the best. You'll like the steak here."

The waitress comes over before I have time to inform him he's wrong.

"Hi, my name's Christina and I'll—"

Brock interrupts our waitress, "We'll both be having the Filet Mignon, hers cooked medium, mine rare. She'll have sides of steamed broccoli and a side salad, and I'll take mashed potatoes and mac n' cheese. Also, she'll have a glass of the Pinot Noir. I'll take a beer, and keep 'em coming." He shoos her away with his hand.

Christina leaves as abruptly as she arrived. I can't blame her, I'd like to leave too. There's no way Will would have acted like that with wait staff. I mentally shake myself. I'm not on a date with Brock to be reminded of how wonderful Will is.

"That was really fucking rude Brock," I state.

He leans across the table. "Nikki, when are you going to realize I don't care what others think of me? Her presence was interrupting me getting to know you."

Awww, he wants to get to know me, I sarcastically comment to myself.

"So, let's start with the basics. Favorite color, band, food, and animal."

I hate small talk, but I don't want this guy to know all my deepest darkest thoughts, so I play nice. Anything to get back to my own car quickly. "Forest green, black and grey. Depends on the day. Ice Cream. Dolphin. Your turn."

He grins at my answers and replies, "Ice cream isn't a food. I like the color red, like my truck. I don't have a favorite band, but I prefer old-school country. We're eating my favorite food, steak, obviously. My favorite animal is a tiger."

"Ice cream is too a food, you eat it, don't you?" I jibe at him.

"Okay Nikki, guess I need to get specific with you. What is your favorite *meal* to eat? One that includes all major food groups?"

He's showing a minuscule amount of intelligence in how he's interacting with me. I want to get back to my car but I let this douchebag drive me here. I have to pretend to enjoy his company for just a little while longer. I ponder for a moment. "I love food, it's all so good. I don't like spice or red meat."

"Only because you haven't had the steak here before," Brock argues again.

I continue as if he hadn't, "I guess authentic Mexican food would have to be my favorite."

"You like Mexican food but you don't like spicy food?" he questions.

"There are plenty of Mexican dishes that don't have to be spicy. Just don't add hot sauce or too much salsa and you're golden," I explain.

Christina brings Brock his first beer and he downs it before she has even left our table. "I'll go grab you another then." She offers and departs.

"Feeling a little dehydrated?" I ask him sarcastically.

He puts the glass down with a thump and looks up at me. "Best beer in town, got to enjoy it when I trek this far out."

I nod my head and let him choose where the conversation travels from there.

Brock continues to ask me dull questions that provide information about me without actually getting to know me on a deeper level. I'm fine with that. I don't want him knowing me more than at surface level.

After a few more unbearable minutes, our food comes out, accompanied by another beer for Brock. I had forgotten that he ordered me a mooing steak, and sides that were entirely green. "Why do you get carb loaded sides and I'm forced to eat greens?" I ask once our waitress is out of earshot. It's not her fault I had a lapse in judgment and agreed to this date.

"Isn't it simple?" he asks me after downing his second beer.

I take a bite of salad because at least I can eat that without wanting to puke, "If it was simple I would have figured it out already."

"Debatable." He jabs, with all the arrogance of his douchebag existence. With a small slur to his speech he explains, "I figured you're watching your weight." Brock throws this out there with the same gravity as if discussing the color of the sky.

I put my fork down. "Is that so?" I ask him so calmly I'm sure it's hard for him to identify that I'm plotting his murder. Tipp is only a phone call away if I need help hiding his body.

Christina slides a third beer to our table. She turns and walks away without another word. I feel envious of her ability to get away from him and wish I had the same luxury right now.

He takes a swig followed by a bite of steak and replies while chewing his food, "I mean, yeah. It's gotta take effort to stay trim."

He didn't grasp that it was a rhetorical question. My first violent fantasy flits across my mind. If I use the steak knife sitting next to my plate and stab him in the junk would I end up wearing orange? A guy can't bleed out from a dick wound can he? I wonder if I could get a lawyer good enough to demand a female judge. Any woman would think I'm completely justified, right?

I think Christina can sense this is a doomed date, and she's returned to check on our meals. "How's everything tasting you two?" She asks cheerfully, with yet another beer grasped in her hands.

Brock reaches to take the beverage from her and with food in his mouth again Brock says, "It's grea—"

"Christina," I interject, "We need the check please. Two boxes as well."

"Oh, I'm sorry," she responds. "Is everything not to your liking Miss?"

I smile reassuringly at her, "I'm sure the steak would be great if I ate red meat. The only thing not to my liking is," I gesture to the barbarian across from me, "Well, my date."

Christina's eyes pop with shock at my blatant honesty. "I see, I'll be right back." She rushes off to gather the items I've asked for.

Brock has finished chewing, his plate is almost empty already. He places his silverware down and wipes his mouth with the back of his hand. With a pointer finger indicating at me, he seethes, "You see here Nikki, I don't—"

His anger would probably be more intimidating if he wasn't blotchy in the face from all the beer he's downed in a mere matter of minutes. I roll my shoulders back and put him in his place. "Brock shut up. I thought I could give you a chance and see if you weren't so bad one-on-one. I was wrong."

"I—" he tries.

"I'm not done yet. Thank you for taking me out to eat. We are never going to be compatible." I pull out my wallet and hand him twenty bucks. "I have no idea how much my food was because you didn't let me see the menu, so here's a twenty to cover the salad I ate. You can enjoy eating the rest of my meal for me, because I have no interest in keeping my leftovers. Are you going to let me drive us back to my car or do I need to call someone? There is no way in Hell I'm letting you drive me while you're drunk." I put out my hand asking for his keys indicating how ready I am to take this situation into my own control.

He sighs and mumbles, "Nikki, wait. Keep your cash. Put your phone away please. I'll, I'll take you back to your car alright?" He gets out his wallet and puts a hundred on the table. "Fuck the leftovers, let's just get out of here." He downs the last of his beer and puts his keys in my outstretched hand.

I don't feel physically threatened by him. He's only been a jerk, but never close to physically abusive, so I think I'll be safe driving back to my car with him.

Brock tries to get out of our booth but stumbles a little. Once he's regained his footing he leads the way out. I connect eyes with our waitress on the way out. She mouths, "Want me to call someone?" while holding her thumb and pinky to the side of her head mimicking a phone. I grin at her and shake my head. Just before I exit the door I sign, *"Thank you,"* to her with my limited knowledge of ASL.

Brock opens the door again for me and I climb into the red truck silently. I start the engine as Brock tunes the radio to a country station. "Honky Tonk Badonkadonk" begins serenading us through the speakers. I know technically it's only Y2K, but something about the way Trace Adkins' voice resonates makes me think it's more old school.

I can't help but smile. What a comical ending to this miserable date. Brock looks over at me as the chorus starts up. I start laughing and we're lost to the hilarity of the situation. We both start singing along with Trace and Brock turns up the music. The four minutes of the song are the best I've spent in Brock's presence. At least I'm no longer worried about him changing his mind and taking revenge about me embarrassing him at the restaurant before arriving at my car.

When the song ends he turns the volume back down and we listen to a few more songs in companionable silence while I navigate the Southern California freeways.

We pass billboards and SDSU on our way. I begin to daydream about how my life would be different if I could have afforded attending a four-year university right out of high school. That's where all my friends ended up. My options were different. I could have ended up one hundred thousand dollars in debt at twenty-two, or I could pay my way at community college by living with Nana and working a full-time job on the side. I'm lost in the daydream of how life would be simpler if my financial circumstances were different. They're not though. At least I have the opportunity to attend college, right? For some people that's as much a dream as attending a four year, pledging a sorority, and getting to live on campus is to me.

I pull Brock's truck into the bookstore parking lot. He doesn't know what I drive and after this date I think I'll keep it that way. I park in the back where there are multiple open spaces to accommodate his truck. I kill the engine and hop out of the vehicle. I don't care if he's going to drive or hop in the back and sober up. All I want is to be done with this evening.

We meet at the end of his truck bed and he starts, "Nikki, wait."

I hesitantly do as he asks. "Brock, I think we both know that was an especially horrible date for both of us."

He rubs the back of his neck like he's nervous. "I know, there's just one more thing I need to know before you leave tonight though."

I'm curious so I bite. "Okay, what's up?"

Without saying another word Brock's hand moves toward me, across the open air between us. I'm watching it approach my body in slow motion but I must be stunned because my reflexes don't work. My eyes follow the trajectory of his outstretched fingers. By the time my brain comprehends where his hand is going, it's too late. He reaches my breast and squeezes it. My jaw drops open and I stand there a silent, horrified, idiot. He gives my breast a second squeeze and retracts his hand from my incredibly invaded personal bubble.

"Thanks, Nikki, I needed to see if they were real before I lost my chance," Brock says by way of explanation.

He walks past me and gets into his truck. I'm still standing there stunned as he pulls through the space and drives off. I stay rooted there in the empty parking space allowing my neurons to catch up with what just happened. Douchebag Brock is indeed a douchebag. No nice guy is hiding in there. He just grabbed my breast to check if it was real. *What the fuck?*

Eleven

True Friends

SLEEP EVADES ME ALL night. I try to shower off the feeling of his fingers on my body but it doesn't help. I lay in my bed staring up at the blank ceiling as my mind relives what I've tried to suppress for so long.

I thought driving Brock's truck back to my car would be fine. He didn't seem dangerous. I should have known better. I don't know why I gave him the opportunity to show me exactly how horrible a person he was. I know it was only a tit grab, but it's bringing back what my ex did to me almost a year ago.

The ghost of Brock's hand reminds me of how Turner's felt against my body. If I close my eyes it's like I'm reliving that night all over again. Tipp doesn't even know he assaulted me. I survived, but don't like the term survivor. I never filed charges because I shouldn't have put myself in that situation. He was my boyfriend. I trusted him. He betrayed my trust. Simple as that.

I roll over and try to find a comfortable position but when I close my eyes, I remember the night I went straight to the shower with all my clothes on. I sat and cried for what felt like hours. When the water turned cold I stood up, undressed, and robotically cleaned myself off. My body didn't seem like my own.

My ex had defiled me. It took months for me to be able to look at myself naked in the mirror again. Whenever I tried, I could feel his hands on my body. I could feel his mouth grazing my skin. I'll never forget the noises he made when I woke up to discover what he was doing to me.

I know Brock only felt me up. It was one breast. Two squeezes. Just his hand. So why was this bringing up my past? Why did his violation of my physical space bring back the memories of my ex? Why didn't I move over to the bar and get Tipp to pick me up? Even Stefan would have been a better alternative than getting in Brock's car.

Brock isn't Turner. Brock isn't Turner. Brock isn't Turner, becomes my new mantra. I need to remember that. What those two did to me were entirely different acts. However, when I close my eyes, their hands blur together in my memory.

Turner is my ex. He assaulted me because I upset him over something small one night. When he sobered up the next morning he came over and tried to convince me he didn't mean it, it wasn't his fault. He's why I don't tell anyone where I live. He's why I can't say I love you to anyone else. He's my most shameful secret. Why is Brock bleeding into those memories?

Gods, I am such an idiot.

I manage to work my weekend shifts in robot mode. There is no joy to experience. It doesn't matter how nice or rude customers are, I am numb to everything around me.

At home, Nana asks if I am doing okay when she sees me, but there's no way I can tell her what happened. I don't want to relive it by telling her, and I don't want to see the pity in her eyes that would inevitably come if I divulge the truth. I tell her I'm feeling off and leave it at that. Not a complete lie, and nowhere near the truth.

At school I go through the motions. I can't bring myself to answer any questions posed by professors, and I don't engage in small talk with peers. I don't like small talk anyway, but I really don't have the energy to pretend with anyone right now.

When I show up to French on Tuesday I sit down in my usual seat and wait for Tipp. She's not going to let me off easy. It's too apparent there's something majorly wrong, and I can't bullshit her because she's the best bullshitter I know.

"Babe, where you been?" Tipp asks cheerfully from behind me.

I don't turn around, I give her a shrug of the shoulder and shake my head.

I hear her movement pause behind me. "Nikki, what's wrong?"

She knows me that well. I remain facing forward with my head hung low.

Tipp walks in front of me and freezes as soon as she sees the look in my eyes. "Veronica Anne Welch."

Fuck, she middle named me. I look up at her with my solemn face.

Tipp immediately takes my hand and pulls me out of my seat. Once we're outside, she takes me to a bench down the breezeway. How can my best friend know so well that this isn't a conversation for listening ears?

"Nikki, what's wrong? You look like you haven't slept in days."

"Well, you're not entirely wrong. I fall asleep, but it's not peaceful," I whisper as tears leak from my eyes.

Tipp leans in and gives me a hug. She's tiny, but she gives a solid embrace. After a few seconds I relent and hug her back. Then the tears start to freely flow. She holds me as my sobs get harder. I'm practiced at silent crying this far into my life. I never wanted to wake my family members in high school when I would cry myself to sleep over stupid shit. Gods, how I wish my high school problems were my problems today. I may be sobbing quietly, but my body is visibly shaking.

Once Tipp's shoulder is drenched with my tears and my breathing calms down I pull back. I have no doubt that my eyeliner is streaked down my cheeks but best friends have to love you even when you're a snot covered mess.

I sniffle right in her face. Tipp gives me a resigned grin and pats my leg with her hand. "Come on babe, let's get you cleaned up."

I follow her to the bathroom and am not surprised at the reflection I see staring back at me. I start the process of rubbing off the evidence of my tears, ruined foundation included. Guess the rest of today will be spent fresh-faced.

"Okay babe," Tipp begins while leaning up against the bathroom sink. "Who the fuck do I need to castrate?"

I give her the first smile I've had since Friday. "Me."

"Bullshit, someone did something to make you feel like this. I want details. Now."

I stare at my hands uncomfortably, take a deep breath, and tell her everything. Tipp listens intently as I tell her about my ex and what he did to me. She holds my hand when I get nervous telling her about Friday night with Brock. When I've wrapped up all the details, she starts cracking her knuckles.

"I'll hold, you punch?" Is her only response.

I shake my head. "I shouldn't have let myself be in a situation like that, it's my fault."

"No, it's fucking not!" She practically screams at me.

I flinch back.

"Shit, I'm sorry," she says as she sees me physically recoil from her. "Okay, what do you need from me? How do we move forward?"

I turn and stare at my reflection in the mirror. With her support instead of judgment, I can look at myself and feel a little less shame. "I just want this all to be behind me."

Tipp doesn't like that, "You do understand what he did to you is considered sexual assault in California, right?"

I turn away from her and decide to wash my hands. They're not dirty but it gives me something to focus on other than her pissed off face. "Yes," I admit begrudgingly.

"Do you plan on pressing charges?"

I turn the faucet off and walk over to the paper towels. Tipp waits for my reply.

"To what avail?" I begin, "You know how it would work out, the jury would ask what I was wearing, they'd blame me for getting in his car, and somehow justify what he did to me because of how I hurt his feelings at the restaurant. If by some slim chance that isn't how they process it, I'm sure his Daddy would be able to pay someone off and he wouldn't have any consequences."

Tipp wants to say something but I cut over her, "If, *if*, that didn't happen, it would get out somehow. I don't want the whole campus to know what he put me through. It was bad enough having to tell you all the details. I don't want to go through that over and over again with strangers listening, judging, and making assumptions about me, okay?" My voice is strained by the time I'm done blasting her with all my pent up thoughts from the last few days.

I can see that Tipp doesn't like what I'm saying, but she also understands. She nods her head. "Fine, so how do you want me to support you?"

"Honestly, I don't know. How about when I figure it out I'll let you know, and for now you can keep being my friend," I offer.

"Bitch, that's never going to change."

"Good, but we're like fifteen minutes late for class right now," I remind her.

"You think you're ready to go back?" Tipp arches an eyebrow at me and holds open the bathroom door for me.

I nod my head and lead the way.

When we get back to the classroom, Madame Krasse gives us a look while continuing on with her lesson. Tipp and I go immediately to our seats and settle into our work quickly. The class is engaging and challenging enough to keep my mind focused for the rest of the session.

As Tipp and I exit the room, I realize I'm going to have to see Brock in a matter of hours. I recently finished spilling my deepest darkest secrets to Tipp. I don't owe anything to Stefan, but I feel as if he'll want to know too. I've brushed off eating lunch with him for too many days now. If I want to build a friendship with him I'm going to have to start reciprocating. I hug Tipp goodbye and tell her I'll be fine dealing with Brock tonight. She doesn't want to leave me, but she has work to get to. It's time to hold my chin up high. I know I fucked up. I put myself in that situation. I can accept my past faults and make sure they never happen to me again.

As I walk to the Griffin Center and approach our regular table I hear a familiar voice call out, "Nik!"

I turn and a genuine smile spreads across my face as I see Will and Stefan walking toward me.

"Hey guys," I greet them with a small wave.

"You've decided we're worthy of your presence again!" Stefan teases.

"Not really," I laugh. "I was minding my own business getting some lunner. You two were definitely stalking me."

Will meets my gaze with a shy grin. "Caught us red handed there Nikki. We've been secretly pining for your company. It's the only *logical* conclusion since our last conversation."

My cheeks immediately flush. I put my bag down at our table seizing the opportunity to avoid answering and ask the boys, "What will you be getting for dinner?"

"A sub." They say in unison.

"That doesn't seem suspicious at all," I accuse while narrowing my eyes at them.

They shrug, put their bags down, and walk off to get their meal. I take a deep breath and steady myself. I can get through a meal with them. They'll tease me, I'll take it, everything will be fine.

Unsurprisingly, it's not fine, and neither am I. Will and Stefan continue their light mocking while I eat, and sometime halfway through my meal I stop replying to their comments. My food goes from tasting delicious for the first time in days, back to bland. Stefan and Will seem to catch on by the time I finish eating.

Once I returned from tossing out my trash Will speaks up, "Hey Nikki, I'm sorry if we upset you—"

"I'm not," Stefan states like a petulant child.

"Yes we are," Will scolds him. "What I was trying to say, before Stefan reminded me what a dick he can be, is sorry if we pushed you too far. We're messing with you and don't mean to hurt your feelings."

I look up from my hands with tears in my eyes. It doesn't count as crying if they never spill over.

Will looks horrified. "Fuck, Nikki. I'm sorry. We didn't mean it."

I swallow, "No, it's not you two. I've been dealing with some shit these last few days. Tipp helped me finally process it, but that doesn't mean I'm over it."

Stefan leans forward, transitioning into a man who looks like he cares. He leans his forearms on the table and stares at me with intent. "You wanna talk about it?"

"Not really," I admit. "I'm afraid if I don't tell you about it now it will get worse in class, though."

This piques their interest.

"You know Brock?"

Stefan is immediately on alert. "Nik, what did he do?"

"I may have had a lapse in judgment after class last week. You know how you were pissed at me for breaking things off with Will." I look Will's direction. "Sorry about that." I continue on. "Brock asked me out."

"And you said no," Stefan states because there is no other sensible option to that question.

"Not quite," I admit reluctantly, while twisting my hands nervously under the table.

Stefan gives me a mocking smirk. "Let me guess, it went terrible and now you're embarrassed to have to see him again?"

I look from Stefan to Will again. "Not quite." I repeat. I feel more confident telling them the truth when I look into Will's eyes. He's not jumping to conclusions or forming opinions without all the details. He's listening. Intently.

Stefan's smirk fades. "What else?" His voice turns icey.

I look to the ceiling, take a steadying breath and make sure no one around us is listening in. When I'm certain our conversation is as private as it can be in a room filled with college students mingling and eating their own meals, I tell the guys, "Technically, he assaulted me Friday night."

They both freeze where they are. I give them some time to process and then ask, "Stefan, I know our friendship is new, but can you not leave me alone in Astronomy this semester? I just don't want him to have the opportunity to be near me again but it's too late to unenroll from the class."

Stefan looks the most serious I've ever seen him. "Nikki, I won't let him within a hundred feet of you if that's what you want."

I feel immediate relief with his support. "That's okay, I just don't want to be alone in his presence again."

I look away from him and notice Will has sat quietly listening to everything without a word. He's clenching his jaw and both his hands are balled into fists.

Stefan notices his best friend too. "You good, man?" he asks and claps his friend on his shoulder. This seems to break Will from his trance.

He clears his throat, "Yeah. I mean no, but yeah." Will looks to me, "You ever need anything let me know. I don't care that we didn't work out. No guy should ever treat you like that again. Especially not now that you're friends with us."

I'm astonished by his statement. "We're friends?"

"You're friends with Stefan, he's basically my brother. That means you and I are friends too," Will clarifies for me.

He stands without warning, picks up his bag, and turns from the table. "See you two later," he calls over his shoulder as he walks away.

"That was abrupt," I chuckle to Stefan.

He's still looking in his best friend's direction. His face seems puzzled. When he changes his focus to me he pastes on a smile and asks, "Ready for class?"

"No," I answer honestly. "Let's go."

The walk across campus ends too quickly and I pause at the top of the stairs leading down to our classroom. Stefan halts as well. He doesn't ask me any questions. He waits like a silent guard until I muster up my courage.

I take a tentative step forward. *One step at a time,* I tell myself. As we enter the cooler courtyard a light breeze grazes my cheeks and refreshes my self confidence. The trees calm my mind and encourage me to find my strength. Birds chatter somewhere above reminding me to find beauty in my surrounding environment. I look over to Stefan with newfound composure and lead the way to our classroom.

As we approach the door, I roll my shoulders back and steady myself. I enter the classroom prepared to show Brock that I'm not affected by his actions.

I look at his table. It's empty.

Stefan and I take our seats and wait for class to begin. Mr. Fitzgibbons enters the room and we hunker down with our tasks for the day. At some point Brock walks in late, but due to his lack of punctuality, he doesn't have an opportunity to interact with me. Thank the gods.

Stefan and I wrap up our work efficiently and turn it in a few minutes early. I see Brock working with his lab partner and my body fills with relief knowing he won't be able to get up and try to interact with me.

We pack up our class supplies and exit quietly while allowing others to finish their assignments.

As we head toward the stairs to leave the Science Complex, Stefan follows me instead of splintering off to go to his car.

"What are you doing?" I ask.

"I think I'll start parking in the structure on Tuesdays and Thursdays," is his bizarre response.

"Because?"

"You know why, Nik. I'm not letting anything happen to you. Brock won't be going anywhere near you. I'm going to make sure of it," Stefan informs me.

"Oh," I shyly utter, "Thanks."

"Don't mention it," he reassures me.

We walk to my car without feeling the need to fill the evening with chit-chat. I have nothing more to say. I wasn't expecting Stefan and Will to be so supportive of my mistake. It may have been a shit weekend, but maybe with some time, and these new found friends, I'll be able to move forward from what Brock did to me.

As I drive home that night I put on some light music. I'm not better but I have hope. Some day in the future, I'll be back to my wonderful, fabulous self.

Twelve

Self Healing

CLASSES WITH STEFAN AND Tipp help me feel better sometimes, but the hardest moments are when I am left alone. In the silence of my car or bedroom is when I struggle the most. It's been almost two weeks since that night and every day comes with one struggle or another.

Basic tasks are challenging right now. I eat because I know that food is required to sustain my body. I drink water to replenish the constant river of tears leaking from my eyes. I haven't worked out since before that Friday night. Luckily, Nana has gone out of town again so I'm able to wallow around the house without worrying her.

Turner raped me. Brock assaulted me. There's a difference.

I go to work. I drive home. I go to sleep. I dream of Brock or Turner. I go to classes. I drive home. I go to sleep. I dream of Turner or Brock.

I wake every morning feeling more tired than the night before. My sleep is restless and I can't escape the demons of my past.

It's a vicious loop I can't break through.

Brock assaulted me. Turner raped me. It doesn't feel like there's a difference.

No matter what, I know I don't want to pursue legal action. Everyone would find out. I don't want to bring further light to my shameful decisions.

Nana will be back this weekend so it's time for a final emotional breakdown. I'll give myself until then to process everything. I can call in sick. My hair can get greasy. I can lie in bed all day and watch movies to numb my feelings. When she gets back I'll work on adapting to life and what it has become.

I decide that Thursday is going to be a mental health ditch day. I text Tipp and Stefan so they don't worry and then turn my phone off.

I plan to sleep in as late as I want on Thursday.

Turns out my body has become accustomed to waking early and I only manage to stay in bed until eight a.m.

I eat a decadent breakfast of buttered toast and then prepare for my day.

I make sure Otis has everything he needs and seclude myself from the world.

Chick flicks would just add insult to injury, so I put in the best action movies I can find. Their quick plot and flashy imagery keep my mind occupied for a couple hours. Eventually, I run out of movies to numb my brain with. That means it's time to force myself to ugly cry. I find the saddest movie I've ever seen, grab a box of tissues, and prepare.

The opening credits for *Marley and Me* appear on the screen.

I snuggle under my cozy blanket with some freshly popped popcorn and wish that I had someone I could trust by my side. I think back to that hug Will gave me so long ago, I bet he's a wonderful cuddler, especially during movie marathons. I sigh remembering that I burned that bridge and ended up on a date with Douchebag Brock instead. One of the biggest regrets of my life right there.

I click play and within five minutes I'm crying. Those silent tears from last week are long gone. Why would anyone write such a sad movie? Dogs are the epitome of pure love on our planet and Marley was such a good boy. I let myself feel everything that's been plaguing me for the last fourteen days. Marley makes sure I keep feeling it— for two fucking hours.

By the time I'm done laughing and sobbing, sometimes simultaneously, I have a headache. I've exposed my raw emotions to the living room. There's a pile of used tissues strewn about in chaos. I laugh as I realize if someone stumbled into this room without context they'd think a teenage boy had been jerking off in here. The popcorn was tipped over at some point during the movie. I scared Otis away with one of my larger sobs.

"That's it," I announce to the house. "I'm done. Those boys fucked up. They fucked me up. And now I'm moving on... Maybe after a shower and a nap."

I let Turner take my innocence. I won't let Brock take any more than the two weeks of processing I needed.

When Nana returns on Saturday she notices I'm a little different.

"You okay sweetie?" She asks at dinner that weekend. "You look a little haunted."

I smile at her and admit, "I felt sick for a good portion of your trip. I didn't eat that much, but I think I'm doing better now."

It's not a lie I rationalize, just an omission of the larger truth.

"I'm glad you're feeling better. How's the semester going?"she asks earnestly.

I catch her up on the relevant details and we have an amiable dinner. She regales me with tales about my cousins and how they're doing in school. It's good to have her home. I think her presence is keeping me grounded in moving past those douchebags and finding my joy again.

On Sunday I go to work and decide I will focus on the positives of life and how to function. There are times when thoughts of Turner and Brock try to creep back into my mind, but I'm choosing to focus on the positives in my surroundings.

In the sandwich shop when I feel the phantom touch of one of their hands, I shake my head and think about the rhythmic chopping of the tomatoes in the slicer in front of me.

When one of my customers has a similar appearance to one of the douchebags, I notice how perfectly four slices of Swiss cheese fits on the sub in front of me.

On Monday, when a truck on the freeway cuts me off on the way to campus and attempts to upset my delicate state of mind, I focus on the feeling of the pebbled steering wheel under my fingers and listen to the wind blowing through my open car windows.

In French, Tipp doesn't bother to ask if I'm doing okay. I appreciate that she knows that I would lie to her. Instead, she brings some of The Goods and we share them like the naughty treat smugglers we are. Madame Krasse begins our lesson on time and I'm so thankful for my Hermione-like characteristics. My internal drive to be a studious student who knows the answer keeps me focused on the work and I don't have to play defense against my brain for over an hour.

On Tuesday, I meet up for lunner with Stefan and Will. They're both smiling as I walk up to our usual table. They look like they're up to something.

Will pulls a sandwich from behind his back and gives it to me. "We know you've been having a rough time, so we decided to buy you lunch."

"Oh how sweet of you," I reply dryly as I take the sub from his hand.

I join them at the table and debate whether or not I want to eat the free food. I already had my sub for the day when I left work, but I don't want to hurt their feelings by rejecting this food. "What kind did you get?" I ask.

"Open it and find out," Stefan cryptically replies.

I pick up the sandwich and realize the bag feels strange. I've wrapped hundreds of subs by this point in my temporary sandwich artist career and this one feels way too lumpy to be made well.

"What happened to it?" My suspicions are growing larger now.

"Will you please just open it?" Will asks me with too large a smile on his face to be innocent.

I look from him to the sandwich. After a few seconds of hesitation, I decide if I open it and it's inedible, I can come up with an excuse to not eat it. I flip it over and undo the tape keeping it together. As I start unrolling it, the guys' grins grow. Suddenly, it breaks in half, and then into thirds. What the Hell is wrong with this sandwich? When there's only one layer left wrapping the "sandwich" I almost drop it. I pick up the last layer and see three rolled tacos. Then Will's grin transforms into a gorgeous smile and he pulls out a bag from his backpack. He gets out all the fixings for me: guacamole, sour cream, shredded cheese, and a side of rice and beans.

I'm not gonna cry, I'm not gonna cry, I'm not gonna cry, I repeat internally.

"You guys," my voice raises an octave. This was so sweet of them even if they presented it as a joke.

"Don't get all mushy on us Nik, eat your food," Stefan pushes.

I do exactly that. I'm still quieter than I would have been a month ago, but I enjoy Will and Stefan's presence. They're both helping bring me back to my usual self and I appreciate it more than they'll ever know.

We finish our meals and Stefan and I get up to head out to Astronomy. Before we leave, Will stands too.

"Nikki," he begins. "It was nice to see you smile today."

Of course that makes me grin again.

Will continues, "I hope with time, and better guys in your life, your beautiful smile will become a more permanent part of your existence."

That makes me blush. "Thanks Will, have a great night." I give him a small wave goodbye and turn to go across campus with Stefan.

I don't say a word on our stroll. My mind is fixated on what Will said. He likes my smile. He likes seeing me smiling. He's noticed it has been missing for a while. That warms my cold, dead, black heart. Even more, his horrible laugh hasn't surfaced since our one and only date. He must feel more at ease hanging out with me when Stefan is around too.

Stefan interrupts my train of thought, "You okay over there, space cadet?"

I blink a few times as my brain processes that he's talking to me. "Huh? Oh, yeah," I respond lamely.

"Right," Stefan draws out.

I don't give him anything by way of explanation. Our evening continues without a hitch, and Stefan stays true to his word by creating a physical barrier with his own body between Brock and me.

Thirteen

Reading Over His Shoulder

As THE DAYS GO on, I start feeling more and more like myself. I hunker down and catch up on my classes. It is rather startling how quickly I fell behind in only two weeks. I am fortunate that Tipp could predict the future and is prepared to help me catch up. She's made copies of her notes and study guides and hands them over as soon as I mention it. Stefan is also assisting my make up work by providing a copy of his detailed notes to help me study for our upcoming exam. I am incredibly lucky that there haven't been any exams during my two week mental hiatus.

Now, the week before Spring Break, professors are all going to be evaluating our academic progress through multiple-guess tests. My bedroom floor has transformed into a tsunami of index cards, open textbooks, and discarded note sheets. Otis has created a nest on the outskirts of the disaster zone of composition notebook paper. The senior, grey tabby cat monitors my progress through the various stacks for a few hours after my Saturday shift.

Tipp's been saying that she wants to stop by on her way to work today so we can catch up. Over the years of our friendship, she's

become accustomed to entering Nana's house through the Granny
Flat's private back door. I look up when I hear the clink of the latch
closing, signaling her arrival.

"Hey!" I shout to Tipp.

As she rounds the corner, I see her smile.

"You finally sound like you!" Tipp cries happily to me. "You're even
doing homework again!"

I grin at her as she enters my room. "I told you, I only needed some
time," I remind her.

"I know!" She shouts as she collides with me in a strong embrace.
"But it's finally true, you're back!"

"Jesus, Tipp, I was here all along, just processing some shit, not on
another planet!" I tease her.

She lets go of me, "Well I know, but it felt like you were. I was
worried."

I put my book down. "Moving on. I'm glad you were able to stop
by."

"Oh, why is that?" Tipp asks as she lays down on my bed. I'd tease
her about making herself at home, but at this point it's expected.

I steady myself. I really hope she's agreeable. "I may have, possibly,
just a lil' bit, fucked it up with Will," I finish with a grimace.

Tipp sits up, sensing the seriousness of this topic's direction, "Well
duh. How did you manage to finally figure it out on your own?"

"Oh fuck you!" I exclaim while grinning at her. "As I was processing
all the shit, my mind kept drifting off to him. Like when I told him
what Brock did he was *pissed* on my behalf. I don't think he's the kind
of guy that would ever intentionally hurt me." A heavy sigh blows
through my lips as I confide in my best friend. "Anyway, I fucked up.
I know that now but I don't know what to do about it."

"Well," she claps her hands together. "First thing's first. How do you know you're missing him, and not the idea of him?"

"Huh?" I scrunch up my nose in confusion.

"How do you know that Will is the specific person you want in your life, versus only wishing you had someone to get your yaw-yaws out with?"

"I'm ashamed to be considered your best friend. Yaw-yaws? We are two grown ass women," I chide her as I walk toward my night stand. I open the middle drawer and pull out my magnificent marbled black, white, and grey Belladix: the prettiest dildo you've ever seen. I point it at her as I explain, "It's called being horny Mom. And Belladix takes great care of those needs. Thank you very much," I finish with a flourish of the dildo and a sassy head tilt in her direction.

Tipp doesn't miss a beat. "I'll restate. Do you miss someone else giving you your orgasms, or is it actually Will you miss? You don't even know him that well, do you?"

She's right, but it feels like I know him on a deeper level, even after our failed first date. It's something about that sweet grin he always gives me. He's my friend but he's always noticing what I need. When he complimented my smile the other day, I nearly swooned on the spot. "I've been hanging out with him a little bit since that date. He's more at ease with Stefan around and I haven't heard that horrendous laugh since," I inform Tipp.

"That's it?" Tipp encourages me to continue.

My eyes roll as I refuse to look at her and admit, "You may have been onto something about me not wanting to get hurt again." I cross my arms and huff a breath waiting for her opinion. "You think I'm an idiot, don't you?"

"No more than usual," She jokes with me. Otis has left my note pile and is nuzzling Tipp on my bed. She scratches him behind his ears while simultaneously burning me.

"He seems like he'd give really good hugs, okay?" I blurt.

"Hugs being a substitution for…"

"Nothing, hugs being hugs. I want a fucking good hug again. He's big, and tall, and strong, and yummy. I just, I know he gives good hugs, and I want another one."

Tipp smirks at me and gets off the bed. "You had me until yummy." She approaches me and raises an eyebrow, "So what are you going to do about it?"

"I think you should tell me," I try.

"No."

"But—"

"No," Tipp repeats, crossing her arms as a visible barrier to my idea. I lean into her side like I do our friendship and she relents.

She opens up and draws me in. "I give good hugs too," she tells me.

"You're tiny, it's not the same." I laugh as she releases me and starts walking out of my room.

"Fine." I sigh,

Tipp walks toward the door. "Well babe, you gotta buck up and figure your shit out. I need to go if I'm going to make it to work on time." She turns to leave.

As Tipp rounds the back of the house to her car, I give a wave out my window.

Alright. I don't want to go back to the dating pool, but I would like to try again with Will. It's time to grow up and strategize a simple plan to get him to give me a second chance. That plan starts with getting Stefan on my side.

I sit in my corner chair and steady my nerves. This is going to be an awkward conversation.

> Hey dude, how's it going?

His reply chimes through almost instantly.

> Good. You haven't texted me in a while. What's up?

I roll my neck hoping to release some tension before typing.

> Straight to the point… I have a question for you.

> And?

I read his message and decide to bite the bullet. Nothing ventured, nothing gained is that old saying. I think.

> Do you think there's any way that Will would give me a second chance?

I hit send and wait. Otis jumps onto my desk and head butts my shoulder, asking me for pets. I pull him into my lap without taking my eyes off the screen. My phone vibrates in my hand. The screen illuminates and I feel a pit open in my stomach as I look at Stefan's response.

> I don't know Nik. You friend zoned him pretty effectively.

I groan to Otis as I'm forced to admit my mistake to Stefan.

> I know. I fucked up. What can I do to make it right?

> It was pretty savage. You're probably going to have to show him that you mean it.

A deep breath of relief fills my lungs. He didn't say there's no chance in winning Will back. There may be some hope still.

> Any recommendations?

"He didn't completely shut me down," I inform Otis. He meows in agreement and nudges my hand to keep petting him. I listen to his soothing purrs as I wait for another message from Stefan.

> I'm not going to do the work for you but I'll help you find the time and you can figure it out for yourself.

I scratch my ear as I try to decipher his message. I finally ask him:

> What does that mean?

> I might know that a group of us are going out to sushi on Friday, and now you're invited. The rest is up to you.

A smile blossoms across my face at this opportunity.

> Oh. Okay. Thanks! When and where?

> Friday before break, send me your address, I'll pick you up.

That causes me to pause. Not many people know where I live and I prefer it that way. If they can't find me, they can't follow me. Not like Turner.

> I can just meet you there.

> You could, or you can ride there with Will and me. Thought this would give you two more time with me as a nervous laugh buffer.

Crap, he's right. Will is more comfortable when Stefan is around. "Okay." I talk it through with Otis, "The reason that I want a second chance with Will is because I know he's a good guy right?"

"Meow," Otis replies, confirming I'm right.

"I can trust them with where we live, right?"

Silence. Of course Otis would chose this moment to be quiet. Why is everyone forcing me to make decisions right now? I reconsider my phone and type out:

> I'll send you my address day of. What time?

I still have time to back out if I want, and Stefan doesn't need to know where I live until I know I'm comfortable with it. Maybe I should ask if Tipp can come along for emotional support. As that thought crosses my mind, I realize it would be a little desperate of me. Well, best friends get to know all the dark details about you right? I open up my conversation thread with Tipp.

> Hey love, you free next Friday night?

I know she's driving to work and will get back to me later. My phone dings and I see it's from Stefan.

> Let's do 6pm.

> Sounds good. See you in class!

I pick up Otis and let him know that I need to resume my homework if I have any shot at catching up. When did we start learning about the solar and lunar eclipses? Apparently in French we've also moved on to ordering food at a restaurant? *Je suis baisée. I'm screwed.*

The time passes slowly as I study. I hear my phone go off from across the room. I extract myself from my piles of books and notes to see who dares contact me in such a tumultuous situation.

Tipp's name is shining on my screen with her response.

> Sorry babe, picked up a double.

"Shit," I say to myself. Looks like I do have to figure things out on my own this time around. Yay me.

> No worries, I'll figure it out.

She has no idea what I'll be figuring out. I'll fill her in on the details of Stefan and my conversation when I see her next. For the time being, I've got to make ordering restaurant food my bitch if I'm going to pass French this term. "L'addition s'il vous plaît'," I practice to the cat. At least he's always here for me.

With exams plaguing everyone, the week before break passes quickly. We're all either studying or worrying about how we did on the test we just finished. I swear the campus gets noticeably smellier from people stress sweating. I did what I could for my exams. It is in the hands of Karma now.

After the shit I've been living through this last month, I'm excited for tonight. I made it to a morning session at the gym. Now I'm busy filling the day with chores and errands to keep the panic about hanging out with Stefan and Will tonight at bay. Following a trip to Petco to get new toys for Otis, a car wash, a quick lunch at a panini shop, and a pointless walk through Parkway Center, I decide to head home. I've got a few more hours to kill, so I decide to catch up on some detective shows with Nana. While fast forwarding through commercials and snack breaks, we chat about life.

"How's your term going?" Nana asks.

She doesn't know about any of the assault problems I've been dealing with, so my answer remains vague. "Pretty good, Tipp has been great in helping me with French and I made a new friend in Astronomy. I'm actually going out with him tonight."

Her interest piques with the word him. "A boy?" Nana asks.

"Yes, but Stefan is just a friend. He has a girlfriend and he's way too pompous for me to ever be interested in him," I explain.

Nana grins at me. "What will you be up to tonight?"

I smile back. She's so sweet and easy to chat with. "We're going out to sushi with a group of his friends. He'll be picking me up in a couple hours actually."

"That will be fun," Nana responds. "Remember, you can always have people over here if you want."

"I know, Nana. If tonight goes well, then maybe I will have some people over, but for now my social circle is almost entirely comprised of Tipp."

"Well let's see what went on in Chicago last week, shall we?" She asks as she uses the remote to select the next show for us. Who knew that my Nana would love watching firefighter and cop shows?

When our episode ends, I excuse myself to get ready for tonight. Nana waves me off and wishes me well as I leave the room. I need to figure out the perfect outfit that communicates I'm sorry, I fucked up, and you should give me a second chance. No pressure, right?

Fourteen

Sushi and Twister, an Uncommon Pairing

As the most recent country hits play on the radio in the background, I get primped for tonight. A good song can always soothe the soul, and my anxious self needs that calming effect right now. I analyze tonight's plans and decide on a half back hairdo so that my locks don't get in the way of eating dinner. My bangs are down and I have my traditional makeup on. Some people think I go too heavy on the eyeshadow, but those people apparently aren't meant to be in my life. To whoever thinks that it's deceiving for girls to wear makeup, do you honestly think that the skin above my eyes sparkles and is a different color than the rest of my body?

The toughest choice for tonight is an outfit. The fabrics that I chose have to communicate the perfect message to Will. I'm sorry. I know I messed up. We should try again. I'm rather adorable, don't you think? Unfortunately, I've never encountered a print that adequately communicates all of those things at once.

I stare at my closet, knowing the time is ticking down and Stefan will be here any minute. I have so many choices but nothing seems quite right.

I grab my favorite pair of jeans. They're black, and technically jeggings, but they look great. Ever since the skinny jean movement came around, I've loved it. I cuff the bottom of the pants up by two rolls because my proportions look better when I do. Now for the shirt. It's still Spring in Southern California so it will probably get chilly after dinner. Guess that's what Will's jacket is for because I need to focus on looking my best, not being weighed down by layers. I settle on a one-inch strap tank top. It has green and white vertical stripes with little daisies popping up all over it. The top tapers in at my waist accentuating my fabulous rack without overdoing it. I finish off the look with some light brown wedges and admire my ensemble in the mirror.

"Pretty damn cute, if I do say so myself," I compliment my reflection.

I glance back at the clock and see that Stefan should be rolling up any second now. I head out to the living room to say goodbye to Nana.

"You look adorable," she compliments me as I walk in the room.

"Thanks!" I reply with a full smile.

Nana hugs me goodbye. "Have fun tonight sweetheart," she says and gives me a kiss on the cheek.

I hug her back and head to the front of the house. My timing is perfect because once I've crossed the 3,000 square foot house I see Stefan's headlights headed down the driveway. I exit, lock the door behind me, and turn around to see he's not alone in his SUV.

I walk down the drive toward his car and motion for him to stop. I approach the driver's side window as it rolls down. Stefan is driving, Will's in the passenger seat, and some girl I don't know is in the backseat.

"Hop in." Stefan points to the seat behind him.

I move around to the back door and get in.

"Hey," I say to the car at large.

Will turns around and makes introductions. "Nikki, this is Mia."

Mia, who is Mia? "Hey Mia, how do you know the guys?" I ask. I mean it as small talk, but it's possible my tone has come across as an interrogation.

She shakes my hand as she answers, "Oh we go way back." She smiles at me. "I just got back to town and wanted to catch up with them, so Will invited me along tonight!"

Fuck, this is not good. Mia is chipper, and cute, and peppy, and well— drop-dead gorgeous. She's slender with fair complexion and straight, dark hair. Her lips form a natural pout that looks irresistible to kiss. Worst of all, Will invited her. However, he's not driving her separately, and they're not seated next to each other. Logically speaking if they were seriously into one another he'd want alone time with her, not to have Stefan along as a third wheel. So, maybe I've still got a chance. *What the hell is Stefan up to telling me this would be a good time to tell Will I know I messed up?*

Play it cool, I tell myself. "Glad to have you along," I say to Mia as if having her along doesn't ruin my plans.

Mia and Will begin a conversation about something someone said in a random class, but I don't really listen. I'm too busy staring at Stefan through the rear view mirror. If looks could kill he would be dead, and probably all of us along with him because he's driving, but still. When he glances at the mirror he sees my expression, he grins at me. Fucking grins. This confirms it, he knew this was a setup. I thought these guys were nice why? Boy was I wrong. I am going to have to get creative tonight apparently.

I sit in the back half listening to Mia and Will talk, responding with the appropriate "Ohs," and, "No ways," half heartedly.

Stefan pulls into a crowded parking lot. In Southern California it always seems that too many people are opening too many shops all in the same crammed strip malls. This particular shopping center has over twenty businesses packed around a grocery store. Stefan circles a few times before happening across another car backing out of a parking spot. His SUV barely fits and we all have to squeeze carefully out of our doors to make sure we don't hit the cars on either side of us. Moments like this make me glad I drive a Beetle. She always fits in these tight spaces.

We all meet at the trunk of the car and I have the opportunity to secretly observe Mia and how gorgeous she truly is. She's got a perfect petite body. I'm five foot seven inches, not a petite part to my body.

No sooner has the thought cleared my mind than Stefan walks up and puts his arm around her shoulders. I tilt my head to the side in confusion. I feel my eyebrows pinch together in the middle. Then something even weirder happens, Mia kisses Stefan on the cheek. With that I pull my head back and am sure I'm making a double or triple chin with my affronted appearance.

Stefan and Mia tear their gazes from one another and look at me in unison. Then all three of them start laughing.

I don't get it. I cross my arms and wait.

Mia's the first to catch her breath. "The guys told me about what happened with you and Will," she starts. "Stefan had the idea of making you think this was a setup just to see your reaction, I have to admit, I'm glad I went along with it. Your facial expressions are hilarious!"

Stefan clears his throat, "Nik, this is Mia, my girlfriend. She's got a week off from Basic so she came home for a few days."

"Oh, hey. Guess it's actually nice to meet you now," I reply robotically with a small wave. I might be back to hanging out with people again, but being the butt of someone's joke has never been fun to me.

Stefan and Mia turn away and walk to Yoka Sushi, leaving Will and me behind.

"Hey, I'm sorry about that," Will tries. "I didn't want to go along with it."

"But you did," I remind him.

He sighs. "Not on purpose."

"By omission you did. You could have told me who she was when I got in the car. I'm here for a second chance, not to be the butt of your jokes for the evening." I start following the direction Stefan and Mia have headed. I don't want Will to see how much his prank is affecting me. My posture may look solid, but inside I feel like a crushed little girl huddled in a corner. I know it was just a joke, but damn that hurt.

"Hey Nikki," Will grabs my hand to get me to stop walking. "There aren't any more plans to mess with you, promise."

I look up at him. I forgot how cute he can be when he's being sincere. "You promise?"

"Yeah," he says, then he smiles. It's one of those beaming smiles that could blind you if you look too hard at it. "So, you're here for a second chance, huh?"

Magically he stops looking so cute with that one question. "Nope." I pop the p for emphasis as I turn away from him.

He follows after me. "Pretty sure I heard that at the end of your tirade."

Oh, he's teasing me now, is he? "Stefan heard I've never been to sushi before and invited me along," I quickly lie.

"Right." Will disbelievingly responds.

We are seated in the back of the restaurant at a table set for six people. Mia sits facing out and looking upon the restaurant, and Stefan moves to sit next to her. I choose the seat opposite Mia and Will sits to my left. This leaves two seats empty, one next to each of the guys. I look questioningly at Stefan and he informs me, "My brother and his girlfriend will be joining us," He informs me.

Fucking shit, I think. The only appropriate response I can manage is, "Oh, cool."

While we wait for them to arrive the boys dive into the menu. I admit to Mia that I've never been to sushi before and have no idea what looks or sounds good. She smiles at me kindly.

As Mia is about to aid me in understanding the menu, Will leans over and asks, "Well, do you know if you like raw rolls or cooked ones?"

I can't help the involuntary facial reaction I have to the idea of a raw roll. My lip curls revealing my top row of teeth and I reply, "I don't think raw fish is going to work out well for me."

"Okay, cooked it is. Is there a type of seafood you don't like?" He asks.

"Not that I know of."

He looks up from the menu and smiles at me. "Good."

With his encouragement and deciphering, we select a couple rolls that sound like something I can stomach. At some point in our menu discussion Stefan's brother and his girlfriend show up. There's also a third person with them.

Stefan introduces everyone, apparently his brother's name is Chuck, his girlfriend is Brittney, and their mysterious friend is Michelle. Brittney ends up sitting at the head of the table and Michelle is on the other side of Will. I don't know if it's the prank Stefan pulled on me in the car, but I'm starting to feel territorial over Will with this new girl.

I catch Stefan's eye and raise an eyebrow at him. Does he know what's going on with Michelle? He raises his hands in a gesture of innocence and shakes his head slightly. I narrow my eyes at him repeating my nonverbal question. He shakes his head harder and mouths, *"Not me.* "If we continue this silent conversation someone is going to notice so I'll have to take his *"word"* for it.

A few minutes later a waiter comes by and takes our order. I am still debating which roll I want to have the most when I hear Will rattle off all three of them, plus four more which we hadn't discussed. Stefan chimes in asking for two orders of garlic edamame for the table, and sweet and sour soups for everyone.

Then Will interrupts and points to me, "Actually, she'll have a miso please."

I watch the guys in fascination, this ordering routine seems like a well rehearsed dance for the two of them.

When the chaos of the ordering concludes I ask Will, "What just happened?"

He explains, "When we come here we do family style, so everyone will share the garlic edamame, we got four raw rolls, and three cooked rolls. You will probably want to stick to the cooked ones."

"What about the soup?"

He gives me a lopsided grin. "You never have hot sauce with your Mexican food."

"And?" I question.

"I have a feeling you don't like hot food. Sweet and sour soup is spicy, so I thought you'd enjoy the miso soup more."

I blush. I didn't know he'd been paying that much attention, or that he would remember. I push some hair back over my shoulder and quietly say, "Thank you."

Will grins at me and squeezes my knee with his hand. Then he joins in the conversation happening at the table around us. My stomach immediately flutters at his simple touch. I'm disappointed he took his hand away so quickly. My knee was the perfect resting spot for it.

By the time our soup arrives I'm feeling a little more comfortable with the group. Will was right; I devour the Miso soup very quickly. He offers me a sip of his, as well. With one small taste I know that sweet and sour soup is not my speed.

Will laughs as I swallow the spoonful of his soup. "Guessing I was right?"

I stick my tongue out like the proper lady I am not, and take a big swig of my Shirley Temple. "If I had a bowl of that I think I'd die. It's *way* too hot for me!"

Will takes his bowl back from me as Stefan eloquently calls out, "Spicy in, spicy out. That's my favorite."

"Always classy Stefan," Will taunts him.

"Anything for a joke!" Stefan replies mid chuckle.

Will remains neutral about that comment. He huffs out a small laugh and continues eating his soup. I realize we've been here talking and hanging out for probably half an hour now and I haven't heard his nervous laugh yet. Thank the gods!

Shortly after we finish our soups, the garlic edamame comes out from the kitchen. *Sugar snap peas smothered in garlicky goodness, yes please!* I feel my mouth salivating as soon as I smell them. The only problem is that I'm not sure how to eat one.

I watch Stefan and Mia for guidance. They pick up one piece and stick it in their mouth and then pull it out. When it comes out it's thinner though. I think they're pulling the peas out with their teeth. *Why did I agree to go to sushi with a large group for my first time?*

"You're looking a little lost," Will says under his breath to me.

"Picked up on that did you?"

He grins at me. Why does he always smile at my sass? "So, pick one up, and use your teeth to pinch out the pea," he instructs, while demonstrating his own directions. I bite my bottom lip between my teeth as I wish part of me could be the snap peas he's sucking at. Before I can get too far down that fantasy lane I pick one from the plate and give it a shot.

I nervously follow along with Will's instructions, hoping I don't make an ass out of myself. I stick the pod in my mouth while holding on to the tip and try to figure it out. After I fail to get all three peas out at once I try just the one furthest in my mouth. As it slips out of the pod I feel triumphant. Then I use the opening to get the other two peas out and place the empty pod in the discard bowl where the others have put theirs. The edamame is delicious and now that I know how to eat it I dive in for a few more pods.

Between edamame bites, small talk continues at the table. Most of the people know one another. Stefan, of course, is the common link. My scalp tingles as I feel Brittney judging me with her boyfriend. It looks like they're trying to be coy whispering behind their hands to one another, but seriously, we all have eyeballs and ears for that matter. I'm glad that they sat furthest away from me because they don't seem like humans I'm interested in getting to know better. Michelle on the other hand? She's way too agreeable to anything that Will says. She keeps leaning into his comments and running her hand up and down his arm like he's a dog she eagerly wants to pet. They've talked about school, work, and other getting to know you topics. Somehow she's found a way to laugh at all of it. I participate in small talk with Mia and Stefan and bide my time.

My nose picks up on an aroma wafting through the restaurant. It's got an earthy base, I'm guessing, from the cooked rice. Layered into it is the savory smell of meat combined with a sweet, almost barbeque scent. My taste buds start salivating before food even reaches our table. I had no idea sushi could smell this enticing.

The sushi comes out. Stefan puts the raw rolls on the table furthest away from me. I get a whiff of the cooked rolls before they reach us.

The serving platter with the rolls Will helped me pick out is placed in front of me. It's accompanied by sweet aromas and wrapped in a deep-fried buttery blanket. I don't know which one to try first. Then it hits me. How will I be picking up this sushi? There are no forks on the table.

I tap Will on the arm to get his attention and, hesitating only slightly, I ask, "Uh, any advice on how to chopstick?"

He already has his held in his hand like a pro. Stefan smirks at me. Mia must be the sweetest woman on Earth because she elbows Stefan in the ribs and tells him to be nice.

Will lets me know my choices. "Well, you have three options: One, we get you a fork. Two, you get a training device for yours. Three, you jump off the deep end."

I look at the chopsticks. *They can't be that hard right?* "Let's try it, no training wheels."

He leans toward me and our arms brush. My skin feels tingly with excitement anywhere he touches me.

"Alright, the bottom chopstick doesn't move. It needs to be secure at the bottom of your thumb joint, and resting next to the nail on your ring finger," he begins.

"Try holding it like a pencil first," Stefan chimes in.

With that, I get the bottom stick situated.

Will continues on, "Good, now the top one will be doing all the work. Pinch it between your thumb and index finger."

"Like this?" I ask showing him my best attempt.

He breathes out a small laugh, "Not quite." Then Will reaches out and takes my hand in his. He steadies my hand with one of his, while his other hand slides my chopsticks further out. I tense at his touch.

My mind flashes to where else I'd like his hands to wander. My neck. My hips. Everywhere. His hands are rough and calloused; best of all, warm to the touch.

Once he finishes fixing my chopsticks he explains, "You'll have better leverage if you hold them further back."

Our eyes lock and he's still holding my hands in his. I can't help but think his large, tender, and strong hands can hold mine all day.

We smile at each other and then Stefan interrupts, "They're chopsticks guys, get a room if you're going to mentally undress one another."

Will drops my hand immediately and coughs in surprise.

I release my bottom lip from the bite of my teeth and feel my cheeks flush at Stefan's call out.

Mia saves me the embarrassment of having to reply to him by telling me which roll is which on the serving tray.

I manage to pick up one of each and put them on my plate before digging in. These chopsticks are a little tricky, but I'm not above using one in each hand if needed.

I can feel Will watching me as I try each piece. I don't remember what's in this one, but I think I see some shrimp. Once I manage to get it into my mouth I'm hit by the various textures. There's the soft rice, the moist sauces, crunchy cooked shrimp and crispy onions on the outer shell. All of those put together are perfection. The decadence of the flavors have my eyes rolling back in my head while I savor every chew.

"Really good, isn't it?" Mia asks me.

I can only nod my head in agreement as I finish off the piece. There's only one left to try, it's also the most intimidating. It's deep fried, and has two sauces on the outside of it.

"Trust me Nikki, just try it. You'll thank me later," Will encourages me.

I didn't know I'd be the source of entertainment for this outing, but half the people at the table are watching me shakily guide this piece to my mouth. *It's only my third time using chopsticks for crying out loud! I* don't *need the pressure of spectators.*

When the flavors hit my tongue I sit motionless for a few seconds. It's warmer than I thought it would be. Then I chew, once, twice, three times. I genuinely don't know if I've ever tasted something this delectable before in my life. I look from Mia, to Stefan, to Will, and then I full on moan. My shoulders sag and my head tilts back as I sit and let my taste buds experience the best foodgasm of my life.

Will watches the spectacle of me enjoying my food and then clears his throat and confirms, "You hate it, don't you?"

I think his voice came out a little huskier there. Were his eyes just lingering on my lips? I swallow the best bite of food I'll ever have on this planet and ask him, "Can we order an entire Tempura roll just for me?"

"Only if this means I'm forgiven for participating in Stefan's stupid joke earlier," Will barters.

"I'd forgive you for running over my cat if it was necessary to experience this food," I tease him.

Stefan flags down the waiter the next time he passes and Will orders the table two more of the Tempura Sake rolls. When they come out he places one directly in front of me. I smile broadly while my eyes bulge out of their sockets in anticipation of having this roll all to myself. I must look like a kid on Christmas morning based off of how the group is chuckling. I don't care. This food is fantastic. Tipp is gonna be pissed she missed out on it.

Once I'm halfway through the roll I realize I'm not going to be able to eat it all. Everyone else has less than two pieces on their plates and I'm still at four. I know this extra Tempura was for me, but I guess I need to share it now. "Hey, do you want a few of these?" I ask Will while gesturing to the food in front of me.

"Don't mind if I do!" Stefan says as he whisks one off my plate with his chopsticks.

"I don't believe that offer was for you," Mia tells him.

"It wasn't," I say as I glare at Stefan. "If I had a fork I'd stab you with it right now."

"Good luck with that Nik," Stefan taunts as he dips the stolen piece into soy sauce.

I pull my plate closer and try again. "Will only, would you like a couple of Tempura pieces?" Then I pointedly give Stefan a challenging look.

Will picks up his chopsticks and takes two pieces from my plate. "Thanks, Nikki."

I pick up my last piece and look at the group. "Thanks for teaching me about sushi tonight everyone, it was really great getting to know all of you." Then I take my last bite of the best sushi roll to exist in this universe.

We split the bill seven ways and get up to head out to our cars. The sun over Southern California has set and, as I guessed, there is a slight chill in the air. Unfortunately, Will didn't bring a jacket with him. I cross my arms as we walk to our cars.

Mia calls out sadly, "I wish we didn't have to call this a night, I'm having such a great time!"

I feel for her, especially since she hasn't seen Stefan in weeks. Then I remember Nana's offer from earlier. "We could all go back to Nana's place if you want?"

"To do what?" Stefan inquires.

"Not sure," I reply honestly. "But she's got a huge backyard, and my room is big enough to fit all of us. Guess I'm offering up the location and you have to figure out the agenda."

"Let's do it," Michelle pops out of nowhere and is apparently invited too. I thought she'd splintered off with Chuck and Brittney when we exited the restaurant.

Stefan uses his key fob to unlock the car. "Alright, everyone pile in, but Mia gets shotgun this time."

That leaves Will, Michelle, and me to figure out seating in the backseat. Will doesn't seem to mind having to sit with two women in a cramped space. He even takes it upon himself to sit in the middle. Right when I am about to worry about his comfort level he lets out a sigh and stretches his arms out behind Michelle and me as we climb in on either side of him. I see a smirk on his face that's usually outfitted on his best friend. He's must be loving all the attention he's getting tonight. Fuck it, if he wants to feel like the man of the hour I can help out his ego. Once I'm situated and belted in for safety I get comfortable and lay my head on his shoulder.

As Stefan pulls out of the parking lot I ask the car, "What are we going to do at my house?"

No one has an answer. After a moment, Stefan, of course, has an idea. "I need to make a pit stop at my house on the way. This will be perfect."

Half an hour later we're pulling into Nana's driveway and parking behind my Beetle. Will's shoulder has been comfortable for the last 30 minutes and I'm disappointed to have to remove myself from his warmth.

I slide off of the seat and head to unlock the front door. I think I hear Stefan say something to Will on their way up the drive, but I can't be certain.

When we enter the house I call out to see if Nana is home. With no answer, I assume she's either out living life or will be keeping to herself for the evening.

Seeing as we're on our own, I lead the group down to the far end of the house which ends in my bedroom. It's got the bed, a large cozy chair for reading, and my desk chair for seating. I could take an additional chair from the dining room, but I've never been against sitting on the floor. As the oldest child, I'm used to sacrificing my comfort for others.

Stefan and Mia end up joining me on the floor. They're at the foot of my bed using it as a back rest. Michelle opts for my desk chair which leaves Will in the most comfortable seat, my reading chair. We all settle in and Stefan pulls a game from Mia's purse.

Twister.

"You expect all of us to play Twister?" I ask incredulously.

"Nah, not all of us," Stefan replies cryptically. "Mia busted her knee up at training, so she'll be the spinner." He presses a kiss to her cheek and continues. "It will be you, Michelle, Will, and me!" His voice elevates an octave at the end, signifying his excitement with this idea.

"I haven't played Twister in years," Michelle begins. "I don't think all four of us adults will fit." She motions between all of us.

It's Will's turn to convince us this is a good idea. "Where's your sense of adventure, Michelle? Half the fun is that we are too big, the competition will be weeded out quickly."

"I'm game," I chime in. "But I have home field advantage," I say as I go to my dresser and pull out a pair of leggings. "I'm going to change so I actually stand a chance. Michelle, do you want to borrow a pair?"

"Nah girl, I'm good," she says waving off my suggestion.

I head toward my ensuite bathroom to change. "Suit yourself."

I have an ace up my sleeves the boys don't know about. I've been a dancer my entire life. I'm incredibly flexible. They might think this will be a quick win, but I can't wait to crush them.

"Right hand red!" Mia announces the beginning of the game from her new spot in my cozy reading chair.

I've got this.

A flick of Mia's finger and the sound of the spinner is the only noise as we all size up our competition. "Left foot yellow."

Easy. I grin at the boys as they seem to have a devious silent conversation about the game. Their eyes dart across the board and back to one another. Stefan's wearing his smirk, and Will's is almost a mirror image. They exchange a quick nod that I don't have enough time to process before our next position is announced.

"Right foot blue," Mia yells out so quickly I wonder if she even spun it again.

"Dear God, please don't fart," I hear Michelle say somewhere in front of me. I look up from my own game play to see Stefan's ass is unapologetically in her face.

"If that's what it takes to get a win, I'll force one out," he taunts her.

"Gross," Mia comments as she flicks the spinner again.

I'm increasingly glad that Will and I are currently facing one another. I don't want to get to know his ass as well as Michelle is getting to know Stefan's right now.

"Why are your limbs so spread out?" I ask Will. His foot is on the complete opposite end of the game mat as his hand. I know he's tall, but that's some reach.

"Strategy," he answers with a wink.

What the hell does that mean?

"Left hand red," Mia announces.

So far I feel like I'm doing some weird side stretch. The boys are already looking unsteady and right as Mia is about to call out another color Michelle falls off the board with an, "Ooof."

"One down, two to go," Stefan declares.

Once Michelle clears the field of play, Mia says, "Left hand green."

I easily move into a squat with my arms spread to either side of my body. Will looks uncomfortable though. "Don't you dare," I hear him threaten. I'm not touching him so I know it can't be me he's talking to. Then I see it, Stefan's arm is snaking its way between Will's legs as he heads for a green dot. Will is spread eagle for the world to see. His strategy isn't making any sense to me. Instead of keeping his game tight and clean he's practically doing a backbend, although when he adjusts it looks more like he's humping the air.

Stefan's head pokes out from underneath Will's body. "Hey Nik, how's it going?" He asks as if we were discussing something as mundane as the weather.

"Uh, hi Stefan. You okay down there?" I ask through a laugh.

"Oh yeah, just lifting a little extra weight to get a good workout in," he replies as he almost picks up Will's body with his own.

"Yeah, right there," Will sighs out as his body is moved by his best friend.

"Babe, choose the next one!" Stefan shouts as Will's weight gets to be too much for him.

Mia flicks the spinner and we wait with bated breaths for her to reveal our fates. "Right foot green."

I don't have to adjust much. They boys, however? They're a giant tangle of limbs. Playing this game with two men over six feet tall was a silly choice, but incredibly entertaining. Stefan makes quick work of Will's precarious position. He merely straightens his legs and Will is picked up off the ground. As Stefan settles into his new spot Will falls off of him and lands with a thud.

"Isn't that cheating?" I ask the group.

"No way! His elbow touched the mat, he's out!" Stefan informs me.

"It's all up to you Nikki, you gotta beat him," Will encourages me. So I do.

"Left foot blue," Mia tells us.

I twist so fast Stefan doesn't see it coming. He is already unsteady from uprooting Will so I take a move from their playbook and stretch my leg all the way across the board. Stefan wobbles. I push him a tiny little bit with my thigh and he topples over.

The room cheers at the literal upending of Stefan. He locks eyes with me. "Oh, it's on Nik."

I glare back at him. "Bring it," I taunt as I stand and stretch lazily.

Will comes back to the game and referees, "I think I'll be between you two again, don't want it getting too dangerous in here."

"You joining Michelle?" I ask.

"No, it is a lot more fun watching than participating," She answers.

We switch up the version of the game this round and put our feet on two different colored circles before any spins are made. I stick to my red and blue corner while the boys sprawl across the mat with one foot each in yellow, and another all the way in blue, I shake my head at them. Typical manspreading.

Mia announces our first position, "Right hand red."

We all bend over easily and put our right hands on a different red circle. It feels like there's much more room with one less player on the board this time around.

Mia flicks the needle and Michelle calls out, "Left hand yellow."

Will's height is his strength in this game. He puts his hand down on the yellow that would have been easiest for me to use.

I see my hand. I see the open yellow spot second closest to me. In order to stay alive in this round Will and I are going to be getting rather close. Of course, that was Stefan's goal the whole time. I curve my body, reaching my left hand toward the yellow. I'm going to have to reach over the top of Will's body in order to get to an open dot. Right before it makes contact with the mat, my stomach is squished against Will's elbow, and his neck and the back of his head are crushed, in turn, by my boobs. I'm in position and Will's in a nice spot too, I'm guessing.

"How you doing there Will?" Mia asks in a suggestive voice.

Stefan snorts.

I grimace.

"Me? Uh, I'm pretty great right now, thanks!" Will calls back from beneath my breasts.

"I would hope so," Stefan taunts his best friend. "Your neck is getting to second base before your hands are!"

Will starts laughing beneath me. I'm barely holding on when Mia calls out, "Left foot red."

The same moment I pick up my left foot to switch positions Will lifts up his entire body. I'm thrown off balance, roll off his neck, and thud to the ground under him. Will moves his foot to the red circle and looks down at me. "Nice try, Nikki."

My cheeks flood crimson and I nervously smile at him. This should feel like a compromising position, but I like being pinned underneath him. I gaze up at Will feeling my core heat as I wonder how much better this would be if there were fewer people around us.

My thoughts have me biting my lip, yet again, and Will's eyes have started smoldering while he's grinning down at me. He holds his body up strongly above me and licks his lips causing me to practically combust.

Stefan chooses this time to nudge my leg, "I need that spot."

I escape from Will's trance and crawl out from under him. I sit leaning against my bed and watch the boys battle to the finish. After a few more moves that I'm not paying enough attention to, Stefan manages to topple Will off the board again. "Another?" the victorious Stefan questions.

"I think I've run out of balance for the night," Will replies.

I shrug my shoulders in response. "I think I'm Twistered out, thanks though."

Neither Mia or Michelle voice wanting to continue. "It's actually getting pretty late," Michelle interjects. "Do you think you could drop me off at home sometime soon?"

With that, the evening ends. I walk the group out to Stefan's car and give Will a hug goodnight. His hugs are nothing short of wonderful. It doesn't last long enough though. I want to be wrapped in his arms for hours, not a mere five seconds.

I retreat up the stairs to Nana's entryway and watch them drive off into the night. As I walk to my room and prepare for bed, I notice for the first time in a while there's a smile plastered on my face. It's definitely caused by Will, and I never want it to go away.

Fifteen

Spring Break

Spring Break brings a much needed reprieve for me. I manage to pick up a few extra shifts so I am doing a seven day stretch of openings. That is going to look nice on my upcoming paycheck, which is perfect because there are some new fantasy releases coming out that I need to stock up. The Twisted Sisters just announced they're releasing another book and they're an immediate buy for me. Colleen Hoover is always producing something new that will make me sob uncontrollably for the three or four days it takes to read. Most importantly, there is a new edition of the *Throne of Glass* series with sprayed edges I have my eye on. That alone will cost an entire extra shift. So worth it. I can visualize them sitting on my bookshelf now. I don't have a problem. I'm aware that my collection will qualify as a library some day, and I can't think of a better goal in life.

Tipp and I manage to set up a dinner date with Nana half way through the week. Nana loves cooking as long as it means socializing in one way or another. Today she made one of my favorite recipes: open faced tuna sandwiches with cheddar cheese broiled on top. Nana has me set up the cushions on the patio for our meal. There's a slight breeze making it the perfect temperature. Nana wraps up in a sweater as I get us all drinks. Tipp is too distracted giving Otis affection to be assisting with anything right now.

Nana picked the perfect spot for her house. She and my Grandfather made plans for a dream house, but then lumber prices got too high and they realized buying would be a better fit. This house was the closest they found to their original dream. It's located close to everything you could want, mountains, ocean, desert. It's all within a 30 minute drive.

Her backyard is about an acre. My Mom and Uncle raised sheep, chickens, horses, and had numerous dogs and cats on this property. As I look toward the slowly setting sun I think of how nice it will be to someday do those things with my future family.

Nana pushes our meals through the kitchen window that opens onto the patio. I walk over and pick them up. The only thing that draws Tipp out from petting Otis is the delicious fragrance of our dinner wafting onto the patio.

"That smells delicious!" She exclaims as she settles in for the meal.

Nana comes outside with her ever present basket of napkins and we all sit at the table, ready to dig in.

As Tipp and I take our first bites Nana asks, "How have the two of you been?"

I let Tipp reply first. "Fine thanks. Work's been busy, which is good for tips."

"That's nice, and school?" Nana continues.

Tipp takes a bite so I interject while she has a mouthful, "I don't even know what classes you're taking other than French with me."

"Whose fault is that?" She teases me. "Classes are good, I'm acing pretty much everything. Currently it looks good for me to transfer to a four year after Fall semester next year."

"You're transferring early?" I ask alarmed. "I thought we were on the same time line?"

Tipp doesn't miss a beat. "We were, until you decided to galavant across Australia for a semester. That kind of messed up your timeline."

I think on that. Australia was one of the best semesters of my life. I learned so many lessons that can't be taught in a classroom. "Yeah, okay. That was definitely a once in a lifetime experience."

Nana chimes in, "Moving to Oregon probably puts a hitch in that timeline too, Nikki." She looks to Tipp and asks with genuine curiosity, "Do you know where you want to transfer to?"

"I haven't settled anywhere for certain. I think my biggest hurdle is choosing whether I want to stay local or get out and explore somewhere new."

"Is SDSU still a front runner for you?" I ask.

"It could be, if I want to stay in town," Tipp replies.

We all enjoy the slight breeze coasting across the patio while we eat. Behind the tree line I see the remains of the stables from the horses and sheep that used to live here. My smile breaks into a grin as I recall that I'm technically living in my Mother's childhood bedroom.

Nana interrupts my train of thought by asking, "Well Nikki, how did your date go the other night?"

I scoff lovingly at her. "It wasn't a date."

"From how cute you looked, I got a different feeling."

How dare she call me out on this! I fake being affronted. "Is it a crime for a woman to care about her appearance when hanging out with friends these days?"

"Only when she denies that she's desperately pining over one of them," Tipp deadpans.

These women. Thinking they know me. It's not like they're my best friend and Nana for crying out loud. "I'll have you know," I begin by pointing at Tipp, "I'm very aware I'm 'pining for him,' as you say. And I'm pretty sure Friday night got us back on track."

"What makes you think that?" Tipp challenges.

"We had fun together," is my lame response.

Nana laughs softly at me. "That's a good place to start."

"See Tipp, Nana approves, and she was happily married for many many years. So, ha!" I finish as I take another savory bite of my tuna sandwich.

"Nana," Tipp starts, "How did you and Nikki's Grandfather meet?"

I know this story; it's one of my favorites. Nana told it to me recently during one of our conversations that began with a ten p.m. hug goodnight and turned into us still talking in the kitchen until two in the morning. Those talks are one of the many reasons I'm glad I moved in with Nana after graduating. I've gotten to know her so much better than I would have otherwise.

"Now that is a long story," Nana says as she looks off into the distance with a smile.

"Good thing I'm not working tonight then," Tipp encourages her to go on.

Nana smiles at that. She readies by taking a sip of her Squirt and then dives into the tale.

"I was attending SDSU at the time, and he was freshly out of the military. I was driving near campus in my convertible and I guess technically I cut him off. I didn't think much of it. People accidentally do that from time to time. Then, we pulled up to an intersection and were stopped at a red light.

"His car stopped evenly with mine and he yelled through our open windows, 'Do you realize you just cut me off?' In those days we didn't have air conditioning so we drove with our windows down.

"I knew what I'd done, but he was being a little confident so I teased him and said, 'Yeah, sorry about that.'

"He yelled across the sounds of our engines, 'I think you owe me a coffee to make it up to me!'"

"He didn't!" Tipp exclaims.

"He did." Nana smiles, reminiscing about the love of her life and continues, "I laughed at him and said maybe next time. I wasn't going to go on a date with him for an honest mistake.

"Then the light turned green and I drove off. I didn't think anything of it and went about whatever I had to do with the rest of my day."

Neither Tipp nor I interrupt Nana. We can tell there's more to come. I continue eating as Nana reveals the cutest part of her story.

"A few days later I was at work in a record shop. I was sorting the records and in walks the same guy. He noticed me and asked, 'When are we going out on that date to make up for you cutting me off?'

"I laughed at him again and informed him, 'That will never be happening.'

"He smiled at me and cockily said, 'Never say never.'

"It was cliche and arrogant. He bought a record I think and then left. I thought that was that. Then he came in again a few days later and asked me the same question. I turned him down yet again and he left the shop. After a third time I was starting to get annoyed. I figured at that point I might as well say, 'Yes,' and prove to him that we had absolutely nothing in common. He took me out a week later. Turns out I was wrong because a year and a half after that we were married."

"So he was stalking you?" Tipp asks.

"No, I don't think so. He always maintained that he happened to come into the store and when he saw that I was working there it was a huge coincidence," Nana defends her husband. "Of course, after he figured that out, returning was intentional. I think it worked out pretty well for him. We were married for over thirty years and now Nikki's birthday is on our wedding anniversary."

I smile at Nana. I never had the chance to meet my Grandfather, but I can tell by how he's talked about by Mom and Nana, that he was incredibly loved.

I clear my throat before asking Tipp, "Can you get Will to do some sort of grand gesture like that for me, please?"

We all laugh at my comment and spend the rest of our meal discussing Tipp's potential college locations.

As we're washing dinner dishes and chatting in the kitchen, my phone rings. I pull it from my pocket and look at the caller ID. It's Will.

We haven't talked since Friday night. I've spent the last three days convincing myself not to freak out over the fact that he hasn't reached out. Now, here he is and I'm staring at my phone like an idiot.

Tipp pushes me with her shoulder, "You going to get that?"

I try to get out of it. "I can let it go to voicemail." *Why does Will make me so bloody nervous? This is not like me at all!*

Tipp yanks the phone from my hand and presses the answer icon, then she holds it out to me with a smug smirk. I'm fucked now. I take the phone from her outstretched hand and flip her off as I leave the kitchen and head toward my room.

I hear Nana warn Tipp, "You might want to disappear now, she's going to be mad at you for that move."

Nana's right. Tipp needs to run and hide far, far away for that little stunt.

"Hello?" I hear Will's voice call through the phone.

"Uh— hi," I stutter out. "What's up?"

"Hey Nikki, I uh," he sounds nervous. "I was wondering if you wanted to go out with a group of us on Thursday night?"

"Like a hang out?"

"Not quite... I was hoping it could be more like a date than a hang out," Will clarifies.

Well this is an interesting turn of events, and hell yes I want to go out with him! I plop down in my reading chair and fidget with the stitching on the arm. "What did you have in mind?" I ask cooly, hiding all of my excitement that's about to bubble over.

"I was thinking I could pick you up, around seven. The two of us could go grab dinner, or dessert, whatever you'd prefer. Then we could head over to the bowling alley and meet up with most of the people from Friday night, and a few others you haven't met yet," he blurts it all without taking a breath.

That stupid smile from Friday night is back on my face and I inform him, "I eat dinner."

"Cool, so Thursday at seven?" He confirms.

"Sounds good Will, I'll see you then."

"Alright then, bye Nikki."

"Bye Will." I hang up the phone and hold it to my chest grinning like a fool. He's improving, he actually said bye this time! It's all about the small victories in life.

I walk back to the kitchen and find Nana doing dishes alone. I ask her, "Did Tipp take your suggestion to flee seriously?"

She looks over her shoulder at me. "Can you blame her? She forced you to do something against your will."

Nana has a point. Guess Tipp will miss the updates about my love life today.

I keep Nana company as she rinses off the last of the dishes and loads them into the washer. I wish her a goodnight and retreat to my room.

I need to fit in a workout and shower before bed. My opening shift will be here too soon and it seems that I'll be needing my beauty sleep this week. I've got a date with Will to fixate on.

Sixteen

Midnight Bowling

LAST WEEK I GOT Will interested enough to give me a second chance. Tonight, I need to seal the deal. I choose one of my favorite tank tops, black with a white skull and some floral accents in a dark blue and silver. I pair it with a brand new pair of skinny jeans and some cute wedges.

On my bed I have my purse ready and a pair of socks laid next to it. While I wait for the time to pass I grab my current read and settle into my cozy reading chair.

I dive into the world of shifters and surprisingly I am able to focus on the content. That's a sign of how good a writer this Raven Kennedy woman is. Before I know it, my six fifty-five p.m. alarm is blaring. *Dammit, it was just getting to a good part. Guess I'll find out what happens later.*

I set my book down and grab my shoes at the foot of my bed. I carefully balance one foot and then the other as I buckle the wedges on. I grab my socks, toss them into my purse, and head out of my room. Nana smiles and wishes me a good night as I hug her goodbye and then I wait on a couch in the front room.

It doesn't take long for Will's headlights to shine through the always open wall of windows.

Will and I meet at the middle of the steep downward part of the driveway that leads to the bottom parking area.

"Hey Nikki." Will waves as he walks up to me.

I grin at him. "Hey Will. Why did you park down here this time?" I ask curiously.

He pulls me into a full embrace as we meet. I wasn't expecting it. Damn, he gives good hugs. Great even. *Those are my descriptions right now? Good and great?* Apparently my brain turns into mush around this guy.

"Hadn't done it before, thought I'd see if I liked it," he answers.

"Well, if it does become a habit, make sure you're parked all the way to the right." I point to the spot next to the long-abandoned basketball hoop that lingers at the back of the drive.

Will walks me to the passenger door, manually unlocks it, and opens it for me. "Why is that?" He asks while holding my door open.

"Nana parks in the middle garage," I gesture to our left. "She needs the space up until the middle spot so that she can back her van in correctly. She can do it with less space, but it's nicer if you park out of her way."

"So you think I'll be coming around often enough to need to know where to park?" He teases me as he closes my door.

While Will walks around the car to his side and manually unlocks that door as well, I have enough time to think up a clever retort, "I dumped you once, and you're here giving me another chance. Something tells me you're gonna want to keep coming around."

"I like your confidence, Nikki," Will compliments as he makes a three point turn and heads down the road into the city.

"Where are we headed?" I ask after a few minutes of contented silence.

"I thought we could head into Rancho and get some dinner at Friday's before we head to bowling. Work for you?"

"Under one condition."

He looks at me quickly while driving. "What's that?"

"It's a requirement whenever I go to Friday's that I get their potato skins appetizer." It's true.

"I think we can make that happen."

I perk up in my seat. "Then Friday's sounds great!"

When we get to the sports bar turned restaurant, Will and I head to a high table in the bar area. I always enjoy sitting where it's lively. People are so entertaining to watch during sporting events.

"Do you like watching sports?" I ask Will.

He puts down his menu. "Nah, I'd rather be playing the sports myself."

"You think you're good enough to go pro?" I challenge.

He laughs, a real laugh, not that milk curdling one from our first date. "Not at all. If I can't go out and play the sport myself I think it's boring to watch someone else do it."

I've never met someone who feels this way before. I lean across the table and ask him in a serious tone, "You mean to tell me you don't spend every Sunday yelling at a T.V. screen?"

"Only if that happens to be the day I'm watching the newest episode of The Witcher."

I reach out my hand and touch his forearm. Will looks from my hand to my face. "You okay?" He asks with concern lacing eyes.

"Just making sure you're real. I don't mind watching sports with others if that's what they want to do, but I really don't care who has the most passing yards in a season." I've never admitted that to anyone before. It feels liberating to say it aloud.

"Can I tell you a secret?" Will asks.

I'm curious now. "Yes."

"I only know what passing yards are because I played football in high school. I don't know much about other sports." He looks a little embarrassed confiding in me.

I bite my lip. I like getting to know his deep dark secrets. "So when you say you're a nerd, you're a full on nerd?"

With a straight face Will says, "Bill Nye the Science Guy is my favorite athlete."

"Ha!" I exclaim way too loud. A couple people near us in the bar look my way. I turn my head, look down and scratch my forehead trying to look less conspicuous. "Don't hate me?" I ask then grimace.

"How could I ever hate you?"

"I've never seen an episode of Bill Nye..."

Will's eyes double in size. He rubs his chin with his thumb, picks up the napkin from his lap and places it on the table.

"What are you doing?"

He sighs, "Nikki, I don't think I can do this." Then he moves to stand up. "You've never seen an episode of Bill Nye?"

I know he's teasing me, but I was scared there for a moment. "Don't do that!" I scold him.

Will smiles mockingly at me. "Tell me you've at least seen Bob Ross?" Then he tilts his head and cocks an eyebrow my direction.

I lean back in the booth and purse my lips. "What if I haven't?"

He stares at me in contemplation. "I guess there's only one thing to do then."

"What's that?"

"I'm going to give the future teacher an education. Cancel bowling, we've got more important things to do."

I half smile at him. Our meal continues with more fun conversations about his favorite video games and my favorite books. Luckily he doesn't ask what I'm currently reading. Sometimes I think it would be easier if I replied, "Fairy porn," to anyone who asked that. Weed out the faint hearted people who wouldn't be able to handle me. I just got my chance with Will back, though. I don't want my deviousness to scare him off.

After a delicious meal, with even better potato skins, we head back to the car. Will is ever the gentleman and opens my door for me again. I sit down and before I can say thank you he aggressively slams the door in my face.

"Well that was—" I began saying to myself. Then it hits me. First my nose crinkles up, then I think I can taste the air. I sit and process what's happening to my environment as Will slowly walks around the car.

The smell grows.

Will opens his door as I start to manually roll down my window.

"You okay?" he asks once he's in and buckled up.

"Di— Did you?" I stutter.

"Did I?" he asks.

"Did you fart when you closed my door?" My voice comes out high pitched with the awkwardness of that question.

His cheeks turn the cutest shade of pink. "Why?"

"Well, um." I scratch my head, and nervously talk with my hands, "Were you trying to fart outside the car so I wouldn't know?"

"Yes. I'm guessing that didn't work since you're asking about it?"

"I think you farted a few seconds too early."

"What!" He buries his head and shakes it back and forth in his hands.

"I think you farted as you were closing my door, and effectively trapped me in here with it." I barely manage to giggle out.

"No..." Will says into his hands in disbelief.

"Yeah..." I confirm much to his horror.

"I'm so sorry, Nikki." His apology is challenging to hear through his embarrassment.

I take one of his hands in mine. "Hey, look at me," I encourage him. "It's okay, we all fart. I do have one question though."

"Yes?" He asks, looking at me hopefully.

"Is your butt okay? Cause that smelled like a rotten meal."

He pulls his hand back from me.

I don't relent. "That smelled like a zebra, that was murdered by a rabid hyena, who then was left out for a week in the Savanna, and picked at by buzzards. That was one of the foulest smelling farts I've ever been subjected to."

"Are you done yet?" He begs while rolling his eyes.

I give him a massive side eye. "No, I think you should suffer at least as long as I was trapped in the presence of the odor emitted by your asshole."

"I'm gonna drive us to bowling now," he says while clicking on the radio. I notice that he turns up the volume a little bit. I think he's trying to drown out my mocking. Poor thing, I'll be sure to remember to bring it up when we're surrounded by all of his friends.

We walk into the bowling alley hand in hand. I notice that my soft manicured hands are encompassed perfectly in his warm, calloused ones.

Will takes us to the arcade where we find Stefan and Mia playing a racing game. Mia is kicking his ass.

When they wrap up the game Mia greets me, "Hey girl! I see that second chances do exist!" She embraces me in a quick hug.

"Hey Mia, hey Stefan," I greet the couple.

"Anyone else here yet?" Will asks his best friend.

Stefan answers, "Chuck and Brittney are already at our lanes, and everyone else bailed for the night. Looks like it's the six of us."

Will shows me where I can get my shoes and we head over to the lanes Chuck and Brittney are at.

"Hey Will," Chuck calls as he sees us approaching. Brittney looks like there's a stick stuck up her ass tonight. Between her whispering with Chuck at sushi and her unpleasant demeanor tonight, I wonder if she's ever actually happy. I let the guys catch up and go to change my shoes. I set my purse down and feel around for my socks. My hand reaches into all the nooks and crannies of my black hole of a bag but nothing feels like the right texture. I start pulling the contents of my bag out and stack it all on my lap. Once it is an empty sack I accept that my aim must have been off when I tossed in my socks.

Will wraps up his conversation with Chuck and sits down next to me to put on his shoes. He notices the pile of assorted items on my lap. "You good, Nikki?"

"No," I reply honestly. I notice his look of concern and clarify. "I'm fine, but I somehow didn't bring any socks. There's no way I'm wearing shoes that have been on a stranger's feet without socks."

"That's not too bad, I thought something was actually wrong," he replies as he finishes tying up his second shoe.

"Did you not hear me? There's no way I can bowl tonight. This sucks." I say as I aggressively shove the pile of items back into my purse.

"Nikki, they've got sock vending machines here," Will tells me with a smile.

I grab his arm in shock, "What! Where?"

"I'll show you," he offers as he takes my hand and leads the way.

A small grin spreads across my face when our fingers lace. I like how comfortable he is with holding my hand.

Will walks me all the way across the crowded bowling alley to a vending machine near the bathrooms. Sure enough it's packed with socks. There are multi packs, plain white ones, black, knee highs, and an assortment of rainbow colors.

"You want black?" Will asks.

I scan the sock collection until a pair catch my eye. "How about those?" I point to a pair of sunset orange socks, striped with a burnt red. They are the most vibrant pair in the machine, and I think they're perfect.

Will smiles at me. "You got it." Then he pulls out his wallet and buys the socks. He bends to pick them out of the machine and hands them to me.

I'm surprised by him yet again. "Oh, thank you. You didn't have to though, I was planning on getting them myself."

"Nikki, you gotta let others take care of you from time to time. I may not enjoy spending ten cents per text message, but I can afford a two dollar pair of socks," he chides me.

I chew the inside of my cheek. I'm really not used to others taking care of me like this. "It's cause of all the money you saved by not texting me, isn't it?"

"Now you understand me." He smiles and puts his arm around my shoulders as we walk over to our small group. I change into my bowling shoes as Stefan and Will input our names on the scoreboard. Only they're not putting in our real names —we all have nicknames. Stefan has dubbed himself Blind Date Master, no doubt because of his success in setting Will and me up. He chose Cutie as Mia's name. Sweet, but plain. He's started typing something when I get an idea for Will's name.

I jump up and whisper in his ear, "Will's name should be Sir Fart-salot."

"How would you know that Nik?" Stefan asks sounding intrigued.

"Dude, you don't want to know."

He laughs at me. "I'm pretty sure I do." Then he types my suggestion on the screen.

The last person to get their nickname is me and I should have seen it coming with this crew. Logical Thinker appears on the scoreboard for the entire bowling alley to see.

"I'm never going to live that down am I?" I whine to Stefan.

Will comes up behind me with his ball selection in hand. "Never, babe. Torturing you with previous life choices seems like the only logical thing to do." He gives me a cheeky wink and places his ball down on the ball return.

I turn to face him. "We have pet names now, do we?"

"I liked how it felt, didn't you?"

He's got me there, but I can't let him know. I try to hide my smile as I tease him. "We'll see." Then I change the subject. "Where are the lightweight balls?"

"How light you thinking Nik?" Stefan asks.

"I have an injury from high school actually. I'll play two games right handed, but anything after that and I start to really suck."

The boys accept my reasoning and Mia chimes in with the answer I need.

"Well, the little kid balls are behind you," she directs me helpfully.

"Great. Thanks." Then I turn on my heel to scout out my ball.

Of course the lightest they have is nine pounds, I can make it work, but the eight pound ball does make a difference. I find the grip size I need, but the ball is neon pink. What a disgusting color.

Mid-walk back to the group, the bowling alley changes right before my eyes. It goes from being bright and lit up for people to set up their areas, to dark with thumping music. Then the black lights flicker on and people's outfits start glowing. I look down to see my shoelaces and the skulls on my shirt are glowing. Also, the annoying pink ball is now practically iridescent in the black light. I like that visual much better than the color it was a few seconds ago.

On my path back to my friends, I walk past Chuck and Brittney. They decided to keep a lane to themselves since so many people were last minute no shows.

I overhear her say, "Who wears high rise jeans bowling anyway?" to Chuck when I'm within earshot.

Guess that confirms whether or not Brittney is a fan. Tipp would bite her head off for a comment like that. That's not my style. If hating on me is what she needs out of life, it shows more about her character than mine. I toss my hair over my shoulder as if I didn't hear her and get ready for a night of fun with Will, Stefan, and Mia.

My first four frames are abysmal, which means my entire game is basically toast. "Hey, the first game doesn't count," I argue as Stefan teases me about my scores.

"Says who?" Mia asks.

"My family. Every time we go bowling. The first game is a warm up game." I double down.

"Hate to break it to ya Nik, we're not your family." Stefan's face turns sinister as he exaggerates, "It's life or death from the first frame now that you live in Lakeside."

Will chimes in, "Those rules don't work for Nikki then. She doesn't live in Lakeside, man."

It's sweet of Will coming to my defense like that. While I'm distracted thinking about his chivalry, it becomes my turn. I have nothing left to sustain my argument so I stick my tongue out at Stefan, turn my back to him, and pick up my ball.

With my first throw I manage to get nine pins down. I wait for the alley to give me my ball back and ignore the guys. I want to stay in the zone, not let Stefan or Will fuck with my confidence.

The ball return spits out my ball; I pick it up and set up my shot. As I swing and release the ball, it feels right. I watch the lane in trepidation hoping that I can get this spare to shove it in Stefan's face. I hold my breath as the ball goes down the lane. It feels like time shifts to slow motion as I watch my ball rotate toward the remaining pin. It barely makes contact, but all that matters is that my pin is down. I punch my fist into the air and pivot to see Will coming at me full speed with his arms outstretched. He picks me up in a massive bear hug and twirls me around like this is the greatest moment of his life.

I laugh in his arms as he puts me down and kisses me on the head. "Great shot, Nikki," he compliments me. A comment like that coming from such a sweet man has me feeling all warm and fuzzy where my black heart is usually located. I'm relieved that blushes don't glow in black light, because if they did my face would be lit up as bright as my bowling ball. I can still feel where his lips touched my hair in celebration. I heat up even farther thinking about where I wish his lips had ended up instead.

I'm glad I decided earlier that pulling my hair back would be the best option because I'm definitely feeling overheated now. My messy bun is at least letting the back of my neck cool off, even if my brain and its fantasies aren't helping.

We settle into the plastic bowling alley seats side by side and watch Stefan get a strike, (asshole) followed by Mia getting a seven-ten split. She impresses everyone when she borrows my ball and gets the spare.

"How?" Will demands to know her secrets.

Mia blushes at us. "My family went bowling a lot growing up, you pick up some tricks when your parents are in a bowling league."

"You ever offer private lessons?" I joke with Mia as Will goes up for his turn.

Will can't be a stranger to a bowling alley. He dries his fingers in the air vent, which I didn't know the purpose of until earlier this evening, and picks up his ball with confidence. I give him my full attention as he lines up the shot. His upper body leans a little to the right, as if he's cradling the bowling ball. He takes a few graceful steps and the ball kisses down on the lane without making a sound. His ball shoots toward the end of the lane with a beautiful curve that I know I'll never be able to replicate. It hits the pins with a clattering explosion of white and red everywhere. When the chaos settles we see he's thrown another strike. That's his second one this game and we're only five frames in.

I had no idea that the right man with the correct skills could make bowling look sexy, and here he is, walking straight toward me grinning from ear to ear. He puts a hand out and pulls me from my chair.

I try to center my fluttering body but it must not have gone so well because I end up only getting seven pins total after my two shots. Who cares, I get to watch Will dominate and chat with the others between my shots. There are plenty of other things in life I can kick their asses at.

At the end of our first game it's very clear who is the best... Me, of course. "Lowest score is winner right?" I chipperly ask the group.

Will puts his arm around my hips as we all stand behind the scoreboard and take in the final scores. "Yupp, just like golf," he teases me as he kisses my hair again.

Stefan is the second biggest looser and Will and Mia are within ten of one another.

"Okay boys, warm up is over, time to put up a bit of a fight," Mia taunts as she resets the board for a second game. "Sorry Nikki, but it's almost like you rolled over and asked me to rub your belly."

I laugh at her. "Oh I'm not here to compete. I was promised free dinner and then we ended up here."

"Really now?" Stefan asks getting back from throwing his first frame. "You gonna tell us about that nickname now Nik?"

"No, she's not," Will answers for me.

"I think I should, your friends need to know the truth about you," I insist.

Will shakes his head at me. "Not this intimately."

I don't care, and start to explain, "So after dinner when we were getting back into Will's c—" Then there's a giant hand covering the bottom half of my face. His thumb is below my chin and his palm is firmly across my lips. Will has physically cut me off from telling this story.

I like his hand. It's rough from his work, but it delicately prevents my mouth from talking. It also has no business trying to shut me up. So, I decide to fight dirty. I open my mouth and lick all the way up his palm.

"Ahhh!" Will exclaims when his brain realizes what I just did. He takes a step back and wipes his hand down the side of his jeans. "What was that Nikki?" he asks with a repulsed look on his face. His eyebrows are scrunched together, his upper lip is pulled up and he's giving himself a double chin with how far his neck is retreating away from me.

I tilt my head and look up at him through my bangs. "I won't be silenced by a giant of a man like you."

Stefan and Mia watch us like we're a tennis match.

"You're up babe," I tell him with an air kiss.

He shakes his head and moves toward the ball return. As he passes me I hear him mutter under his breath, "You're so damn sexy when you get feisty like that."

I smile at his back and beckon Stefan and Mia toward me. As Will shoots his shot I tell them about getting crop dusted and then hot boxed by Will's deadly gas earlier.

When Will's finished his frame with only eight pins down, Stefan meets him and claps a hand on his shoulder. "Way to show Nik exactly what she's signing up for if she dates you!" He practically shouts at Will.

"If only Brittney was nearby to tell Nikki about the blanket incident," Mia teases Will.

"Oh no, does his gas have multiple stories lurking around?" I ask the group. Before they can tell any more embarrassing stories about Will, I get up and play my frame.

As our second game wraps up everyone talks about a third. I back out and say that my wrist has had enough fun for one night. I honestly didn't think we'd be here for this long.

I happily watch the third game. The three of them play quick paced and are well matched. It could be anyone's game until Stefan gets three strikes in a row. That jumps him to the lead and Mia and Will struggle to catch up. By the end of the third game, we're all satisfied and ready to head home for the evening.

After we trade our bowling shoes out for our street shoes and put our balls away, I thank Mia and Stefan for letting me tag along.

"Looks like we'll be seeing you around a bit more then?" Stefan asks Will with a leading smirk.

Mia tells me, "I have to fly out on Tuesday, so make sure these two knuckleheads don't get into too much trouble while I'm gone, okay?" Then she pulls me in for a hug.

"I'll do my best," I promise as I hug her back.

We leave the bowling alley together and head to opposite ends of the parking lot once outside. Will and I walk to his beige Toyota Camry. It gets him from point A to point B but, "Why does it have to be beige?" I intend to ask it, but my words come out more as a whine.

"What do you mean?" Will ponders.

I pause our walking right next to the passenger side and look up at him. "I *mean*, why is your car the ugliest color known to mankind?"

He leans past me and unlocks the car. As he opens the passenger door he replies, "Because it was the color of the car that my Uncle was selling." Then he closes it for me. I pause my breathing for a second and decide I'll need oxygen at some point on this drive home and I might as well test the air now. I take a miniature inhale. The air isn't pungent. I quickly and silently thank the gods as Will is getting into the driver seat.

"Fine, I guess that's an acceptable reason for an ugly colored car."

He starts the engine and pulls out of the parking lot. "What do you have against beige?"

He does not know the can of worms he's opened. My soliloquy begins. "If you're going to be a color you need to fully commit. Beige is the worst color out there. It's what all dead plants wither to. The color boring cookie cutter houses are painted. There's no personality or differentiation with it. One shade of beige is the same as another shade of beige; depressing and lacking soul."

Will is confused. "A color can have soul?"

"They can have depth. Don't get me started on pastels either. If you're going to be a color, make it vibrant and out there. I hate being born in April only because it makes everyone think I must lllooovvveee pastels. They are an insult to real colors."

He chuckles at me. "Any other quirks I need to know about?"

I smile in return. "There are plenty, but I can't scare you off too quickly now, can I?"

He takes my hand in his and rests our entwined fingers on his thigh for the remainder of the drive to my house.

When we're getting close I ask him, "Can you pull in behind my car this time? I don't want your headlights to wake up Nana."

"Sure thing," he replies.

Will pulls into the drive and goes halfway down before parking and killing the engine. I open my door and walk behind his car to go into my house. Will grabs my hand and pulls me toward him. When my body is flush against his, he stares into my eyes and says, "Thanks for a fun night Nikki. I think this second chance is going to work out pretty well for us."

I'm glad it's dark so he can't see me blushing again. "Thanks for the second chance, I hope you're right."

Will tucks some of the wisps of hair that have fallen out of my messy bun behind my ear and leaves his hand resting on my neck. His other hand lands on my hip and guides me to lean against his car. "You said your Nana's room is across the house from here?" He asks.

That's not the direction I thought this was going. "Yeah, why?"

He looks down at me with hooded eyes. "I don't think you're going to want an audience for this."

Then he kisses me. He holds me possessively and it makes me feel cherished. Will's kiss contradicts his hold on me. It's as if he's afraid of scaring me off if he goes too quickly. He gives me an exploring peck, then two. When I've had enough of him being a gentleman, my hands find his chest and pull him closer.

This is all the encouragement he needs. Will pushes me against his car as he deepens the kiss and we take what we need from one another. The hand on my neck helps him angle my mouth to the perfect position for his height. His tongue brushes across my lips asking for my permission to enter. I open willingly and we explore one another.

The hand on my hip travels up to my neck and applies the tiniest bit of pressure on either side of it. That small flicker of dominance excites me in a way I haven't experienced before. All too quickly I'm letting out a small moan as Will continues to familiarize himself with my mouth.

I think Will fears he went too far because he pulls back. He rests his forehead against mine. We're both panting.

Will takes a step back from me and smiles. "We need to stop there."

I'm biting my lip and shake my head in disagreement. "We don't have to." I don't want this to end. Will's domineering persona has me feeling hot and bothered. I need more of him.

He pinches my chin between his thumb and forefinger. "We do Nik, because the things I want to do to you? They won't be happening for the first time where your Nana can look out a window and see us." He pauses and then adds, "Or hear us for that matter."

I close the distance he tried putting between us. I push my breasts out just enough to graze across his pecs and taunt, "Promise?"

"Fuck Nikki," he growls at me. "Go inside before I pick you up and put you back in my car. I'll see you soon, okay?" He asks, clearly at the limit of his control by my excitement to his threats.

I lick my lips. "Night, Will." I push onto my tiptoes and give him a soft kiss.

I saunter past him and go to the back entrance on my side of the house. That quick makeout session better be the sole content of my dreams for the next month. I haven't felt this happy to be alive in too long. As I close the door behind me, the sound of Will's engine turning over fills the silence. I walk down the hall to my room and hear that Will's car is still idling outside. I put my bag down and unbuckle my shoes in the dark. Then I turn on the light to get ready for bed. It isn't until my bedroom lights up that I can tell Will's car has started backing down the drive.

I'm still excited from that kiss. That was a fucking great first kiss. One books wish they could write about. Belladix is gonna be getting a workout tonight.

Seventeen

Getting to Know You

The rest of Spring Break wraps up quickly between my shifts, working out, and hanging out with Will.

We've been exclusively hanging out at his sister's condo. I'm not ready for Nana to meet him just yet. It's been relaxing because his sister and brother-in-law are out of town on vacation right now. I usually make it over to his house by six or seven so Will has enough time to shower before I show up. Due to working so many opening shifts I've already had dinner by that time. Will heats up whatever leftovers he has lying around and we socialize. Will and I realized that we have overlapping dinner breaks every Tuesday and Thursday. I asked if he'd be interested in spending those times with me, and of course he said yes.

He's introduced me to The Witcher and reruns of Game of Thrones. I had no idea how much I could hate a fictional character until I met Joffrey. I've loved plenty of fictional boyfriends over the years, but never have I wanted to jump through the pages and erase someone from existence like I do with him. He makes most other villains look like sweet teddy bears.

After an episode or two I typically start feeling tired and need to head home in order to get up early enough for work so I head out. That's how it's been all break. I'm rather bummed that his sister will be getting back on Monday. I don't think we'll have the same laid-back environment when we have to hide in Will's room for any semblance of privacy.

In our secluded hideaway I can feel myself falling for him. The sweet way Will always asks if I need anything, or the way he's always touching me, just endears, him to me more. He doesn't have me guessing at what he's feeling, it's written all over his face. I adore spending time with him so much it has me worried that things may be just a little too perfect.

That worry is assuaged when I remember that I still haven't told Will about Oregon. I just got him back though, and I don't want to derail things by bringing up a problem that's so far down the road.

Unfortunately, Spring Break ends too quickly to explore concerns of the future any further and we're thrust face-first back to reality whether we like it or not.

My first class back has Tipp in it. She's been in Hawaii with her family and impossible to get ahold of since dinner with Nana. I get to class a little early and hope she manages to do the same as I pull out my supplies for our lesson.

The door bursts open and an impressively tan Tipp walks into the room.

"How are you so tan this quickly?" I ask her in greeting.

She takes off her sunnies. "I was in Hawaii babe, that's what happens."

I feel jealous heat prickle at the back of my neck. "Maybe to you! The rest of us mere mortals would burn to a crisp being in the sun for a week straight."

She smiles at me gracefully, sliding into her seat. "Sorry I've been MIA, we just landed last night. So, how did the rest of your break go?"

"I went on a date with Will." I blush thinking about how that night ended.

Tipp stops rummaging around her bag and looks at me intently, with her elbows on her desk and her chin propped on her fists. "You have my full attention. Tell me everything."

I bite my lip, remembering how natural and right everything felt. I quickly fill her in about dinner, the crop dusting and everything else. When I get to our kiss Tipp dances in her seat and squeals at the top of her lungs in excitement for me. This is enough to draw the attention of our peers that have trickled in since the story began.

"Shhhh, not everyone needs to be listening," I hush her.

"Oh, who gives a fuck?" Tipp says too loudly. "They wish they all had sex lives as fun as yours."

I bury my head in my hands, refusing to look around the classroom to see who heard her say that. "Making out with him once doesn't qualify as a sex life."

"Fine. But the way he put his hands on you? That's the kind of man that knows what he's doing." She starts fanning herself thinking about my nonexistent sex life.

"Get your own man to fantasize about," I tease her.

"Already got my own harem babe. You have no idea what Henry Cavill and Sebastian Stan do to me every night in my dreams. If I'm lucky Zade will even show up in my nightmares." She winks at me with her final name drop.

That's my best friend folks. "Simping much?"

She scoffs, "No judgment. You have Belladix, and now Will. I have my men. We're all happy."

I love Tipp, she's the best, most ridiculous, and sexually voracious woman I've ever met. I lower my voice conspiratorially and lean closer to her. "I haven't even told you the best part yet, bitch."

Her eyes widen, "You fucked him on the first date? Way to get some!" She exclaims while holding her hand up for a high five.

"What are we bros in Vegas? I haven't had sex with him yet."

Tipp picks up on my slip of the tongue. "Yet?" She prompts, shimmying her shoulders with no shame.

"Yeah, we both know it's probably going to happen, but the best part is his laugh."

"I'm not following."

I shake my head and sigh. "Remember that horrible laugh, the reason I broke up with him in the first place?" I ask her. "Well, I didn't hear it once, all the times we've hung out. I'm so relieved that laugh was a fluke."

Tipp glares at me then repeats one word, "Time*s*?" placing an emphasis on the s.

Shit, I hadn't told her about the rest of break yet. My face grimaces as I admit, "I may have gone over to his house every night since then..." I look anywhere but at her.

"But you still haven't fucked him?" Tipp's one track mind is way too fixated on my vagina's lack of action.

"I'm getting to know him first. It will happen in due time," I placate her.

She points at me. "And you'll call me the second it's over and tell me all the details."

"No."

"It's what a best friend would do."

"Guess we're not best friends then." I wink at her.

Tipp gasps and clutches imaginary pearls as Madame Krasse calls our attention to begin the lesson for the day.

Once class has ended from P.E. for Elementary Educators on Tuesday I head to the Griffin Center. This has become one of my favorite weekly routines: hanging out with Will and Stefan before Astronomy.

I chose a seat with an unobstructed view of the social center and pull my work out while I wait for Will's class to end. I have a little over two hours before he's free, so that's plenty of time to get a chunk of French homework done.

I startle when I feel a hand on my shoulder. I follow the hand and see the owner's face. Will. I break into a grin when I see him and he kisses me hello. It feels so natural, like something we've done a thousand times, even though every time our lips meet it feels like butterflies are flitting around in my stomach. I can't help but feel joy and excitement in his presence.

As he sits down he asks, "How's it going, Nikki?"

"Apparently I was in the zone with this French work; it's going pretty good."

"Well I don't want to mess up the middle of your assignment. What do you want for dinner?" He offers, "I'll go get it while you wrap up your problems."

I feel guilty that he's always buying me food. "I can buy my own dinner," I protest.

He takes my hand in his. "I know you can, but I want to get it for you. So, what will it be tonight?"

I sniff the air seeing if it will lead my stomach to a decision. Seconds tick by but there's nothing pungent enough to sway me.

"Indecisive?" Will confirms.

I nod. "I feel like I've had everything from here over a hundred times this semester, I wish there was something different."

"How about chicken nuggets from Chevron?" Will suggests.

I look around the Griffin Center looking for what he's suggested. "That's not at the food court?"

"Nah, it's on the South side of campus, but that's only a five minute walk."

I haven't made it out there before and I tell Will as much.

"Alright, I'll leave my bag here and get some nuggets. What kind of sauces and drink do you want?"

I smile at him. "You're the sweetest, can I get ketchup, and ranch please? I'll take a tea of some sort if they have it."

"I'll be right back," he says as he leans in for another kiss. His hand holds my neck again as I look up at him. Will's lips taste like sunshine on a winter day and the hustle of the center fades to the distance as he kisses me. He lingers a little longer than I expected and he starts to deepen the kiss.

I push him back from him with a giggle. "You can't do that here," I admonish him.

He leans down and whispers in my ear, "Why not? I like the idea of leaving you here wanting more." He gives me a final peck on the lips and heads off to get our dinner.

I try to focus on my homework again, but that bastard has made it impossible for me. He's right, I do want more. *Dammit.*

I roll back my shoulders and internally lecture my vagina for mentally blocking my homework abilities. She doesn't care. At this rate my time would be better served scrolling through my phone. So I put away my books and do exactly that.

Will returns quickly and the smell emanating from the bag he holds is exactly what I didn't know I wanted. He pulls out two to-go boxes followed by two teas, one green and one black. "I wasn't sure which you'd want so I'll drink whichever one you don't."

I pick up the green tea and explain, "Thanks for dinner Will, but black tea has too much caffeine for me to drink this late at night."

"Duly noted, enjoy your dinner Nikki." He hands me my box and I dig in.

As I bite into my second nugget Will asks, "Do you have plans next Friday?"

I swallow and think about it. "I'm not sure, why?"

"I've really enjoyed hanging out with you this week, and I'd like you to meet my friends. They're having a game night."

I'm surprised by his invitation. "I thought Stefan was your best friend?"

He chuckles. "A guy can have more than one friend."

I shrug. "True. What time and where?"

"Stefan's house, it's our usual spot. I don't know the exact time. Probably in the evening, some of them have jobs that go until five and six, so after that. You can invite Tipp if that would make you feel more comfortable," he finishes.

That's sweet of him. "I'll check and let you know soon."

At the mention of Stefan's house I realize who's missing and ask, "Where is Stefan?"

Will finishes his bite before answering, "Mia had to fly out today, I think he's going to barely make it to class on time."

"Why didn't he text me?" I ask.

"He and Mia have had a lot of *'catching up'* to do." Then he winks like I needed more of a hint to understand what that means. "He's forgotten to do a lot of things this week."

I grimace. "Do I want to know why you know these details about your best friend's sex life?"

"Oh I don't know anything for certain," he pauses and takes a drink for effect. "If I had to be away from you for three months and then you came home again, I imagine we'd both be forgetting about eating, personal hygiene, or texting other people."

His blatant admission of attraction has my heart thumping. "I'd love to sit here and hear all about what you'd do to me, but I don't think that's an acceptable reason for being late to Astronomy."

Will watches me grab my bag and gather my trash.

"Leave it," he instructs. "I'll bus our table."

"You buy me dinner, and clean up after the meal? You are one of a kind, aren't you?" I ask as I approach him. Even seated he's almost taller than me. I put my hand on his cheek and lean over ever so slightly to kiss him. I meant for it to be a soft goodbye kiss, the kind that will be a routine with every parting and greeting we have, but Will has other plans. He pulls me closer and holds me in place with his hands on my hips. After a minute I pull back and look into his eyes.

He earnestly asks, "You going to be okay at Astronomy without Stefan there?"

This puzzles me. I haven't had to think about Stefan as my human shield in a while. I tilt my head from side to side as I decide. "Stefan won't be around for the rest of my life, I think I can handle Brock tonight if he tries anything."

"I won't be leaving campus for a while yet, you let me know if that changes okay? You can even waste ten cents and send me a text message if you want."

I smile at him, give him a peck on the lips, and start my trek across campus.

Stefan doesn't make it to class on time and Brock unfortunately see's Stefan's absence as an opportunity to talk to me again. "Hey Nikki, looking good tonight," is his repulsive conversation opener.

"Thanks, Brock." I don't look up. I minimally engage. *Please take a fucking hint.*

Then I feel his hand on my back. I shoot out of my desk and stand up straight. I demand, "What the fuck do you think you're doing?" It's loud enough for the rest of the class to hear.

"Jesus, Nik, I was saying 'Hi,'" he claims.

"First off, it's Nikki or Veronica to you, and secondly, when's the last time you touched Jarod as you were greeting him?" I mention another classmate by name so at a minimum one person in this room will be focussing on Brock right now. I'm livid that he had the audacity to put his hand on me again.

He puts his hands up in fake innocence and takes a step back. "Message received."

"I doubt it," I mumble as he struts back to his seat a row behind me.

Professor Fitzgibbons begins our lesson and I perch on the edge of my chair. My leg is tapping anxiously and my hand is holding my pencil in a vice grip. I hate how one guy can take me from feeling so happy hanging out with Will to nervously searching the doorway for my security blanket to arrive. I copy down what's on the board, but my brain doesn't focus on anything other than the repulsive feeling of Brock's hand on my body again.

Stefan shows up a few minutes later and I feel my hackles lower now that he's nearby. Spring Break has passed, so there are only seven more weeks of me having a class with Brock. I can do it, I think.

Eighteen

Unexpected Escort

WILL AND MY WEDNESDAY schedules don't work together nicely so we settle on a quick evening catch up via the phone. I feel like I'm back in high school waiting on the guy to call me, lying on my bed as we talk, a stupid smile plastered to my lips every second I get to be near him. This doe-eyed, love-struck puppy is not a good look for the cold black-hearted persona I present to the rest of the world.

On Thursday I meet the guys for dinner. This routine has been a welcome addition to my semester. Stefan is acting a little somber. His head is resting on his forearms folded beneath him on the table. I haven't seen this guy slouch since I met him, so not a good sign. I'm guessing it's because Mia is back at Basic.

Should I approach him cautiously, or get the tough talk over with? I'm not sure what he needs at this moment. I sit down next to Will. He puts his hand on my leg and I lean into his presence at my side. We're physically connected, showing our mutual exclusivity, without peacocking it to everyone around us. His thick and steady hand almost wraps around the entire top of my thigh. That's especially impressive, because I'm curvy. My legs are not skinny, and he's dwarfing their presence with just five fingers. His possessive touch brings back how he kissed me after midnight bowling. I want to know what else his hands can do. What other sensations they can make me experience. I feel warmth starting to pool in my core. My bottom lip starts to draw between my teeth before I get a grip and mentally slap myself. *Snap out of it! Okay, focus Nikki, Stefan needs a friend right now, not a horndog.* "How long before you get to see Mia again?"

Stefan looks at me slowly, his eyes are missing their usual glint and I think I screwed up mentioning her. "I fly out to see her the day after term ends. Thirty five days to be exact."

I grin at Stefan. "Okay, how adorable is it that you know exactly when you're going to see her next. Also, thirty five days is nothing. We'll keep you busy enough to barely notice, right Will?" I look to his best friend for assistance in lifting Stefan's mood. I can't stand when people are sad, it triggers the eternal optimist in me.

Will clears his throat. "I mean we'll hang out and everything, but I'm not offering to service you. That's what Big Bertha is for."

This makes Stefan's face change: a tiny, one sided, beginning baby grin is pulling at his cheek.

"You're in an open relationship?" I question, confused.

That creates a full blown dimpled smile from Stefan. He laughs lightly and asks, "I haven't introduced you to Big Bertha yet?"

His tone has me nervous... Why would any woman let him call her Big Bertha? Is she modeling her name off Fat Amy? "No..." I nervously answer.

Stefan whips out his right hand and makes a fist. It hovers in the air about the same height as his head and, to my horror, it starts talking.

Stefan positions his thumb below his fingers making an improper fist. He makes a voice impersonating a woman's and talks out of the side of his mouth, "Hi, I'm Bertha."

I look from Stefan, to Will, and back again. I say in disbelief, "You named your masturbating hand? And made her talk!"

Will squeezes my leg, I don't know if it's in support or razzing.

"Want to see me do a trick?" Bertha offers.

"No!" I project and put my hands out in a bracing gesture. "I don't want to know what Stefan thinks a trick is with you."

The guys laugh at me and Bertha disappears. I accomplished my goal because Stefan isn't moping anymore, but at what cost? I never needed to know Stefan calls his masturbating hand Bertha.

Stefan steeples his fingers on our table. "Thanks Nik, I needed that."

I purse my lips. "I'm not sure if you're welcome."

Will leans over and kisses my cheek. His hand hasn't left my thigh this entire conversation. I feel comforted by his presence and that's what I need after what Stefan just subjected me to.

"So Nik, how you been?" Stefan asks, thankfully changing subjects.

"You have been a little oblivious this week, guess I can forgive that," I goad. Then I sigh. "I hate to admit it, but when you were late to class on Tuesday, Brock tried to interact with me again."

Will's face remains neutral, but his hand stiffens on my leg. That small action tells me all I need to know about how much he cares for me. "What did he do, Veronica?"

Oh shit, he just full named me, while demanding an answer. If we weren't discussing my former physical assaulter, that would be hot as fuck. I swallow. "Nothing really. He just put his hand on my back, but why would he think he can touch me? Ever."

"Nik, I'm sorry I was late. I didn't think something like that would happen," Stefan apologizes.

I put a hand up. "Dude, you needed to take Mia to the airport, there's nothing to be sorry for." It's not his fault Brock is denser than a pile of bricks.

Will speaks up sounding protective, "We need to get him to back off."

"Agreed," Stefan chimes in.

I nervously laugh, "Okay guys, you're not going to teach him a lesson like some stupid T.V. show."

"That's not what I had in mind," Will answers mischievously.

"Do share," Stefan says while leaning in conspiratorially.

Together the three of us hatch a plan. We need to make it clear to Brock that I'm nowhere near the realm of available, let alone interested in him.

An hour later we're walking across campus ready to set things in motion. I hope it works. I'm feeling nervous for a multitude of reasons. What if Brock isn't early to class? What if I'm overreacting? What if it works and he leaves me the fuck alone?

Will takes my hand in his. "I know you don't need a man to protect you," he comforts quietly enough that Stefan doesn't hear on the other side of me. "But I'm glad you trust me enough to try this."

My hands are getting sweaty from nerves. I take my hand out of his hold and hook it in the crook of his elbow. Will adjusts seamlessly like we've done this plenty of times before.

Stefan interrupts our moment, "I'm gonna hang back so you two can do your thing. I'll come down the stairs a bit after you so I can give a play by play of Brock's stupid face when he sees you."

I perk up at that, "Yes please!" I can't wait to hear how we crushed his douchebag ego.

Will and I descend the steps leading down to the classroom and I put on a lighthearted, giggly persona that I don't feel in my soul.

Halfway down the stairs Will asks, "Do you see him?"

I scan the courtyard and see Brock seated facing the stairs. He's leering directly at us with his arms crossed. Internally, I shiver at how pissed he looks right now. Externally though, I look up at Will with a fake flirtatious smile and answer, "Yeah."

Will is looking back at me, and I swear the *romance* exuding from us could be captured in a movie. "Perfect," he growls like a predator ready for a hunt.

I already told Will that my class was in the first room to the left of the stairs. He leads us that way and pulls me into a slightly recessed corner. It gives the illusion of privacy because it's shaded, but if you're looking, like Brock definitely is, you can see everything that's happening within its depths.

Will pushes me against the wall gently. He leans his forearm on the wall above my head and holds my hip with his right hand. I bite my lip and look up at him.

"Ready?" He asks for my permission before continuing with our plan.

I nod my head, unable to speak. *This may be for show, but can he do this again when he means it, please? And where there aren't witnesses? That would be great.*

Will starts kissing me. It's slow and tortuous. He kisses me like he has all the time in the world. I feel his soft lips caressing mine and his hand flexes on my hip. I lace my hands around the back of his neck. It's a good thing the wall is supporting all of my weight because I feel like I'm floating.

Then he nips at my bottom lip with his teeth. That's something he hasn't tried before. This may be a show to thwart Brock, but my body reacts to Will's. I smile against his lips and open my mouth to grant him access. His tongue slips in and strokes mine.

We continue making out for a while and then Will surfaces for a breath. He nuzzles into my neck and asks, "Do you think that was enough?"

I slightly shake my head. It could have been enough, but when a man can kiss like that, who would want to stop?

I feel his cheeks break into a devious smile as he kisses his way up my neck. I tilt my head back again to make sure he has room to do his work.

His hand leaves the wall and grips me by the throat. He removes his lips from my skin and I swallow back a whimper. "Remember, you asked for this," he warns.

Even though we planned this, the sheer possessiveness of his kiss steals my breath. He uses his grip on my neck to move my mouth into the perfect position. My hands slide down and rest on his chest. He's completely in control, and it feels... it feels like jumping and knowing that he'll always be there to catch me. He could swallow me whole right now and I'd die happy. Horny, but happy.

Will lessens the intensity of the kiss. He finishes it with a gentle peck of his lips against mine. I involuntarily let out a soft sigh and he smiles at me in response.

He strokes his thumb just below my jaw line. Will's voice turns gravelly and his potentially dominant side slips out, "Now be a good girl and get to class before you're late."

I'm dumbstruck, he's never tried that before. I don't know if I like it. I bite my lip and challenge him, "What if I don't want to?"

He uses his thumb to pull my bottom lip from beneath my teeth. "Then I guess you aren't actually a nerd. You're just a little slut in disguise, aren't you?"

My mouth drops open. First, did I like that better than being called a good girl? *Is there a degradation kink hiding somewhere in me?* Second, I can't keep tonsil tagging this man in the science building. Mr. Fitzgibbons could walk by any minute and I don't want him to see *this*. I say nothing in response to Will.

He kisses my forehead. "Call me on your drive home tonight, okay?"

That releases me from his spell. I go on my tip toes and kiss his lips lightly and whisper, "Thanks Will," before heading to class.

I enter the classroom with a giant grin on my face. Stefan glances up and pretends to be disappointed in me by shaking his head, while simultaneously giving me a covert thumbs up.

I intentionally change up my route to my desk and walk past Brock. He notices and bitterly spits out, "Geeze Nik, I get the picture. You've got a boyfriend now."

I stop mid-step and pivot to look at him. I tick off points with my fingers as I lecture him. "One, my name is Nikki or Veronica, not Nik. Not to you. Two," my head weaves a little with my sass, "Do you get the point? I'm not yours and I never will be. You don't get to touch me. Ever again. Period." I over-pronounce the final word.

He must be dense because he looks surprised at what I say. He crosses his arms and turns his back to me. As I round his desk and walk up to mine I hear him mumble under his breath, "Whatever. Ver-on-i-ca."

That makes my smile even bigger.

"Hey! How's it going?" I chirp to Stefan.

He slides closer to me and says in a hushed tone, "Nik, that was something else. I had to walk in here before I got secondhand horny."

I nudge him with my elbow. "Oh shut up, you knew it was coming."

"From my view, I don't think I was the only one cumming."

Nineteen

Game Night

It's Friday and I'm at work, I'm not supposed to be. My days off this weekend got mixed up, something about another employee wanting a vacation. It all works out in my favor because I can sleep in as late as I want tomorrow. That will probably be needed, because tonight I'm meeting the rest of Will's friend group. I know Stefan already, and Will told me that Chuck and Brittney will be there too. Which means that there will be two people there that like me, and two people there that definitely don't. Hopefully Will and Stefan have more sway in the group than Chuck and Brittney.

"Should I wear high rise jeans to accentuate my hips?" I ask Tipp while I'm driving home from my opening shift.

"Girl yes!" She yells through the speakerphone.

I chuckle. "It's a good thing my bra is holding the phone up, if you'd been in my ear I think I would have temporarily lost hearing!" I taunt her excitement and continue, "Ugh, I'm gonna have to wash my hair again. I'm barely going to have enough time to get everything done before tonight."

"Smell like a sandwich?"

I roll my eyes at the steering wheel. "When do I not smell like a sandwich these days? I have to keep an entirely separate bag to put my dirty work clothes in when I change for class. The other day I sat down in French and that guy Alex that sits next to us? He smelled the air and then said, 'Mmmm, it smells like sandwiches in here.' I almost died."

"He didn't!" She yells this down the line too.

"He did! It was mortifying. I really hope he doesn't know I was the one perfuming our classroom."

"Okay yes, you do need to wash your hair then."

I pull into Nana's drive. It's barely noon, but a three a.m. wakeup for work means you get to nap whenever you want to. I ramble off my to-do list to Tipp. "Shower, eat, nap, get cute, survive meeting the guys."

"You got this babe." It's the first quiet thing she's said in this conversation. That unnerves me.

"You don't sound so confident."

"You just told me to stop yelling!" Tipp yells at me.

"That's better. You going calm had me worried." I laugh as I tease her. I hit the lock on my key fob and head into the house.

"Bye, bitch!" Tipp screams for emphasis.

"Bye, love."

As I leave the foyer and enter the kitchen, I see Nana has recently put the finishing touches on lunch and left a plate for me on the counter. Next to it, there's a note in her perfect previous-teacher penmanship.

Nikki,

I hope tonight goes great. I'll be out for a while shopping with Laura. Our practice starts at six tonight and I don't think I'll make it home between then and now. Be yourself and I'm sure they'll love you. Talk to you when our paths cross next.

Love always,

Nana

I don't deserve a Nana as wonderful as she is. She is the sweetest, most diplomatic, nurturing woman I've ever met. People should be jealous of how wonderful my Nana is. I keep notes like this in a keepsake box in my room.

I unwrap the tinfoil from the plate to reveal my favorite: a crispy chicken caesar salad. I take Nana's note and the lunch to my room and sit at my desk while I eat. The weather is turning. Blooms are showing up on previously naked tree branches as Spring continues to warm the air. I'll be expected to put away all my cozy sweaters and knee high boots soon. San Diego is too hot for those anyway, but I sweat a little extra to embrace the cute outfits of Fall and Winter. I watch the breeze blow through the trees lining Nana's driveway and listen to the birds chirping outside my window as I devour my salad.

When I'm finished, I tuck Nana's note into my keepsake box and take my plate to the kitchen. I check the clock: one p.m. I backwards plan the afternoon to Otis who has joined me while I wash my plate off.

"If Will picks me up at five-thirty tonight, then I need to get up at four, just to make sure I have enough time to get ready." I dry my hands and pick Otis up. I continue as we walk back to my room, "I'm guessing it will take me about an hour to shower, settle in and actually fall asleep which means I'll get a two hour nap when all this is said and done." I put Otis down on my bed and he meows his agreement to my plan. "Okay buddy, stay there and I'll be back in just a bit. Gonna cuddle me for an afternoon nap?"

Otis heads to the unused side of my double bed and starts kneading the pillow. I pet under his chin in his favorite spot and he purrs. I take this as commitment to company for my nap. I turn on a four p.m. alarm and close my bedroom door. Tonight will be here before I know it.

At five I get a call from Will. "Hey, slight problem with our plans tonight"

Seriously? I spent my entire afternoon getting ready for tonight, I swear, if he's canceling on me...

Our relationship is too new for him to notice when my customer service voice kicks in. "What's up?"

"I had to stay late at work and I just got off," Will explains. I hear rustling from his end of the phone.

"So, what's the problem?" I don't understand. He's off now, and there's still an hour before we're supposed to be at Stefan's.

"You haven't seen me when I get off a shift before, have you?"

What does that mean? I arch an eyebrow, as if he can see. "Why does that matter?"

He chuckles. "I'll spare you the details, but I need a shower before we hang out tonight."

Will. Showering. Those are some details I'd like to hear. "I'm not afraid of details about you showering." I chew my cheek as I torment him.

He groans and bites out, "Nikki, if we're gonna make it to Stefan's without being late I'm gonna need you to meet me at my place. I'm sorry. But with only an hour we'll be lucky if I can make it home, clean up, and get to Stefan's on time."

I wave my hand in the air. "This whole conversation is you asking if I can meet you at your place instead of you picking me up?"

"Yeah, I'm so sorry."

Why does he feel bad about this? Life happens. It's not like he had a choice about staying at work or not. "That's no big deal Will," I calmly reply. "I'll head over in about fifteen minutes, okay?"

He lets out an audible sigh. "Perfect, if I'm not out of the shower yet my sister can let you in."

"Sounds good, see you soon."

"Thanks Nikki, can't wait." He ends our call.

There's no way I want to get stuck making small talk with his sister while he's naked and soapy. Nope. She'll be able to read my mind or some weird big sister voodoo. I'll head over in twenty minutes. That will give Will plenty of time to get home and wash off. Thankfully I'm always ready early, which means I don't have to scramble to finish up.

I go to my cozy reading chair and kick up my feet. Twenty minutes is plenty of time to figure out what is going on with Tink and Hook. I think Tink is my new plus sized icon. She's petite, hex her for being short, but she owns her curves in every outfit she tailors for herself. Otis climbs onto my lap and we get lost to the world of smut for a couple pages.

Forty minutes later, as I walk up the sidewalk to Will's sister's condo, I call out, "Sorry I'm late!"

"No worries, it's work's fault anyway. You couldn't have known you needed to be ready early," he reassures me. I make it to Will and he wraps his arms around my waist pulling me in for a hug. His hugs really are the best thing since sliced bread. Combine that with his freshly showered smell and I fold into him eagerly.

Will goes to pull back but I ask, "Just one more minute?"

He chuckles and grips me tighter. "Anything for you."

We stand there in the setting sun of Southern California and I bask in the comfort of his strong and safe embrace. He smells of woods and citrus. He's wearing a graphic T, jeans, and Converse. It's a little nicer than his typical boardshorts, but not fancy. My three-inch heels help my head fit perfectly in the crook of his neck.

Eventually, I release him and we kiss hello. It's soft and familiar. I wish Will would deepen it, but we do have places to be.

He grabs my hand with a familiar warmth that wraps around my palm and we head across the street to his car.

I use my free hand to scratch my ear, "I won't lie to you by omission."

He uses the key and unlocks my door. "Oh?"

I get in and pull my door closed. I stare directly ahead, stiff as a board. It's a little toasty in his car, but the air conditioning will turn on soon enough. As Will rounds the hood I brace to tell him the truth. I hope I don't upset him. Previous men have gotten mad at me for less...

Will gets in the driver's seat and immediately blasts the air. The breeze soothes my apprehensiveness and I let out a slow, deep breath.

"Nikki, what's going on?" Will asks, sounding worried.

I turn in my seat and look at him. "I wasn't late because I was still getting ready," I blurt out in one breath.

This makes Will smile. "Why were you late then?"

I ring my fingers and I whisper at an inaudible level, "I was reading smut."

Will takes my hands in his. "Nikki, I can't hear you."

I bite my lower lip and stare at the ceiling of his car. The ugly beige ceiling of his car. I staccato my words. "I. Was. Reading. Smut."

Will's thumb strokes the back of my hand reassuring me. He hasn't tensed, his grip on my hands hasn't tightened, and his smile hasn't morphed away from a sweet one. "Babe, I don't know what that means."

Shit, now I have to spell my crime out to him. I could beat around the bush, but if this is a deal breaker we might as well get this conversation out of the way before I have to survive meeting his group of friends.

"There's a nice way to put this, but I'm not going to use it. I was reading porn. Guys watch it, a lot of women read it."

His eyes start to twinkle along with his smile, "You're late because you were reading erotica?"

I pull my hands out of his. "No!" I whisper-shout. "Erotica is bodice rippers, men degrading women. Smut," I clarify with indignation, "Is about women embracing their sexual desires. Smut is women getting what they want out of sex. Smut is women being degraded if it's their kink, and they always have a safe word." I think I'm finished but my words keep flowing uncontrollably. "And they have a Dom who respects their needs. And the best smut is written by women. Oh!" I point my finger in the air to emphasize the importance of this upcoming thought, "They also, ALWAYS, have an orgasm."

There. He knows it. I'm a crazy, smut reading whore. I have let my freak flag fly. I mentally prepare myself to be dumped and tossed to the curb.

Will's hand gently caresses my cheek. He lovingly pulls my face to look at him. "Nikki, you're late because you were reading a book that happens to be smutty?"

"Yeah," I quietly admit.

Then he leans across the center console and kisses me. His soft lips brush along mine in the sweetest temporary embrace.

I break our kiss in confusion. "You're not mad?" I ask, puzzled by his reaction.

His hand drops from my cheek. He rotates his body back into his seat and puts on his seatbelt. Then he inquires, "How could I be mad at you? You're adorable."

My cheeks warm with a blush. "No one's ever been accepting of my reading habits before. Their responses are usually demeaning and hurtful."

Will's face flashes with anger. It flickers so quickly before fading to his usual carefree expression I barely notice it. "You're dating me now, Nikki. You should never feel lesser than anyone again. What's more, you're reading a fucking book. How many of those assholes from your past have even picked up a book in the last calendar year?"

Well, look at this knight in shining armor. He's technically in a beige Camry, and it's not exactly sparkling, but he's standing up for me so gallantly. Will keeps showing me more and more reasons I'm glad he gave me a second chance.

I haven't replied to his kind words so he puts a hand on my thigh. He hasn't started driving yet. "Nikki, if we have any chance getting there soon you've got to put your seatbelt on."

"Oh!" I squeak out and buckle up. I lace my fingers with his and he drives us to Stefan's house. I can do this. If I just told Will one of my deepest, darkest secrets, getting to know the guys won't be too bad, right?

Once we're on the main road Will squeezes my knee and asks, "What exactly is happening in these smutty books of yours? Any fantasies we'll need to recreate later?"

I laugh at him and start to explain the *Wicked Villains* series. Turning the bad guys good and the good guys bad, Katee Robert is a mastermind. Tink and Hook? They're the best so far.

By the time we get on the freeway, Will's face is a little pink. I don't know if he was ready for the summaries I've provided. There's an infinite amount of smut out there. I haven't gotten into monsters yet, but I did accidentally read one once. I've told Will the deepest taboos I've stumbled across. I've yet to read a smutty book that was too much for me to handle. *Haunting Adeline* almost sent me over the edge, but Tipp read it too and we processed with one another as needed. I think that's where I started to lose Will so I dialed my descriptions back to more consensual books.

I've just wrapped up my description of the Twisted Sisters' books when we pull up to Stefan's house. With a quick glance I notice Will's pants are looking a little tighter.

I go to open my door when Will says, "I need a minute."

The grin that cracks across my face hurts my cheeks. I pressure him to admit his problem with a mock innocent voice, "Why ever would you need a minute?"

He covers his face with a hand and scrubs it down his mouth and chin. Then he cracks his neck and turns to me. "Because Nikki, you just spent a fifteen minute drive telling me about all the sex scenes that you've read recently and how much you liked them." His voice darkens as he growls at me, "That does things to a guy."

I swallow and try to bite down my smile. He looks so miserable over there. It's adorable. I shake my head. I'm not going to make this any worse for him, but then Tipp's voice pops up in the back of my mind. My left hand slowly unbuckles my seatbelt and my right prepares to unlatch the door as my mouth is possessed by the devil. My voice turns sultry as I goad him, "Imagine how much worse it would be if you knew which of those scenes I wanted to act out with you." I unlock the door and hop out before he can grab me and keep me in his car any longer. Apparently I want him suffering tonight as much as I am, only in a slightly different way.

I lean on the trunk of Will's car as I wait for him to get out. I boost my confidence going into this unknown situation and assess my outfit. I'm in signature wedges, the best heels one can wear in Southern California. I have on the same pair of high waisted jeans that I wore to the bowling alley, cuffed two rolls at the ankles, of course. My top is flattering, showing off my figure without being too revealing: forest green complimented by large brown earrings. Hopefully Stefan's house is cool inside because my bangs are styled, my hair is down, and I don't want to overheat under its length and weight.

As I'm brushing my hair over my shoulder I hear Stefan's front door open. "What are you doing down there Nik?" he calls from the front porch. It's an entire flight of stairs above the street where we're parked.

"Waiting for Will," I project back hoping I'm loud enough for him to hear.

Stefan waves off my comment. "Leave him, he knows the way. Come on up."

I look to the car behind me and see that Will hasn't moved to head out yet so I walk off toward Stefan's stairs. At the top I take a deep breath and steady myself. I have no idea how many people I'm about to meet. I think to myself, *just be yourself, if they don't like you that's their problem, not yours.* I don't want to walk into this situation alone, but I also didn't think that through before making Will's situation harder in the car.

Stefan has gone back inside by the time I reach the top. I reach for the doorknob when I hear Will behind me, "Don't let the dog out."

I startle at his sudden presence but feel my body relax with relief knowing I'm not flying solo anymore. When did he get out of the car, and how did he get up those stairs quickly and silently? "Oh, hey. Thanks," I reply as we head inside.

We enter a mostly clean house. There's a large grey sectional to the right of the open concept living room. Behind me on the wall is a T.V. with some sort of video game on the screen. I see a couple of guys with controllers in their hands, intently focused on whatever they're playing, which gives me a moment to get the lay of the land.

To our left there is a pool table and I see Stefan and Chuck holding pool sticks. Behind them is a kitchen island with barstools and a couple of women are talking in hushed tones in the kitchen. I recognize one of them as Brittney.

Will puts his hand on the small of my back and guides me to a room that is straight ahead. We enter and he instructs me, "You can put your purse in this room, it's Stefan's and no one else should be coming in here tonight."

"Thanks."

Will kisses my head once I've tucked my purse out of the way next to a shelf. "Let's go meet everybody then." He laces my hand with his and we walk back to the living room.

We head over to the kitchen first. It gives off eighties vibes with wood stained cupboards, square tiled counters with matching backsplash, and a linoleum floor. The appliances are all white. With that being said, it appears like a kitchen that has been well used, seen many memories, and is clean enough to eat from.

Will motions to the two women talking by the sink. "You already know Brittney, and this is Stefan's mother. We all call her Mrs. Edwards."

I stick my hand out to Stefan's mother. "Nice to meet you Mrs. Edwards, you have a lovely home."

She shakes my hand with a tight smile. "Good to meet you, Veronica. Stefan and Brittney have told me all about you." I have a feeling that Brittney isn't a fan of me for whatever reason. How much does that matter though? This isn't Will's mother.

I decide to fight Brittney's fire with my own sickly sweet lemonade. "Stefan's been a great lab partner for me in Astronomy this semester. He really is a wonderful friend."

Mrs. Edwards' icy demeanor cracks a little bit at my compliment toward her son, "Well, that's great to hear. You two go on and have some fun."

I don't need her approval, but I get the feeling that sucking up a little bit by praising one of the boys she raised can't entirely hurt.

Will leads the way to the pool table and nods his head at Chuck and Stefan as we walk by. "No introductions needed here," he says as we head to the group of guys on the couch.

I wave hello to them both as we pass by.

Two of the guys are playing a cartoon fighting game. It looks like two figures in a fighting ring flailing about aimlessly, but from the commentary of the third guy, it seems that one of them is in the lead. When the fight ends the guy with glasses pumps his fist in the air.

"I take it he won?" I ask Will.

"Yeah. Guys don't start a new game. I want you to meet Nikki," Will says over the din of the television. The third guy grabs the remote and turns the entire system off.

The other two grumble at him, but he doesn't seem to notice. He stands and his height is the first thing that strikes me, he's at least six feet tall. *Are all these guys massive?* He has a kind, genuine smile and caramel colored skin. He takes a step toward us and reaches out his hand. "Hey Nikki, I'm Tyler. It's great to meet you and finally put a face to the name of the girl Will won't stop talking about."

His comment has me blushing. I shake Tyler's hand and ask Will, "You won't shut up about me, huh?" Then I look back at Tyler. "It's nice to meet you, too." He heads over to watch Stefan and Chuck as they wrap up their game of pool.

The two guys on the couch haven't moved. I'm guessing Tyler was raised with a few more manners. The male on the left has freckles, pale skin like he spends a little too much time indoors, and an innocent face. He waves to me.

"Nikki, this is Mark," Will motions to him. "And Sean."

Sean is wiry, has glasses, and short dark hair. He does nothing to acknowledge my presence.

Meeting Tyler felt natural, but Mark and Sean's lack of enthusiasm has me feeling uneasy. I plaster on what I hope is a convincing smile and follow Will's lead.

He pulls me back to the middle of the living area. "Let's see how the game is going between Chuck and Stefan. You've been warned, Stefan always looses to his brother and it always pisses him off."

I appreciate how he's trying to lighten the mood after an awkward hello with Mark and Sean. Brittney is chatting animatedly with Tyler, so Will takes me to a barstool to watch the match.

The two brothers are well suited. They're both down to one ball left to sink, plus the eight ball. As we start watching, Stefan narrowly misses sinking the last remaining striped ball. The angle is minutely off and it ricochets away from the corner pocket. Chuck laughs mockingly at his brother and takes his shot. Unfortunately for Stefan, while missing his shot, he also left the cue ball in the perfect position for his brother.

Chuck sinks the last solid ball and declares for the eight, "Left corner pocket." He motions to it with the cue stick. He sizes up his shot quickly and sinks it confidently.

Stefan is effectively defeated. The brothers shake hands as if their mother has instructed them to.

Brittney runs up to her boyfriend and hugs him. In baby talk she says, "Good job baby. You beat him again!"

I've never heard a grown woman use baby talk to another adult before. As I'm wondering if my brain has short-circuited, I hear Chuck respond in the same baby talk, "Thanks, baby. You're the bestest."

Have I left reality and entered a fifth dimension? Why are two grown ass adults using baby talk? Is this a kink I haven't heard of yet? I make a silent prayer to the smut gods, *Please never let my smut writing queens use baby talk as a kink. I'll take monster romance before that. Or at least have a good content warning so I can steer clear. Amen.*

"What do you think?" Stefan asks as he puts his cue stick away and reracks the balls.

I don't think and reply honestly, "Disgusting."

Will looks at me surprised and Stefan says, "Wow, way to insult a man's home within the first five minutes."

Everyone is staring at me now. "No Stefan, not that!" I apologize quickly. "Sorry I meant like that was a rough loss. Not sure why, *'Disgusting,'* slipped out there."

Stefan checks me over with a side eye. "Right."

Will cuts in, helping to remove everyone's attention from the massive foot I've shoved down my own throat and am currently choking on. "What's the plan for tonight?"

Tyler chimes in, "Mr. Edwards is picking up the pizza on his way home. Then some games from what I hear."

"He'll be here any minute," Mrs. Edwards calls from the kitchen. I didn't know she was still down here. Then I see that she's gathered ten cups and an assortment of drinks from the fridge.

"Come over here Nik," Stefan beckons while heading toward an opening in the wall I hadn't seen on first glance. I leave the comfort of Will's presence and follow Stefan around the corner. "Which games would you be most interested in playing?" he asks as he turns on a light and shows me a pile of games on a dining room table.

The room itself is crowded with storage and piles of unfinished laundry. I force my eyes to focus on the games in the corner nearest us and point to a tiled version of Rummikub. "I've played that one with my family before, so I think it will be best since tonight is about getting to know everyone, not a new game."

Stefan smiles as he picks it up. "Perfect. Hey Nik, glad you came tonight. Just be warned, we're pretty cutthroat with games in this house. Anyway, Will's been itching for the opportunity for the group to get to know you."

I don't think much on what he said other than the fact that I didn't know this mattered so much to Will.

I ask Stefan in hushed tones, "Is it normal for him to bring a girl to meet the guys before his own family?"

Stefan stops and pulls me deeper into the unused dining room. "He hasn't told you?" he quietly asks.

"Told me what?"

"You're the first girl he's brought to meet the group. Ever."

My mouth drops so fast I feel my jaw pop in shock of the sudden movement. I point to my own chest and demand, "Why me?"

Stefan lightly chuckles. "I told you months ago, I think you two are perfect for each other. My guess is Will thinks so too."

He picks up Rummikub and leaves me alone in the dining room to process that. In the middle of a strangers house, and I have now learned that this is the most important test I'll take and I've already succeeded in making a fool of myself.

This is starting off swell.

I roll my shoulders, crack my neck, turn off the dining room light and head back out to the group. They're all standing around the pool table talking now. I scan the group for Will but I can't find him.

Brittney calls out, "He's in the bathroom Nikki, come stand by me."

I'd rather use said bathroom with the door open in front of all these boys but I can't be a complete bitch. Luckily, Tyler is standing next to her and he shuffles to the side to make room for me.

"So we're having pizza again?" Britt asks the group, turning up her nose.

"What's wrong with that?" Sean asks.

"Nothing really, but would a salad kill you?" She asks, then alludes to something more sinister. "And you know how Will gets when he eats pizza."

Chuck, Sean, Mark, and Stefan all laugh.

"That's right! How did I forget about that?" Stefan chortles.

I know Britt is intentionally bringing up something I don't know about to get under my skin. I've hung out with mean girls before. I know how to handle her catty behavior, so I consciously take Britt's bait and ask, "Alright guys, who's going to fill me in on this embarrassing story about Will?"

Chuck raises his hand. "Me! Me! I love this one!"

The rest of the group yields to him.

Brittney wraps her arms around Chuck as if she needs to stake her claim. He gently pushes out of her grip to better use his body to tell the story and that action brings me smug satisfaction. I have no interest in Chuck, especially if Brittney is his type, but he just swatted down her embrace in front of everyone. I want to be a woman who supports other women, but something about Brittney has burrowed under my skin and it's starting to feel like an abscess.

He's cleared himself an entire side of the pool table to tell this story. His hands are dramatic and aid the narration as he dives in. "So, Will has a small problem. He loves eating pizza with us, but his body doesn't always agree with that choice. One of the first times he came over we all had pizza. We were playing games and hanging out; there was nothing special about it."

Stefan is already losing the battle of holding back his laughter as his brother tells this story.

"It must have been winter because Will and Brittney were sitting under the same blanket once we had finished eating. It was a big blanket. So, anyway, a bit after eating Will gets up from the couch to go to the bathroom. That boy needs the toilet after eating, let me warn you now, Nikki."

I scrunch my eyebrows at Chuck's comment. "Noted?" *Where is this leading?*

He continues, "Anyway, once we hear the door click to the bathroom Brittney says in her adorable teeny, tiny, cutie, pootie, wittle voice, 'Guys, I think he farted.' Then she dips her head under the blanket and when she pops back up it looks like she's about to puke. 'He definitely farted,' she confirms, throws the blanket and bolts off the couch."

I think the story is going to end there, but Chuck keeps going. "When she threw off the blanket she released the gas that had been contained."

Mark, Sean, and Stefan are all solidly laughing right now. Tyler has been smiling with me, but his lack of reaction is making me think he hasn't heard this story yet either.

"Nikki, you don't understand the level of foulness that fart contained." Chuck points to the part of the living room with the sectional. "We had to completely evacuate that half of the living room. When Will came out of the bathroom we were all huddled in the kitchen. He had no idea what had happened."

At this moment Will sneaks up behind me and asks the group, "Hey guys, what are we talking about?"

Everyone, including me, busts out belly laughing at his timing. Will's eyebrows arch in confusion. He slides his arm around my waist and waits for me to catch my breath.

Tyler is the first to sober up and explains to Will, "Chuck was regaling us with the tales of your flatulence."

Will immediately knows what story has been shared and defends himself, "Well if you didn't order the greasiest pizza in town then we wouldn't have this problem."

I snake my arm around his waist and give him a squeeze. I want Will to know that his friends aren't going to frighten me away. They might convince me to never have pizza with this man, but this silly story is their way of showing they love him.

Through the kitchen we hear a door slam and a man's voice calls out, "Pizza delivery!"

The rest of the group disperses to the kitchen for dinner and I linger back with Will.

He takes my hands and quietly asks, "Please tell me that story isn't going to scare you off?"

I balance on my tip toes and give him a kiss. When my feet are planted securely on the ground again I assuage his fears, "As long as that doesn't happen every time you eat."

His face melts into a relieved grin and we join the others in the kitchen.

Stefan jeers, "No pizza for Will, he's only allowed salads."

"Shut up man," Will pushes his best friend away from the pizza.

We each get a few pieces and a soda to drink. Since we're the last ones to get our food there aren't enough seats left for us. Stefan notices and offers me his. I accept and listen to the lively conversation around me as we all eat our fill.

Will seems at ease with this group. They must have been friends for a while. I learn that Sean works as a line cook in Meghan's kitchen, at the casino. Mark works at the amusement park in a department adjacent to Will's, and Tyler is in school to be some sort of doctor.

When the catch up conversations begin to lull, Stefan brings out Rummikub. This signals everyone to clean up their spots to make way for the game. At some point in the banter, members of our group left. I only notice because there are now enough barstools for all of us. I do a mental head count and notice that Brittney, Mrs. and Mr. Edwards have all disappeared.

"Will Brittney or your parents be coming back?" I ask Stefan curiously.

"Nah," he says as he grabs my paper plate for me. "Mom and Dad do their own thing, and Brittney doesn't play games with us."

Chuck confirms Stefan's statement with a nod. I think it's odd that she won't play games with them, but that's her own business.

The tiles are spread across the counter and we all work together to put them face down. "Does everyone know the rules?" Chuck asks the group.

We all answer with a version of, "Yes."

Will whispers in my ear, "Are you sure you know the rules?"

I don't know why he's so worried. "Yeah, I've played with my mom before."

With that we all pick up our tiles and begin searching for runs or like numbers to start the game. I set out my tiles and watch the others. Chuck, Stefan, and Sean seem to have changed their demeanor. Their faces are now sinister and serious. Chuck pops his knuckles like he's gearing up for a fight. Sean stretches his arms and shoulders and twists his neck. Stefan's changed completely. The Border Collie friend I knew has been replaced with a Doberman. His smile is gone, replaced with a ferocious mask of predatory intent.

I wiggle in my seat, a little nervous at the shift in the four men before me. I'm glad that Will, Mark, and Tyler still seem normal.

Chuck is the first to have enough points to play.

Soon enough every person has started a set in the playing field except for me. We cycle through the group of players one more time before I speak up.

"I thought you needed fifty points or more to begin the round?"

The group laughs at me as if this is an absolutely absurd remark.

"I thought you knew the rules," Sean teases me.

"I do, but you're starting with fewer points than I've learned with. So how many do we need to begin?" I reply calmly. I'm competitive, but I don't want to seem like an over zealous rule follower this early in the night.

"The rules state that we need thirty points, and they can be from any combination of tiles that fit."

If that's the case I've been sitting on plays this entire time. I've been stuck at 47 points for two rounds waiting to draw one perfect tile so I could start being a threat. I don't believe the guys, but I don't want to be a problem. "If you say so," I say as I finally play my tiles.

We continue the first game and it wraps up in two more moves by Tyler. Luckily, I was able to play most of my tiles and I didn't have to eat too many points. It feels like we finished that round too quickly though. At least compared to the games I've played with my family.

We all tally up our points with near silent concentration and announce them. I'm in the middle of the pack with Stefan being the leader with the fewest points, and Mark having the most.

We flip all the tiles over and shuffle them in an unorganized clanking mess. I ask over the din, "Are we playing with your rules then? Of starting at thirty points?"

Stefan answers me, "Those are the game rules, but if you're so certain Nik, we'll play a round with your rules."

I don't want to cause a scene. I was only trying to figure out how many points we needed before I gave myself an unnecessary handicap again. "I'm just checking, we don't need to do what I remember," I offer sweetly.

Stefan's nostrils flare like he's sensing a challenge. "Oh no Nik. We'll play your way. Right boys?"

I see Sean and Chuck's smiles morph into devious sneers.

"Fifty points it is," Chuck backs his brother.

They're all acting so differently than when we arrived. We ate pizza and had fun but as soon as this game came out it's like they've turned into a pack of hyenas looking at a corpse, fighting over who gets the tastiest bits. I'm starting to feel like I'm the butt of some joke between them.

Will's hand lands on my shoulder and he gives it a light squeeze. He whispers to me, "They're like a dog with a bone when it comes to games. They're cutthroat, but you get used to it." He kisses me on the cheek and goes back to shuffling the tiles about the kitchen island.

We draw our beginning tiles and try to find a configuration that adds up to fifty points. The game starts with Stefan since he's now in the lead.

He's unable to play and lays it on thick. "No where near fifty here," and stares at me as his hand draws a tile to add to his reserve.

Tyler and Will go next, quietly drawing tiles without commentary.

I draw and it moves to Chuck's turn.

"I'm at 32." He glares at me and draws.

Sean follows suit with a scowl in my direction.

We're back to Stefan and he gets meaner, "Sure glad we listened to Nikki's suggestion here." He draws a second tile.

No one is able to play this round of turns and I'm certain that I fucked up. But I didn't know. "Guys I'm sorry, I didn't know," I try to apologize to the group.

Stefan picks up his third tile and snarls out, "You thought you knew better than the rules Nikki. We're playing by your rules now, how's that going?"

I feel the back of my eyes start to sting. What happened to my nice friend? Why is he being such a dick right now?

Tyler, Mark, and Will have been silent this entire game. It's me against three guys. They're all being assholes and I really wish I had never said anything at all.

I draw again, I'm one tile away from being able to play. I need two more points, that's it.

"Love your rules, Nikki," Chuck sarcastically jibes at me as he draws a tile. "Oh finally, I can play NEXT time," he gives me a dirty look as he adds it to his hand.

Sean's the most vicious with his commentary. "Real smart one you picked Will."

He glares at me as he adds yet another tile to his hand.

Will finally has something to say. "Sean, shut the fuck up. You can be a dick about the game and the rules, but don't you dare insult Nikki's intelligence."

Sean flicks his eyes to Will and nods. He doesn't offer an apology and Will doesn't force one either.

I make a fist under the table. I push my nails into the palm of my hand as hard as I can to focus on anything other than the overwhelming need to cry right now. I've never been made to feel so small for such an insignificant mistake before. Will isn't saying anything to get the rest of them to back off either. He told me earlier I should never feel less-than, but I sure as shit am feeling that way now. I just need to make it through this game and excuse myself to the bathroom when it's over. Someone please be able to play already.

When it comes to my turn I suggest, "Why don't we start the round over? I was clearly wrong."

The three laugh at me. Actually laugh. Stefan sticks to his new prick personality. "You modified the rules. It was a great idea Nik, really wonderful."

"Yeah Nik," Sean chimes in. He shouldn't be calling me Nik, only Stefan and Will can get away with that, but I don't think I can correct him without even more hatred being thrown my way. After butchering my name he continues, "This is the best game I've ever played. Absolutely no action. Perfection." Sean concludes his mocking with a chef's kiss.

Stefan's turn provides a minuscule amount of relief for me. He plays and I hear two other people say they'll be able to play now. We spent so many cycles gathering tiles that the game is over within two plays by every person.

I don't care about my points. I excuse myself by quietly mumbling, "I need the restroom," and getting up from the table.

I can feel the three of them glaring at my back as I walk to the bathroom. A tear breaks over the dam right before I make it to the door. I rush in and lightly close the door and lock it behind me.

I turn on the faucet and lean my hands on the counter. As I stare at myself in the mirror silent tears stream down my face. *If that's how Will's friends play a game then I don't think I want to be a part of this group. I made one innocent mistake and they're making me feel so inferior for it.*

I count to ten twice and then focus on slowing my breathing. There are no tissues on the counter so I grab some toilet paper and dab the evidence of my crying off my cheeks. There's no trash can. I open the toilet, drop it in, and flush. Now I actually need to wash my hands. I dry them with the washcloth and give myself a final look in the mirror.

They'd have to be blind to not know what happened in here. My eyes are bloodshot and my Irish heritage has my cheeks shining red and splotchy. Hopefully they're too self absorbed to notice.

I walk back to the kitchen counter and they tell me I'm still in the middle of the pack, Tyler has pulled to the lead this time.

I don't care. I won't sit down again. Instead I choose to stand behind my chair, almost next to Will. I tell him, "I need to leave after this game, I have to get up early in the morning for work." I don't know if I told him I didn't have a shift tomorrow. I don't care if he knows I'm lying. I need to get out of here.

"Gonna join in?" Tyler asks, giving me a sympathetic one sided smile.

"I think I've had enough for tonight, thanks." I'm only polite to him because he wasn't a dick like the others. It wasn't his place to defend me, that's what Will should have done.

I silently repeat to myself, *Don't cry. They don't deserve to see your tears.* Over and over again until the game finally wraps up.

Will pushes back to leave as soon as the totals are tallied. I don't know who won, I don't care. However, my mother did raise me to be a gracious guest. I look at Stefan and say with minimal emotion, "Thank you for having me over tonight." I turn on my heel and head out of the house and down the stairs without saying goodbye to the rest of the group.

Will manages to get to my car door first and opens it for me. I hold my tears back.

"You okay?" he asks once we're on the freeway back to his place.

"Fine," I deadpan. My face is turned to look out my window. I don't want him to see any errant tears that manage to escape.

We drive the rest of the distance in silence. My surroundings begin to blur and I realize it's my eyes trying to let the crying begin. I swallow back my emotions. I can make it to my car. Ten more minutes.

Will parks in his usual spot and I immediately get out of his car. I walk down the street toward my own car and he catches up to me.

He grabs my arm and tries to stop me. I pull it angrily from his grasp.

He follows me to my car. "Please Nikki, can we go upstairs and talk about tonight?"

"Now you have something to say!" I yell at him too loudly for the peaceful night that surrounds us.

"Nikki I'm sorry, I just— please come upstairs and talk to me," he practically begs.

I turn from him and get in my car. I don't hug him. I don't kiss him. I turn on my car and drive off without another word. If Will had something to say it should have been in my defense to his friends.

I feel betrayed and let down. That was Will's friend group. He should have stood up to them for me. Is this the way he'll eventually treat me?

My tears spill over immediately after I turn off of Will's street. They continue my entire drive home. When I pull into Nana's driveway I see that she's still up so I sneak into my room through the backdoor. I don't want to worry her with how I look at the end of this date. My tears continue to stream down my face as I get ready for bed. They only dry up once I've drifted to sleep.

Twenty

A Helping Hand

WILL CALLED ME 6 times over the weekend, but I let it ring through to voicemail every time. He even sent me ten-cent text messages asking if I was okay and if we could chat. I left them all unanswered. He told me his friends could be dicks about game rules, but now that I'd experienced their behavior first hand there should have been a more serious conversation about it beforehand. Will did stand up to Sean when he insulted my intelligence. I'm guessing that cruelty when it's game related is acceptable to them, but when the insults became personal Will drew a line. I needed a couple of days to decide if I could forgive him.

The next week I didn't hide from Will and Stefan, not like I did when Brock assaulted me. I sat at our table for dinner with the guys and ate in silence. They tried to push me into having conversations after eating with them but I made up excuses; having a lot of homework to catch up on and studying for our looming finals.

Will walked with Stefan and me to the science complex but when he tried to splinter off just the two of us I refused and headed downstairs to class.

By French on Wednesday, Tipp has had enough of my avoidance tactics. "Either tell me what happened or I'll go find Will and ask him myself," she demands after a particularly silent class with me.

I try deflecting. "I have to get to English."

It doesn't work, "Great, that gives us fifteen minutes to walk together and catch up."

I sigh and roll my eyes at her in exasperation. Best friends are so annoying. They think they know you and that talking shit through with them will help. Gross.

I cave and give her a speedy recap of the evening and what Chuck, Sean, and Stefan were saying to me. She chews the information over and offers, "Ready for an annoying, brutally honest but you need to hear it, best friend moment?"

Shit, we only pull that when we're not going to like what the other has to say. I stop walking and place my feet in a bracing stance as if her words will be physically jarring to me. "No. Say it anyway."

She crosses her arms and glares at me as she admonishes, "Will should have stood up for you, you need to talk to him about that if things are going to go further. Yeah, they were being assholes, especially when you remember it was your first time getting to know any of them. Also, you're being a little too sensitive."

That last one stings, but I know deep down, hiding behind my heart, probably in the pit of my stomach, that she's right. I pull Tipp into an embrace. I give her a little attitude, "Thanks Mom. I don't need an escort all the way to class though."

She pats me on the head, laying it on thick. "I'll check in that you did your homework and talked to Will about this in a couple days." Tipp turns on her heel and struts off to wherever she needs to be next.

I keep going toward English and pull out my phone. I dial Will and get sent directly to voicemail. He's at work. I leave a message. "Hey, uh, can we chat today when you're off work? Let me know. Okay, bye." My voice came out more reserved than normal, but he hurt my feelings and needs to make up for it before we're good again.

In the middle of class my phone vibrates in my pocket. I pull it out to see proof of Will spending ten more cents on me.

> I should be home by 5. Come by whenever class is out.

Our professor must have sensed our class was over learning before we walked in. For the first time this term he dismisses class early, thirty minutes at that. I could mingle to kill time but I want to get the conversation with Will over and done with. Maybe he'll get off of work a little early too? I decide to head to his complex and wait however long it takes.

When I get to Will's I knock. Meghan promptly opens the door and invites me in.

"Hey," I say nervously. I haven't had a one on one conversation with her before. "Has Will made it home yet? I didn't see his car out front."

She returns to the kitchen as she answers me, "Not yet, but he'll be here any minute. Pull up a seat."

I head down the hall and put my book-bag in Will's room, then hop on the barstool across from Meghan. She's cooking something that smells cheesy, and oily, and like comfort food.

I inhale deeply. "Mmmm, what are you cooking?" I ask.

She smiles at me. "My version of a grilled cheese. Do you want one?"

"Yes, please," I answer immediately, resting my hands on the bar counter, observing her cooking technique. "What makes it your version?" I inquire curiously.

She pulls some ingredients out from the fridge and explains, "I put garlic salt and a few other ingredients in it, takes it up a notch."

I nod my head. I don't necessarily understand since I'm a horrible cook. "I think Will told me something about you being a chef? Do you make anything like us mere mortals or is all of your food elevated a degree of deliciousness?"

"That's sweet of you," she says through a grin. "Speaking of Will, how did things go last week at Stefan's?"

I pull my hands into my lap and fidget nervously with them. "I'm actually here to talk to Will about that. They were pretty awful, honestly."

Meghan places a grilled cheese in front of me and I start ripping it into bite sized pieces. She tilts her head to the side as she watches me.

I explain, "My mom and I usually eat them with split pea soup so I always rip my grilled cheeses into small pieces."

"Makes sense," Meghan replies nonchalantly. "I had a feeling Stefan's house didn't go so well," she confides in me.

"Why?" I ask popping a bite of grilled cheese in my mouth.

"After you left that night I overheard Will on the phone. He must really like you."

That surprises me. "Why do you say that?"

She pulls her own food off the skillet and answers, "Because that night when you were upset he called Stefan as soon as he got up here. He was pissed. I've never seen them fight before, in all their years of friendship. But I heard him say that Stefan was being a dick on purpose and he knew it."

I stop chewing my food, mesmerized by what she's revealing about her brother.

"He ended the phone call by saying that if Stefan ever hurts you like that again their friendship will be over. He told Stefan that he will choose your relationship over their friendship if that's what it comes down to."

I am speechless.

I had no idea that he stood up for me. "Why didn't he tell me he did that?" I ask Meghan.

"My guess? He's not the greatest about showing his emotions, but he definitely cares about you." We hear footsteps climbing the stairs. "Thomas is working tonight, so that's Will." She picks up her plate and drink. "I'll leave you to it." She heads to her room for the evening.

I take another bite of the grilled cheese as Will's key enters the lock. I have so much to think through and no time to process.

He opens the door and freezes when he sees me. "You came?" he questions sounding surprised.

I pivot on my stool and nod at him with a small grin.

Will crosses the room in three steps and wraps me in his arms. He squeezes me, as if confirming that I'm not an illusion.

I wrap my arms around him. He may be an idiot who didn't stand up for me in the moment, but I guess he needed time to process things too.

I inhale deeply and start coughing. "Oh gods you weren't kidding about needing to shower when you're off work. You smell like gasoline."

Will lets me go quickly. "Sorry babe, working with go carts will do that. I'll go shower, but you have to promise not to move."

I turn back to my food and take another bite. Once I've swallowed I admit, "I can't make that promise."

His face falls.

I can't keep him stressed for long. "After I finish this I want to relax and a barstool isn't a good place for that."

"Don't do that to me," Will chuckles with a release of bated breath. "Fine, when you finish eating you can get cozy in my room, sound good?"

I nod, too preoccupied with my snack to respond audibly.

As I close my eyes, savoring Meghan's talented cooking, I feel Will lean over my shoulder. When I open them to see what he's up to I am startled to see him leaning over my plate, fingers ready to take a piece of my snack.

I yank the plate out of his reach. "Uh-uh."

He snaps his fingers shut on air, getting none of my sandwich. "Please?" He asks so nicely, puppy dog eyes included.

I roll my eyes at him. "Only because you asked nicely. One bite." I hold my plate of pre-torn grilled cheese out for him.

Will takes the largest piece off my plate and pops it into his mouth. He chews slowly enjoying Meghan's cooking skills. "Living with her has some serious perks," he says sheepishly. "I'm gonna hop in the shower, then we'll talk, okay?"

I smile at him in agreement.

Will leans in to kiss me. He's slow and unsure as he closes the distance between us. Besides the relieved hug, he hasn't touched me since he got home. This kiss doesn't change that much, only our lips delicately meet for a moment and then he stands up and walks straight for the bathroom.

I finish my grilled cheese slowly and make my way around the island to the kitchen. I hand wash my plate and the pan that Meghan used to cook our food, then I wash the sink and wipe down the counters; it's the least I can do since she fed me.

When the kitchen is spotless, which wasn't hard to accomplish, I head to Will's room and lay down on his bed. It has two pillows, a grey duvet, and smells like him. I pull a pillow out from under his comforter and sink my nose into his woods and citrus scent. I kick my shoes off and snuggle onto the bedding as I wait for him to finish his shower.

I startle awake to Will caressing my arm. His hair is wet from his shower, but he's wearing sweats and a graphic t-shirt.

I grin sleepily at him. "Guess that morning shift took more out of me than I thought."

He leans over and kisses me again. This time he's more deliberate with his actions. His arm slides over mine and stops on my back. His body settles on the bed next to me and he pulls me closer to his large frame. I fit perfectly against his body.

Once he's satisfied with how close I am his hand travels to my cheek and holds me close as he deepens our kiss. I hope his tongue never tires of exploring my mouth. He makes me feel like a forbidden fruit he can't get enough of every time we make out.

Mid kiss I have a sudden intake of breath and he breaks our mouths apart. "You okay?" He asks while stroking my lips with his thumb.

"I didn't come over to make out with you, we need to talk."

That completely removes any sexual tension between us, effective as a firehose. Will sits up and folds a leg to steady himself.

"You're right." He grabs my hand and pulls me up to face him.

I go crisscross applesauce and wait for him to continue. I need to hear what he has to say about game night first.

He doesn't let go of my hand. "Nikki, I know I fucked up. I should have stood up for you in front of the guys, not after the fact."

"I agree," I say nodding my head.

He sighs, "I'm sorry I didn't. But I want you to know that I did call Stefan right after you left. I told him what he did to you was unacceptable. He said he won't do it again."

He doesn't know that Meghan already spilled the beans about this. He also left out the detail where he told Stefan that he'd choose our relationship over their friendship. I don't need that from him though.

"Do you think he'll respect that boundary?" I ask with trepidation.

Will stares into my eyes, "If he doesn't there will be consequences. I don't think he'll want to deal with those."

"Then it's settled. I won't forgive or forget because he hasn't apologized for his actions, but I will move past them." I lean across our tangled legs and give him a peck on the lips. Another thought crosses my mind. "I may eventually forgive Stefan, but that's only because we had a relationship before he was a jerk. I doubt I'll ever like Sean. I'll tolerate him, but I will never be friends with him."

Will smiles at me. "That's fine, I don't really like him either."

I stand on my knees and go in for a hug. Will wraps his arms around my middle and pulls me down on top of him as he lays down. We lay wrapped in one another's arms for a few heartbeats. I relish his embrace. I was mad at him and his inaction but I didn't want things to end between us. Will is the sweetest guy I've ever dated and minus this one mistake things have been wonderful. Also, minus that I may have dumped him once. But beyond those two issues it's been picture perfect.

Will loosens his grip and tells me, "You're welcome to hang out, but I need to get some homework done before my classes tomorrow."

"Study date?" I ask, smiling at him.

"You okay on the bed, or do we need to move to the table?" he asks, moving to his desk chair and turning on the computer.

I spread out like a starfish, "Bed please, it's really comfy."

Will's gaze is fixated on me, "You're gonna have to stop that."

"Stop what?"

His voice drops. "Stop looking so good in my bed Nik. You're going to make it incredibly difficult to get any studying done."

I tuck my legs into the fetal position trying to look less appeasing to him. Will bites his lower lip, and moves his hands to brace getting out of his chair.

"No," I quip, sitting up to show how serious I am. "Either you do your homework or I'll have to leave."

"You wouldn't," Will challenges. He stands and leans his hands on the edge of the bed boxing me in.

"You forget yourself, Will. I am a straight A student. 4.0, the works. Homework gets done or I leave."

He hovers over me and I have to engage my core muscles to keep from folding back onto the bed. He can't win this round, I want to stay and be near him for longer. Will bites the air in front of my nose then abruptly stands and walks back to his desk chair.

I open my books and settle in for a study date in Will's cozy room. Before I put my noise canceling headphones in I hear him mumble, "Should have worn the grey sweatpants."

Twenty-One

Finals are Coming

THE FOLLOWING TUESDAY THE planets must have aligned, or some astrological anomaly like that, because Tipp, Will, Stefan, and I are all on campus at the same time. Tipp gave some excuse about a class being canceled but it wouldn't surprise me if she was ditching in order to drill Stefan about what happened a couple weeks ago at game night.

He never apologized, but I think that's the type of guy he is. You know the kind, they always think they're right and if they ever get caught red handed, 100% wrong, no way around it guilty, they brush it off and pretend it never happened. I've moved forward and Stefan hasn't been a prick since that night. I also haven't hung out with the group again.

As we approach the Griffin Center Tipp asks, "So when are you going to tell Will about Oregon?"

I push a heavy breath through my nostrils. *Why must she keep bringing this up?* "I will soon, okay? I need to find the right time."

She quips, "Or is that the excuse you have for keeping the truth from him?"

We round the corner and see the guys sitting at a table chatting. I plaster on a fake smile and reply to her. "I'll figure it out. For now, can you just be chill about it?"

Tipp rolls her eyes at me and takes a seat next to Stefan. "Hello boys," she draws out dramatically.

I sit next to Will and our group settles into a natural banter.

With finals looming in the near future, we're all feeling a bit like the Starks of Winterfell anticipating the approaching Winter. The conversation remains lighthearted at our table. Comparing who has the toughest final, who needs to cram the hardest and such. Stefan chooses a lull in conversation to bring up our Astronomy extra credit assignment. "You gonna take Fitzgibbons up on that Balboa Park bonus work?"

I shrug. "I hadn't thought too much on it honestly. I think it depends on what my work schedule is and how nervous I am once I see the study guide for our final."

Tipp puts her hand on mine. "Babe, they don't speak Nikki fluently yet."

"Haha, funny," I say with no humor in my voice.

The boys have looks of confusion plastered to their faces. I think it might be my favorite facial expression that Will wears. He looks entirely too cute when his eyebrows draw together and his head tilts to the side like a puppy trying to understand a new command.

Tipp begins, "What Nikki means is that she feels confident. She knows she'll ace the final and probably end up with like a 96% in the class. But she'll decide to do the extra work at the last minute just to make sure."

I don't know where she gets off thinking she knows me that well. I frown and suck my teeth at her. "No. You missed a detail. I won't want to go alone to something I've never been to before so I'll end up begging you to be my wing woman. My academic stress makes you smarter."

This makes Tipp laugh at me. "Not this time bitch. I've got plans."

"You don't even know what night the Balboa Park thing is!"

"Doesn't matter, I'm busy."

My eyebrows shoot toward the ceiling. She's never turned me down before. "Well then, just know that if I fail out of community college now it's entirely your fault."

The guys have been watching our banter silently this entire conversation. Will speaks up when Tipp and I finally come up for breath. He not so subtly asks Stefan, "Do you understand what's happening here?"

Stefan snorts. "No idea, you're the one with two sisters."

"They only call one another bitch when they mean it, I don't think Tipp means it seriously right now."

I take pity on them and explain, "She's the only human allowed to call me bitch, it's a long story about how we first met."

"You love it, bitch!" She always shouts that word too loudly when we're in public.

"She did break my heart and soul just now. Looks like I need a nerdy date in a couple of weeks for an extra credit assignment. You game Will?" I nonchalantly ask him on a date. A nerdy date at that. *Dear stomach, this is not an appropriate time to fall out of my butt.*

Will doesn't need any time to think through my invitation. "Let me know when and where."

My innards find their appropriate locations and my face breaks into a gigantic grin. I've never dated a guy that didn't bitch or moan about doing something school related with me. Check off another pro for Will.

As I'm grinning at Will like an idiot, Stefan asks Tipp, "You hanging around campus much longer?"

She shakes her head, "No, I gotta head out to get ready for work."

"Can I walk you to your car?" Stefan offers.

"Um, sure?" Tipp shoots me a perplexed look as she gathers her stuff.

We say our goodbyes and I tell Stefan I'll meet him in the classroom. Looks like Will is my company for the trek across campus tonight. He grabs my hand and we head off to the science building.

As we're walking, something clicks for me. I'm five foot seven inches. I love wearing heels. I have a loud personality. I've always wanted to feel smaller than the guy I was dating but it had never been accomplished before. Sure, I could be a few inches shorter. I've had fewer muscles, probably in every relationship, but I've never felt small. Will isn't particularly huge. I think he's around six-three. He carries himself with an assured confidence, not arrogance, but it makes me gravitate toward him. He isn't afraid to be himself no matter how dorky that may be. He makes me feel small, without making me feel little. Every time I'm in his presence I want to fit next to him, just to have relief from being the dominant personality in the room.

Will clears his throat. "You might want to let Tipp know that was planned, Stefan's not hitting on her or anything."

I squeeze my hand in his. "Why would you two do that?"

He looks down at me and I see a slight tinge of pink on his cheeks. "I wanted to get you alone for a few minutes," he admits.

Nevermind, confused Will isn't the cutest. Embarrassed Will is my new favorite. "You've got me all to yourself for about six more minutes, then we'll be at the science complex." I hope he appreciates how precise a person I am: that won't be changing over time.

Will pulls me to the side of the pathway and we stop walking. He holds me by my hips. My arms naturally loop behind his neck and I wait patiently for whatever he is nervous to bring up.

He leans in and gives me a gentle kiss. "I was wondering if it would be possible for you to get your shifts covered this weekend?"

"Why would I want to do that?" I ask him, my curiosity piqued.

He moves his hands from my hips, up my sides and rubs along my upper arms nervously. Then he bites his lip and admits, "I want to take you out of town for the weekend."

That surprises me, but before I can say anything he continues, "I know we haven't been dating for long, and it would make sense to wait a couple weeks longer but with finals approaching I know you're going to get busy and—"

I interrupt him with a kiss. His words fade into my mouth and I feel his body relax under my arms. Will wraps his arms around my lower back and pulls my body flush with his. Before we venture into an indecent level of a public display of affection I take a step back from him.

"You're right, it's now or two months from now. If I can find coverage for my shifts, I'm game. Where are we going?" I pull out my phone as I say this, ready to put my shifts up for grabs on the store's group chat.

Will takes my free hand and we head toward the science complex as he tells me his plan. "I was thinking we could hang out in Anaheim for the weekend. I have to work Friday, but we can leave around five that night. Dinner at Downtown Disney, then Universal Studios on Saturday. Sunday is free currently if there's anything you want to do before we come back for classes."

I bite my lip. Those plans sound fun, but I'm more excited for what he's not mentioning. Sex. *It's about damn time.*

I try to play it cool, "Yeah, that sounds fun. Any reason you chose Universal over Disney?"

His cheeks flush again. "My mom gave me two passes to Universal for Christmas and it's about time I use them."

I give him a slight shoulder check. "Look at you, big spender!"

Will takes my teasing in stride. "Well be a good girl and get those shifts covered so I can be a big spender and book our hotel."

I crinkle my nose at him in response.

"Too much?"

"No," I say, shaking my head. "I'm already a good girl. I get good grades, and I don't break rules. That's not a kink for me." Then I lean up on my tip toes and whisper in his ear, "Calling me a dirty little slut might work out better for you." I nip his ear with my teeth as I lower down from my tiptoes.

I hear Will take a sudden intake of breath in response. I'm excited for this weekend and apparently that's making me a little naughty.

We're at the top of the stairs to the science complex now. I descend a few quickly to get out of Will's reach. There's no one around us right now and that emboldens me. "Don't fantasize about this weekend too much tonight." I bite my lip and watch his face morph into a grimace of agony.

"You really going to tease me like that?" Will calls as I go down the stairs.

I turn left to enter our classroom and halt when I see Brock waiting for me. I thought he'd gotten the message with our plan last week. Stefan said he watched Brock's face get pissed when he saw Will and me making out.

I cross my arms and wait for him to say something.

He flashes me his arrogant smirk and bites out, "I get it okay, you have a boyfriend. You don't need to keep rubbing it in."

That isn't what I expected Brock to say to me. I don't deign to respond. Instead, I walk into the classroom and by the time I sit down next to Stefan there's a broad smile affixed to my face. Everything is starting to work itself out.

Tipp freaks out, naturally, when I inform her of our plans this week-end. The only thing she said that stuck with me our entire twenty-minute conversation is, "You're gonna fuck aren't you?"

Duh.

New couple, weekend away, at a hotel. That equals sex any way you slice it.

The problem is, before I talked with Tipp, I was excited to simply hang out with Will in the real world without the interruptions of work or school. After talking with her, my vagina is thinking for me.

On Wednesdays, I typically head over to Will's house once he's off work. We usually get a few hours of homework done in his room, eat dinner, and catch up on T.V. or a movie. I'm growing increasingly comfortable being around his sister and brother-in-law. Maybe after this weekend, I'll be packing overnight bags once or twice a week.

Now I'm sprawling across Will's bed, supposedly doing homework. In reality, my brain is too busy fantasizing about what Will and I will be doing to one another in two days time to actually count as being productive.

My pen hasn't touched the paper in front of me, and instead is circling my lips as I daydream about Will. I hope he's the type to take charge, throw me down, and show me exactly how much he worships my body.

My legs are bent at the knees and they start kicking back and forth perpendicular to the bed as my brain wanders further down it's lust filled escapades.

Maybe I'll get lucky and he'll have his own toys to accompany our fun. Is he more of a ropes and bondage guy? Oh shit, what if he's vanilla? *Don't think that Nikki, the only way he's vanilla is if he's never tried better sex before.* I can always fix that. Hmmm, what would a good safeword be with Will? As I've been running through these pure and chaste thoughts, my bottom lip has become sucked below my teeth. Impossible to know how that happened.

"I'm not going to get enough homework done before this weekend if you keep looking at me like that Nikki." Will's voice impedes my speculation of how adventurous sex will be with him.

I wasn't expecting to get caught and I'm damn sure I look guilty. I avoid Will's eyes and find a very interesting corner of his bedroom ceiling.

Will closes his laptop and rotates in his office chair to look directly at me.

There's nowhere to hide from that burning gaze.

I swallow and track his movements with my eyes.

Will slowly stands and stalks toward me with the grace of a predator hunting its prey.

I can hear my heartbeat in my ears. Is he anticipating this weekend with as much exhilaration as I am? He gets to the edge of the bed and then walks past me. What the hell? Where is he—

Will's hands grab my hips from behind. He flips me over and pulls me toward him in one swift motion.

I'm so startled I let out a high-pitched squeak. Will cuts off any more surprised noises from me by crawling up my body and settling between my now spread thighs.

I try sitting up to meet him but he pushes me down with one strong hand. In the other, he grabs my wrists and pins them above my head.

I'm entirely at his mercy now, and it thrills me.

He hasn't even kissed me yet and I'm sopping wet for him.

Will braces his weight with his free forearm and proceeds to lay claim to my mouth. He starts off slow but I encourage him to deepen it. We're sucking and nipping at one another. I don't know where my mouth starts and his ends.

I can feel his erection growing against my thigh. When his hips start rocking against me, I let out a low whimper that I hope is quiet enough for only us to hear. We freeze for a moment waiting to see if Meghan or Thomas heard anything.

When it seems that the coast is clear Will's hands start investigating my curves thoroughly. He caresses my hip and slides up my side to my breast. His hand tucks under my tank top and caresses my nipple causing it to peak at the contact.

A knock comes from Will's bedroom door. My eyes pop open in shock and Will freezes above me. "Dinner's ready," Meghan calls through it.

Thank gods she didn't open it.

Will removes his hand from my shirt and rests his forehead on my neck. We both let out resigned sighs.

"This is why we're getting a hotel for the weekend," Will's husky voice quietly informs me.

He rolls off me and we sit up on the edge of the bed together. I look in the mirrored closet across from us and make sure that I don't have premature sex hair.

"We can't go out there just yet," he informs me.

I look at his crotch and see proof of exactly how ready for Friday night he is.

After a few minutes Will is decent enough to appear in front of his sister.

I cover for him. "Sorry, needed to wrap up a homework thought before I lost it," as we leave his room and see Meghan and Thomas seated at the table already. Truth is, my thoughts are going to be obsessed with Will for the next two days of torture. I can't wait to see how well he works in the bedroom. If his size is any indication, it will be a gloriously long Friday night.

Twenty-Two

Lust Filled Gazes

REALITY SUCKS. THAT'S THE cold hard truth. When Will and I chatted yesterday before Astronomy we made a logical decision. I hate logical decisions.

Instead of heading to Anaheim tonight and staying in a hotel we decided to stay over at his sister's condo for a night. Reasoning? It's twofold, he's a broke community college kid and having enough money for tuition next semester takes priority over two nights at a hotel. Secondly, I had to switch shifts with our Friday opener this morning in order to secure my last minute days off on Saturday and Sunday. Which means I'll be too tired too early to enjoy anything tonight, dinner or otherwise.

We'll still be sleeping over for the first time tonight. There will also be chaperones, in essence, on the other side of his bedroom wall. No kinky fuckery for us tonight.

I really wanted an orgasm from someone other than Belladix tonight. Now she won't even be able to help me out.

I have a few hours after my shift before heading over to Will's for the weekend and use it to take care of business. I do laundry and pack the sexy undies. Thongs are dental floss for your ass; lace is where it's at. I shave where needed and landscape accordingly in other areas. I don't have the time, patience, energy, or desire for my netheryaya to look like it's prepubescent.

The twenty minute drive to Will's is killing me. I want to see him. I can't wait to be around him for an entire uninterrupted weekend. It takes every ounce of willpower not to speed as I cross the suburbs of San Diego's metropolitan area. There won't be any self control left to keep me from jumping Will's bones tonight. Shit.

When I walk through the condo's front door a bucket of ice water is dumped on my head. I see Thomas and Meghan sitting on the couch watching T.V. They're home. There will be no funny business tonight.

Fortunately, I'm feeling exhausted from waking up at three a.m. for work. Will and I excuse ourselves from the living room quickly to cuddle in his bed.

When I've finished brushing my teeth, I remember that Will and I haven't slept in the same bed before. That means he's never seen me in pajamas, and I have no idea what he sleeps in either.

Will is lounging on top of his bed when I enter his room.

I close the door quietly behind me and put my stuff in my bag. I slowly approach the bed and when I look at him it's apparent he's been tracking my every move. I ask him shyly, "What do you wear for pajamas?"

His lip is going to be bitten raw at the rate that it's been accosted by his teeth this week. He releases his bottom lip and seductively answers, "I typically sleep naked."

My whole body flushes with that admission. I can feel it reflected in my warming cheeks. A tiny, "Oh," pops out of me.

"But tonight isn't typical, Nikki." Will pats the bed next to him. I climb onto it and he says, "I'll wear boxers tonight. I don't want you to be uncomfortable sleeping next to me."

"You won't have to do that forever," I rush to apologize.

He hugs me to him. "If you need me to, I'll wear boxers for you every night for the rest of our lives." He licks his lips as he asks, "I know I'll see soon enough, but what are you wearing for pajamas tonight?"

"Turn around while I change so you can find out," I instruct him. Will doesn't move.

I whisper so that his sister can't overhear us, "I'm not getting naked in front of you right now. There's no way we'll be able to keep our hands to ourselves if I do that."

He chuckles in response. "Nikki, I'm not going to turn around because that wall," he points behind himself, "Is floor to ceiling mirrors. That wouldn't be respecting your privacy."

I look at his closet doors and notice my mistake. "Can you close your eyes then?" I ask, feeling slightly self conscious. Having sex is one thing, watching me change is a different level of vulnerability.

"I want you to be comfortable babe. I'll go brush my teeth and get ready for bed in the bathroom. I'll knock before I enter the room again and if you need more time just let me know." He kisses me on the cheek and leaves the room.

That was incredibly sweet of him. Shit like this is how you tell a man from a boy. We both want sex, but he respects me enough to let me decide when I'm ready to move through these physical milestones.

When the door clicks shut I change out of my street clothes and put on a fresh pair of cute, and cozy, black lace panties. I pair them with a black sleep tank top. It's loose fitting and reveals the perfect amount of cleavage. The hem barely extends beyond my ass. I picked this exact outfit because it's the perfect ratio of sexy to comfortable. Other women would have probably brought lingerie, but I work at a sandwich shop. I don't waste money buying underwear to make sexual partners happy. I buy items that increase my self confidence and feel luxurious against my skin while doing so. Besides, the goal is for all of the clothing to be removed from my body sooner or later. Will isn't going to care if I bought it for five dollars or five hundred.

I lift the grey duvet of Will's bed and get under the covers. If I thought his bed smelled good when I was lying on top of it, I was mistaken. Being under his covers is the closest to Nirvana I've been.

Shortly after I'm settled I hear his soft knock on the door. It cracks open and I see him slowly stick his head in, giving me plenty of opportunity to call out if I hadn't been ready yet. When he sees I'm under the covers he gives me a lop sided grin and enters the room. He's wearing grey sweats and nothing else. His chest is broad and chiseled, the perfect combination of muscles and tanned skin. He walks across the room and puts his clothes in the hamper in his closet. I watch the muscles ripple across his back shamelessly as he does so. Then he turns off the light and I watch his shadowy figure lift up the duvet and slide under the covers next to me. Somehow his proximity makes the euphoria I was feeling even stronger. Will sweetens the deal even more by pulling me close and cradling me against his body. I'm the perfect sized little spoon to his big. Once we're tucked in snug his hands start roaming. They wander across my side and end up at my neck. He takes my chin in his hand and gently forces my head to twist and look back at him.

"Nikki, I'm going to touch you now. If you don't like it, all you have to do is say stop." Will's voice is quiet and stern. He wants this, and I want to give it to him. I think.

"What about your sister?" I whisper with concern.

He lowers his mouth to my ear and breathes onto the shell of it, "I guess you better be quiet then."

I shudder as his breath grazes my ear and arch my body into his.

That's all it takes.

Will bites down on the side of my neck with just enough pressure to sting without a lingering pain. I sigh as silently as I can as his hand travels down to my underwear line.

His fingers trace the barrier between my flesh and his for a few moments.

"Lace, Nikki? You're going to be the death of me. Please tell me they're black too." Will moans into my neck.

I roll onto my back and smile up at him in the dark of his bedroom. My fingers tangle into his blond locks and I pull his lips to my own. Before our lips meet I tell him. "As black as my heart."

Will growls and descends onto my lips with a consuming kiss. His hand is traveling again and he cups my core possessively once and rests there.

I grind my hips into his hand urging him to continue without breaking our kiss.

Will's fingers snake below the line of lace and brush against me, exploring. One finger dives into my folds to find how soaking wet I am for him. He strokes me, fully coating his finger before going deeper. Will breaks our kiss and braces up on his forearm above me. He watches my reaction as his finger slowly pushes inside of me.

My chest arches, my breasts almost spilling free as his finger starts pumping inside of me. "More," I beg him, knowing one finger won't be enough to get me off.

Will's face breaks into a devious grin as he nods and I feel a second finger join the first. He pumps rhythmically in and out of me while watching how I react.

My nails dig into his forearm, clinging to the release his ministrations promise.

I feel his fingers curl inside of me hitting that perfect spot. I'm about to call out when I clamp a hand across my mouth to muffle the noises that are growing increasingly harder to suppress.

"Like that?" He whispers to me.

If I reply with my words there's no way they'll be quiet. Instead I take his hand and move his fingers to my clit.

Will immediately picks up on my directions and moves. He kicks the blankets off the foot of the bed and kneels before me. His hands slide under my ass and he pulls me to the edge of the bed. He pulls my underwear down my legs with expert precision and tucks them into the pocket of his sweats. My legs end up on his shoulders. I'm granted the beautiful image of his face grinning down at me before he starts to devour me like a starving man. His tongue licks me with a perfect rhythm and I'm flying high again.

I lay there forcing myself to be quiet while wishing I could scream my pleasure for the world to hear.

I feel my body start to shudder as Will's tongue draws me closer to the edge of oblivion. He must notice it too because he takes those two fingers and slides them back inside me. His mouth breaks contact with my clit and he looks up at me with a salacious grin.

His fingers thrust inside me with the same rhythm as before but this time they're accompanied by his tongue on my clit. The two combined topple me over the edge in a matter of seconds. I bite the back of my hand to keep from crying out as my breathing catches in my throat. My body seizes up around Will and my free hand grips him by the hair. I pull up on him enough to hear his lips pop off of me. His fingers slowly slide out and he lets me lay there as euphoria surges through my veins.

Will gently kisses up and down my thighs as he waits for my breathing to slow.

When I can breathe through my nose again I prop up on my elbows and look down at him. He smiles up at me like the cat that got the cream.

"Pleased with yourself?" I tease him.

He licks his lips before replying. "Oh very. You taste delicious, Nikki."

I point at him and arch my brows. "I swear if you say I taste like honeydew."

His brow furrows. "What?"

I sigh. "Nevermind, can you come back up here?"

Will stands and I stare at his obvious erection. I reach for it wanting to repay the favor but Will pushes my hands back. "This is about you. Lay down, let me fix the sheets." He slides one of my legs into my underwear followed by the other.

I finish the job as I blink back my surprise at how he's delaying his own gratification. I flip over and slide back to where I was before all of this happened. I lay on my side as Will fixes the sheets above me. He crawls into his side of the bed and pulls me back to his arms. One orgasm is not enough. The way this man was kneeling before me, licking his lips, has me wanting to do so many more things, to, and with him.

Will pulls me back to being his little spoon and he grabs the remote and we catch up on the latest episode of The Witcher.

I fall asleep before the beginning credits have finished. I only know Will gets out of bed once I've dozed off because later I feel him get back in and cuddle up to me. That seems sweet in theory, but he's way too warm to cuddle with while sleeping. I push him away and only let him hold my hand as I fall back asleep. In the morning we can chat about how hot he is. For now I enjoy sleeping near his safe presence enveloped in his woodsy aroma.

I wake up groggy the next day. It must be late in the morning because the bedroom is saturated with sunshine peaking through the slats of Will's blinds. My hand reaches out to find Will. Once he's located I roll over and scuttle next to his large, warm body. In the chill of the dawn his thermos of a body is welcome on my cold hands and feet.

As I settle into his side, I feel Will start to stir. His voice is scratchy with disuse this early in the day. "Good morning, beautiful." He kisses my hair gently and snakes an arm under me to pull me closer.

We lay like that for a few minutes enjoying one another's company in the stillness of a new day.

Much to my disappointment, Will untangles his limbs from mine and gets out of bed. I glimpse his morning wood and it makes me wish we'd been able to go to a hotel last night. Instead of leaving the room and going to the bathroom like I thought he would, Will uses his index finger and thumb to part two of the blinds and looks out the second story window. Rather quickly he lets them snap shut and turns to me with a wicked grin on his face.

"Thomas and Meghan are at work."

That earns a smile in return from me. "How do you know?"

Will walks back to the bed but doesn't move to get in. "This unit is above the carport. They have tandem spots and neither of their cars are below. We're alone, Nikki," he tells me as his eyes transform from their peaceful sea blue to dark stormy waters.

I meet his hungry eyes with an excited hitch in my breath. I start scooting across the bed, moving away from him. "Such a shame we need to get ready to leave. Don't want to hit that horrible San Diego weekend traffic." I flip over to crawl off the bed but before I can manage it Will's grabbed my ankle.

He pulls firmly once, enough to move my entire body, but it doesn't hurt.

"Ahhh," I squeal out in shock. No need to be quiet when you're home alone.

Will is on top of me in the next second. He uses his forearms to bracket my body underneath his. Last night when he came to bed I didn't have time to fully check him out when he took his shirt off. I've felt his taut stomach when we've hugged, but there was always a barrier of a shirt or jacket. Now, my hands glide across his skin unhindered. He's lean and muscular from his work as a mechanic. My hands slide down his back and stop at the waist of his boxers. I stick one finger in his bottoms and then I pull them out an inch or so and snap them against his skin.

Will growls at me in response. "If you want those gone, let me know." His eyes have turned molten with desire. It feels like he's staring at more than me as a woman. It feels like he sees and understands my entire being.

Will lowers his body to the side of mine and pushes his thick thigh between my legs. I roll toward him and he pulls me in for a kiss. Our mouths open for one another automatically. Our tongues dance together and I feel myself grow wet for him.

His hands roam across my body and locate mine. One at a time Will removes my hands from caressing his body and pins them above my head with one of his. "Keep those there, understand?" Will demands.

I nod my head as I bite my lip in anticipation for what he plans to do next.

Will stands and goes to the foot of the bed. *Oh no, please don't have a foot fetish!* We should have talked about kinks first. I have to pick my head off of his bed to see what he's up to, but I do as I'm told and don't move my arms. Will kneels at my feet and starts peppering kisses across my legs. His hands massage their way to my lace panties. I let my head lay back and enjoy the tingling sensations he's creating with his lips and fingers. We may have fooled around a little bit last night, but this is a new experience. It's sensual. He's taking his time and drawing it out this morning.

When his face is at the apex of my thighs he pauses. I look down at him again. I think he's waiting for my permission. "Yes," I huskily moan out as I plead for him to continue.

He takes an agonizingly long time to hook his thumbs into my underwear. I start to use my legs to pick my ass off the bed, but he beats me to it and lifts me with his strong hands. Once my underwear is gone it should be smooth sailing, but Will is evil. Slowly, torturously so, he drags them down my legs, kissing along their path as he goes.

When my sex is bared and my underwear is discarded somewhere on the floor Will stops again. His hands are on my thighs and his mouth is mere inches away from my core. If he doesn't hurry this up, I will stop following his directions and take control of this situation.

"Nikki," he sighs out, sounding as if he's in pain. "If there's anything you don't want to do, say the word. It doesn't matter when or how you change your mind, okay?"

I nod.

That's not good enough for Will, "I need to hear you say it. To make sure you understand me. Your pleasure is my number one concern here." He hasn't moved an inch. His hands have tightened ever so slightly on my legs, but he's waiting patiently for me to give him my verbal consent.

Why is that hot as fuck? I try to respond but I think I've forgotten how to talk. I lick my lips and try again. "Yes."

With that one syllable Will transforms before my eyes. He pounces on me like a drowning man in the desert. My head whips back and my spine arches off the bed from the sudden onslaught to my clit. This time I'm free to call out, and I do. My clit is still sensitive from last night. It heightens every lick of his tongue and every suck of his lips.

Will surfaces for a breath and praises me, "Look at you, glistening for me and we've barely begun. What a good little slut."

If I wasn't wet before I'm a fucking waterfall now. His words go directly to my core.

Then his fingers spread me wide and he inserts one.

That's cute, but let's be honest, I can barely feel it. "Give me another," I demand. I'm getting to give all the directions I wanted to say last night and it makes this that much better. When his second finger slides in with the first I let out a moan I can feel down to my toes.

I lay there and let this man worship me. After a few minutes it's no longer enough. I'm not close enough yet, and his dick needs some attention now. I break his rules and take my hands from above my head. I sit up and grab him by the chin.

"Your turn," I direct him. I pull Will up the bed by his chin, and he listens to my silent commands as if we've been doing this dance for years.

I push Will down next to me and straddle his hips. Will's hands wander my body as I get situated on top of him. My bare pussy sits flush with his cock. There's only the barrier of his boxers between us. He pinches my nipple through the thin fabric of my sleep top. I'm so hot and aroused now, the fabric has grown uncomfortable against my bare nipples. I pull it over my head and toss the clothing somewhere in the room. Who cares where it lands.

Will freezes and stares at my now naked body. His eyes devour every inch of me. His calloused hands feel the dips of my hips and the valley between my breasts.

The only emotion that crosses his face is utter adoration. "Fuck Nikki, you're a Goddess," his gravelly voice compliments me.

I lick my teeth. He's definitely the good boy in this relationship. I reward his compliment by grinding on his hard cock.

Will sits up and grabs my neck urging me to kiss him again. I do just that and torture him by continuing to rub myself across his junk. When we're both out of breath I pull out of his grasp and sit up.

"I don't think so," Will growls and with one hand and a split second he's flipped me onto my back again. Before I have time to register the position change, my thigh brushes against the bare skin of his hip. *Where did his boxers go?* I look down to investigate and see they're no longer attached to his body, that's for sure.

His penis looks even bigger than it felt. I reach a hand out and give it a tentative stroke. It's rigid, ready to do some damage, yet silky, soft, and delicate. A complete oxymoron of a body part. I stroke him again. This time Will's hips slightly thrust forward and his tip nudges my entrance.

He freezes again, with his member right against my outer lips he stares at me and waits for my consent.

I beam at him and breathe, "Yes," answering his silent question.

"Thank fuck." Will lets out a groan as he thrusts inside of me. My juices help him slide in to the hilt on the first try. Will lets out a shaky breath and gives me time to adjust to the fullness of his girth.

I nod for him to continue and Will begins pumping into me. He starts off slow, getting to know my body and all of its nonverbal communication. We're moaning and panting together as one being.

I bite his neck and shoulders and he hisses as I make it slightly sting. I love a man that can handle a few love bites.

When we're both getting close Will pulls out and flips me onto all fours. How this man can fold my body into whatever shape he needs with ease is beyond me.

I brace against his headboard as Will pounds into me with force. This new angle has him hitting deeper inside me. His penis is rubbing against my interior wall perfectly and I'm getting closer with every thrust.

"Fuck yes, right there!" I shout out in encouragement.

Will slaps my ass and moans between his thrusts. "Are you my dirty little cumslut?"

Then he starts picking up pace.

I stop bracing with one my hands and reach between my legs. I start circling my clit and feel my interior walls tightening. "Yes, just for you," I moan out, "Fuck me harder. Use me!"

With two more thrusts and a loud moan Will cums deep inside me. While he's riding the wave of his orgasm still seated within me I rock my hips back and forth drawing out his pleasure.

When he's had enough Will pulls out of me and falls onto the bed next to me. Seeing such a strong man reduced to a spluttering pile solely because of my body is such a power trip.

I relax on my side and start messing with him. I flick his nipples with my tongue. I bite his pecks gently, or at least gently for me. Then I fold on top of him and listen to his erratic heartbeat beneath my ear.

I didn't come, but I got close. That's better than most guys manage. Besides, he got me off last night, it was his turn now.

Will tucks his fist below my chin and brings my lips to his. When we separate his gaze is still heated. *Damn that sounded like a good orgasm from my perspective, is he ready for round two?*

"Nikki, we both know you haven't cum yet." Then he pushes me down on his bed and he's on top of me again. "How do you want it today, babe?"

Internally I'm screaming in excitement. *He's asking what I like?* No guy has ever been intelligent enough to make sure I get to cum. Belladix is usually how I get to finish, but only once I've gotten home. Will is different. I inform him, "Well, without a vibrator you're gonna have to focus on my clit."

With no hesitation his hand is between my legs. He fingers enter me for some lubrication and then heads back to my clit. Too quickly I'm writhing and moaning beneath his touch. He finds the perfect angle and I freeze.

"Right there," I whimper.

Will stays right there and increases his ministrations. His mouth finds my nipple and he sucks and bites it. His actions have my eyes rolling into the back of my head.

"Cum for me baby," he encourages me.

I grip Will's hair with force, not letting any part of him budge except his wonderful arm pumping so quickly it's practically vibrating against my clit. With a few more strokes of his fingers at that perfect angle I fall over the edge. I scream as my orgasm hits me.

With the verbal confirmation of my climax, and my now limp body next to him, Will gently removes his hand and holds me to him.

We both lay there enraptured with one another's bodies. He gently strokes my arms and chest with the tips of his fingers. They're so delicate against my skin they feel like miniature fireworks with every graze in the afterglow of my orgasm. When we're both breathing normally again, Will untangles himself from me and gets off the bed. I hear a rustling of clothes and Will leaves his room. I'm too satiated to investigate.

The sound of a cupboard opening, a sink turning on, and beeping come from somewhere in the condo. A few moments later Will comes back into his room. I halfway open one eyelid and see he has a small towel in his hand.

I brace my body on one elbow and look up at him. "Did you warm that for me?" I ask.

"Of course, do you want to clean up or do you want my help?"

Okay, what the fuck? He gave me an orgasm and he knows about proper aftercare?

"Um, I know you just had all of you all over me, but I don't want you cleaning up our juices from between my legs." I'm a little embarrassed to be shy about this after what we just did. It feels like a different level of intimacy.

He holds out the towel to me. "No worries." I take it from his hand and then Will turns his back to give me added privacy.

"We should get ready for today and head out. I would wait in a four-hour traffic jam if it meant having sex with you, but now we've had sex and I don't particularly delight in the idea of a four-hour traffic jam as penance." Will suggests while averting his gaze from me.

I efficiently finish mopping up our mess and ask, "Where do you want this?" about the towel.

He puts his hand out for it again, "I'll wash it when we get back," and chucks it into his hamper. "We should check on Aurora too before we leave. She could use a bathroom break. Who knows how late Thomas and Meghan will be at work today."

"Okay, where's her kennel?" I ask while locating my underwear and putting them on.

"Their room."

"Let me get dressed and then I can get her," I offer.

"Sure," Will agrees as he starts pulling out items for his overnight bag. I roll my eyes at him. Leave it to a guy to pack the morning of a trip.

I still have to do my hair and makeup for today so I ask Will, "Do you want Aurora to hang out with us while we finish getting ready?"

"I think she'd like that," he says smiling.

Once all my bits and bobbles have the appropriate clothing on I head out of Will's room. My mother always taught me to knock on a closed door, so I do it out of habit. Knock, knock knock, then I let myself into Meghan and Thomas' room. I do a quick once over. When my eyes land on the bed, I freeze.

Twenty-Three

No Headphones

Thomas.

Thomas is home.

Thomas is sitting in the middle of his bed.

Thomas has Aurora in his lap. He's scrolling his phone. He doesn't even have headphones in.

Thomas. Heard. Everything.

"Oh, hi. I uh... I was just checking on Aurora. Clearly she's fine." I robotically tell Thomas. Then I back out of the room, close the door, and burst back into Will's room.

He looks up from his bag with a curious look. I stand there like a gasping fish out of water.

Will walks around his bed and leans over me clutching my forearms in his hands. "Babe, what's wrong?" He sounds worried.

In an inaudible whisper I tell him, "Thomas is home."

"What? Is Aurora okay?"

I take a shaky breath. I try swallowing but there's no saliva to lubricate my vocal cords. I point to the shared wall with the master bedroom and whisper shout at Will, "Thomas is home."

His face breaks into the biggest smile.

I'm humiliated. "How are you smiling about this? It's not funny."

His lips form a barely straight line as he placates me. "Actually, it's hilarious."

I smack his bicep, and continue with my whisper-shouting, "Your brother-in-law just heard us having VERY LOUD sex. He didn't have the T.V. on or headphones in!"

Will can't restrain himself anymore and doubles over in hysterical laughter. I stare at him in disbelief. How is he laughing at a situation like this?

Thomas heard everything!

I stand there waiting for him to calm down but there doesn't seem to be an end to his entertainment.

I'm done. I opt out of this situation. What have I done to deserve humiliation like this? We were fucking loud. Oh my gods, Will followed through with my degradation kink. I will never be able to look his brother-in-law in the eyes again. I can never come over here again.

Thomas will tell Meghan. They're married. Married people have no secrets, right? Nope. Fuck that. My mind is spiraling full force through the abject horror I'm feeling. I have an embarrassing sex story now. I never wanted to be someone with an embarrassing sex story...

Will wheezes a breath and I jump off the derailed train chugging through my mind. I try to calm down.

"I need to go into the bathroom, can you please check the hallway to make sure Thomas isn't out of his room?" I ask Will. I will not be running into him after this incident.

Will pulls on a shirt. "You're kidding, right?"

I don't respond. Instead I wait for him to understand. Will rolls his eyes at me, kisses my forehead, and checks that the coast is clear for me.

As I walk past him into the bathroom he tells me, "You're crazy." The only reason I let him live after calling me a name is because he says it with a smile. Also, he did give me an Earth-shattering orgasm.

I do my hair and makeup in record time and slink across the hallway back into Will's room. When all my belongings are back in my bag I tell Will my plan. "Okay, make sure he isn't in the living room. I'll go downstairs and wait in your car."

"You can't even wait in here for me to get ready?" Will asks incredulously.

I sigh, irritated that he doesn't understand. "Please, you're a guy, it's not the same for you right now."

He pauses his packing and comes over to give me a hug. He lifts my chin forcing me to look at him. "Nikki, Thomas has had sex before, you really don't need to worry about it. But if it makes you more comfortable, here." He gets his keys from his pocket and puts them in my hand. "I'll go check that your path is clear."

I escape the condo without running into Thomas and wait in the car for Will. He comes down within fifteen minutes and we head out to Anaheim.

When we're on the freeway Will turns off the radio and puts a hand on my knee. Will breaks our silence, "So, Thomas came out of his room after you left."

I hold my breath. "What did he say?"

"Not much," Will informs me. "He gave me a high five and then asked that if we're going to have morning sex in the future to please make sure the condo is empty first." Will squeezes my knee one more time and I have to check my pulse to make sure I didn't just die of embarrassment.

"There's only one logical choice left," I tell Will. "We're never having sex again."

Twenty-Four

Window Shopping

WILL KEEPS HIS EYES focused on the freeway before us as he asks, "Dogs or cats?"

That's a tough one, so I mull it over before answering. "I know I loved the dog I had when I was a kid. But I've only had cats since I was in elementary school."

"You like Aurora, don't you?" Will asks me.

"That's different," I object. "Aurora is your sister's dog."

"What?" He pretends to be confused.

"Ha, ha, ha. You're so funny."

Will moves his hand to my thigh. It seems that he always wants to be touching me. His physical contact is warm and reassuring. I could get used to this being where his hand goes while he's driving us around. Will clarifies his question. "What do you think about her size?"

I scrunch up my nose, "Not a fan. If you want a dog that small, just get a cat."

"You thinking Great Dane or something more in the middle?"

I sigh as I contemplate. "Honestly, I've never thought of dog sizes. I loved my German Shepherd growing up, so maybe that size? How about we settle on cats *and* dogs, sizes to be determined?"

Will takes his hand from my leg and holds it open waiting for me to put mine in his. When I do he pulls my hand across the car and kisses the back of it. Then he laces our fingers and rests our arms on the middle console. This man is giving off serious Golden Retriever vibes right now.

"There is one thing I know for sure about dogs." I'm nervous to tell him, but it's something we need to be agreed about for our future together.

"Yeah, what's that?"

I ramble, "I know she's your sister so I'm sorry if this upsets you, but I don't think it's fair that Aurora is locked in the condo for ten hours at a time without a bathroom break. When have you ever gone that long between peeing?" I hope he doesn't hate me for that.

"What would you do differently?" Will asks.

I've been thinking about this for a while. "I wouldn't have a dog before living somewhere it could have a yard."

He quickly glances at me. My lip has worried itself between my teeth. Then he clarifies, "What you're saying then is no yard, no dog?"

"Yes."

He mulls over my statement for a moment before replying. "No yard, no dog. I accept your conditions, Veronica."

I blush when he says my full name. Only one more subject to broach with him. This one could be the deal breaker. "I have one more requirement."

"Nope, only one rule allowed about our future. The rest is up to fate," he teases me.

I laugh at him.

I know this would be the perfect time to bring up that I'm moving to Oregon next summer, but I don't want to ruin our weekend away. I weigh my options and chicken out at the last minute. He'll learn about my Oregon plans, just not yet...

"Okay. But seriously, though." I pause for dramatic effect. "Can you please promise to never buy a beige car again?"

Will's mouth drops open. "You hate it that much?"

I cross my arms and prepare to defend my own stupidity. "No, I appreciate that you have a car that's getting you from point A to point B and that it was a smart financial investment to get this one used from a family member. But," my voice puts emphasis on the last word. "When you get to buy a car in the future, if you could please not choose beige again, that would be fantastic." I'm crazy. He officially knows it. I hate the color beige.

"Does white work?" He asks while watching the traffic surrounding us on the freeway. A smart choice considering we're on a freeway with crazy California drivers. I roll my eyes even though he can't see them.

"Technically, that's an improvement. Although white is the second most boring color on the planet." I say, running my words together.

"I've never met someone with such strong opinions about colors before," Will says with an amused laugh.

Shit, my brand of insanity actually gets worse. "I don't feel this strongly about colors I like. Just the ones I hate."

Will shakes his head at me, saying nothing.

We finish the drive to Anaheim discussing our likes and dislikes. We talk about our childhood pets, best friends, and families. I'm enjoying getting to know him on a deeper level so much, that I'm disappointed when I start to see signs for Downtown Disney parking. I decide I'll be the official DJ for our future adventures because Will's taste in music is lacking, to put it nicely.

Between the two of us reading signs and paying attention we make it to the parking lot without struggle. When our doors open, our ears are immediately accosted with Disney music. Will asks me to take a picture of the parking section we're in so we don't forget. We officially enter Downtown Disney and I take in our surroundings as we wander our way to the shops, hand in hand.

The sun is shining its last rays of the day, casting an orange glow on the shops. My favorite part about walking around public spaces in Southern California is the different languages you hear. I see families interacting with one another and have no idea what they're saying to each other. It's almost comforting to my psyche to hear people communicating in a tongue that I don't understand. It's soothing, like listening to instrumental music. I can't reproduce it, but I can appreciate it. Walking among these strangers hand in hand with my sweet man I feel at peace.

I look up at Will and he grins down at me. Our lips meet in a quick kiss while continuing to walk the shopping center. My heart feels so full with the way that he reminds me he cares through small gestures.

I see an art gallery to the side and pull Will towards it. Before we enter, I admit one of my guilty pleasures to him. "I love walking through shops where I know I'll never be able to afford to buy anything. It's fun to see how other people live."

As we push past the heavy bronze trimmed door of the gallery I notice a couple about our age at the register. I hear the sales lady give a total in the five-digit range. I don't think that will ever be my reality, but I can still have an appreciation of the artistry on display here.

We quietly wander the aisles of prints. Some are framed, others are copies with more reasonable price tags. When I see a print of Belle from *Beauty and the Beast* lying in a meadow reading a book I pause to admire it.

Will stands behind me and wraps his arms around my stomach. His chin is on my shoulder and he kisses behind my ear. "You like this one?"

"Yeah, she's the only princess with an affinity for reading."

"Maybe someday you'll have it," Will suggests.

I shrug and start walking the gallery again. My goal is to be a teacher; that's not a career with money. I doubt that art will ever make it home with me. Besides, it won't do my emotions any good to dwell on things I'll never be able to reasonably afford.

We exit the gallery and continue our meandering through the shops. My neck is always on a swivel walking around public places. Being a woman, it's something I have to do to ensure my safety. I squeeze Will's hand as I remember that he's with me which calms some of my tendencies to survey my surroundings. Out of habit though, I observe what's going on around us as we continue our stroll through Downtown Disney. Instead of searching for potential threats, I focus on the positives around me. I see a child having a temper tantrum about a souvenir. Their mom is clearly overwhelmed and the dad is absorbed in his phone. I look to the other side of the outdoor shopping center and see various people sporting different sets of Mickey ears and occasionally I catch someone in Cosplay. A grin pulls at the side of my mouth as I take in the scene unfolding before us.

As we near the end of the walk I see our destination. The Rainforest Cafe. We enter the gift shop at the front of the restaurant and the ambiance changes immediately. The bright neons of the shops luring you in are replaced by shadows and jungle noises. The restaurant is able to seat us immediately and we're taken up two flights of stairs. We follow the hostess to a part of the building I've never been in before. She seats us in a recessed corner and it feels like we're the only people here. Our table is against a railing that looks down over the forest scenery. Far in the distance I can hear the animals coming to life for their show, signaling the top of the hour.

As I'm taking in our environment I feel Will's leg brush against mine. I look to him and smile. His desire to always touch me is continuing beyond the car. I hope it never stops. My chest feels warm and fuzzy, like I'm wrapped in a sherpa jacket, but it's actually his touch.

We both end up devouring burgers for our dinner. I'm not one of those girls that orders a salad on a date. Where do you think these curves come from? I try not to look at the bill's total, but I see it. I also notice Will tips twenty percent to our waiter. He was polite to him, and remembered to say, "Please," and, "Thank you." I remember my mother saying it's important to watch how others treat wait staff, eventually that's how they'll be treating you too. Another box that Will has checked without knowing he was being assessed.

We join hands again and descend the stairs back to the strip. When we come out of The Rainforest Cafe, the sun has set. I can hear a live band in the distance and the crowds have thinned out. In typical Southern California fashion, there's a breeze that has me slightly chilled. Neither Will nor I thought ahead to bring jackets. Guess I'll be a little cold until we make it to the car.

When we get to the halfway part of the shops we find the band. I've never heard of them but they're playing rock music and I like the beat and melody.

I ask Will, "Want to listen for a bit?"

He nods and leads the way through the crowd gathered. Once he's found a good spot he pulls me in front of him and we enjoy the live music together.

After a few songs I have to wrap my arms around myself trying to fight off the chill created by a light breeze. I think Will notices because he leans down to my ear, "Want to head to the car?" My neck prickles with goose bumps as his warm breath coasts across my skin. I want my whole body to be wrapped up like that.

I nod my head in response. With the music's volume, he wouldn't be able to hear my words anyway.

When we break away from the crowd, Will doesn't keep hold of my hand. Instead, he brings me to his side and wraps an arm around my shoulders, increasing what's in direct contact with him. "Sorry I didn't bring a jacket," he apologizes.

I lace my fingers in his hand and hold him tight. This man just said sorry for not being cold earlier. I turn my head toward the shoulder he's resting our hands on and kiss the back of his. "I'll be fine until we get back to the car," I assure him.

We get to the hotel after another twenty minutes of driving. This puts us closer to Universal Studios for the morning.

I admire the lobby as he takes charge of our reservation. There are gorgeous pictures behind the reception desk that remind me of some of my favorite book characters; because of their contrasting blue and red backgrounds. Behind us and across the lobby there is a bar with ample seating stretched across two floors. It's late and they've adjusted the calm lobby music to reflect popular beats for people to try to talk over while they're drinking. As I'm watching people living their lives around us I spy some employees wheeling a baggage cart to the elevators. I'm surprised that Will booked us somewhere so nice. I would have been happy staying at a cheaper place, but I appreciate his spoiling. We head to the elevators and I see a couple dressed very differently than we are. Her Louboutin red-sole pumps cost more than I make in a week, not to mention the rest of her outfit. I feel the familiar pang of jealousy that other people have so many beautiful things before remembering myself. We need to make the best of the hand we're dealt. If I want Louboutin's I can save for a few years, though why I'd do that I'm not sure. For now, I need to focus on the wonderful man next to me, and all the privileges my life really has.

The elevator ride to our floor is quick. Will takes the lead in finding our hotel room. When he opens the door, I get excited. His bed at home is only a double. That's fine, we fit. Barely. He's six-three and I'm five-seven. It's rather snug on his bed. This hotel bed? It's a king. There will be so much room!

Will stows our suitcases and I sit on the side of the bed watching him. He comes over and brackets me in with his arms. He kisses me gently and suggests, "It's expected to hear random strangers in a hotel. You know that, right?"

I know what he's implying, but going along with his train of thought would be too easy. "Good thing I brought earplugs," I reply, pretending I don't understand him.

A smile lightens his face as his calloused hand wraps around the side of my neck. "Nikki," Will tries to seduce me, "We both know you're not that naive."

I bite my bottom lip. Followed by a gasp as my right hand splays across my chest. "Whatever do you mean?"

Will pushes me down onto the bed. I grin up at him, still playing coy. "Do you want to jump on the bed?"

He bites my neck. "Not quite." He growls, licking his way up my jawbone.

That has me releasing an involuntary moan. My legs kick up from the edge of the bed and wrap around Will's waist.

His arms reach under me, supporting my back and he picks me up. Will walks across the room and holds me against a wall. I can feel his erection growing between my legs.

I tangle my fingers through his hair as he kisses his way down my neck and buries his head in between my breasts. When he surfaces for air, Will grins greedily at me and moans out, "Thank God for low cut shirts and a well endowed chest."

He tries to lower his head for more, but I stop him. I drag his face to mine and kiss him passionately.

Will breaks our kiss and stands there panting in front of me. Somehow he hasn't put me down yet. "Nikki," his lust filled voice begins. "You up for round two tonight?"

I want to be. My libido wants to be. But my vagina isn't on board. I gnaw on my bottom lip and look at Will anxiously. He gently puts me down, keeping me pinned against the wall.

Will unlaces my hands from behind his neck and holds them in his. "Was this morning not okay?" His brows pucker together in the middle. He looks so concerned about my well being.

I smile at him reassuringly. "No, this morning was absolutely wonderful." I fidget with his hand and find a part of the ceiling to stare at. I admit to him, "You, uh, you're just a bit larger than I've had before."

I hear him huff out a chuckle.

I look up at Will and see his face has broken into a wide grin. I guess if I had a penis like that to compliment, I'd be chuffed too. I continue on, "My vagina is a touch sore right now. I don't want to literally be walking funny tomorrow at Universal."

His shoulders are vibrating with barely contained laughter. "Shower and a cuddle then," he offers.

I go on my tip toes and give him a peck followed by a bear hug. "That would be perfect."

Twenty-Five

Universal Studios

I WAKE PRIOR TO the alarm clock's blare. I turn it off before the bellowing noise has the opportunity to ruin a pleasant morning. The only part of us touching is my foot, securely tucked under one of Will's legs. He's lightly snoring somewhere across the giant bed. I reach out to find his torso and am met with an empty bed.

I groan into the morning silence. *I just want to cuddle my mountain of a man!* Maybe a king bed is too large after all. I lay there questioning how badly I want to snuggle him when I hear rustling. Will slides under my arm and I roll over to meet him.

I drape my leg over his pelvis and rest my head on his chest. Will kisses my hair and I know he's at least partially conscious.

I squeeze him. "Mmmm, you feel like a thermos."

His breathing pauses beneath me. His gravelly morning voice asks, "A thermos?"

I nuzzle into him. I can't get enough of his broad, strong body. I hope I get to cuddle him like this for the rest of my life. "Yeah, you're so warm, like a thermos."

He tucks a hand under my chin and guides my face to look at him. "Nikki, do you mean I'm warm like a fur-nace?"

I roll my eyes. *Duh, why is he clarifying?* "Like I said, a thermos."

He picks up his head and kisses me. "No babe, not a thermos. You drink out of those."

"I've been saying the wrong word?"

"Yes, you mean furnace, with an F."

I'm shocked. I sit up and pull the blankets back with me. It's cold in our room, but I barely notice. "Cool, I'm going to go die of embarrassment now." I make to get out of the bed but Will grabs my hips and pulls me back to him before I gain much ground.

"It's cute, babe. I'll happily be your thermos." He tells me as he holds me to his chest.

I lay my hand on his lower stomach and where I should find the edge of his boxers, I feel only skin. I reach a little lower and brush against his pubic hair.

Will makes a rumbling sound deep in his chest.

"Oh, I'm sorry. Did you sleep naked?" I ask confused, my voice comes out a little high pitched with shock.

He lifts the blankets and looks down his body. I take a quick glance too. Sure enough, he's laying there in nothing but his birthday suit. His penis is thick with morning wood.

Will puts the sheets back down. "I wasn't when I went to bed. Guess I kicked my boxers off in the middle of the night."

"Oh," I squeak.

He chuckles. "See anything you want Nikki?"

"Hmmm." I think about it. "Not really."

"Ouch." Will clutches his chest pretending to be wounded.

I smirk at him. "I saw something that's already mine."

That excites him. Will rolls me onto my back and lays on top of me. He grinds his erection between my legs, the only thing separating us is a tiny piece of fabric, yet again. "Oh really now?" He challenges.

I reach between us and stroke his penis. "It's responding like it's mine already."

Will gently thrusts his hips against me as I continue massaging him. "Can you blame me?" He moans, "That feels fantastic, Nikki."

His audible pleasure has me getting wet instantaneously.

"Can I rip these panties off of you?"

I giggle, my pace unrelenting. "No, they cost fifteen fucking dollars."

"I'll buy you new ones," Will growls as he yanks on my underwear. They split down the seam with one effortless tug and my sex is bared to him.

I gasp. "You're gonna buy me two pairs for that. They were my favorite!"

His cock notches right outside my entrance. "Nikki, I'll buy you fifty pairs if it means we get to fuck again."

With his penis in the perfect position I push it inside of me, making Will's dreams come true.

Will takes the lead from there. His hands grip my hips and he pulls me down the bed impaling my body on his rock hard cock. I scream in ecstacy. I'm still a little sore from yesterday morning and he is the biggest I've ever had. Those two things combined makes me uncomfortably full, in an euphoric sense.

Will continues thrusting into me while devouring my breasts. He pinches a nipple with one hand while sucking and biting at the other. I writhe beneath him, somehow needing more.

Then Will pauses. "Don't move," he demands as he gets off the bed.

I don't listen. I partially sit up and brace my upper body on my forearms beneath me. He walks over to his overnight bag and rummages around for a couple seconds. Then he straightens and walks back to me. The view of this large, confident, and well hung man has me salivating. He's all mine.

When he gets closer I see a small black object in his hand. He clicks one end of it and I hear it start vibrating. "You brought a toy?" I ask him, excited at his forethought.

"Did yesterday morning teach you nothing?" His voice is deep and sultry. "My pleasure is worth nothing unless you're equally satisfied."

I'm too stunned to say anything. I smile stupidly at him and wait to see what happens next.

Will drops to his knees and begins worshiping my vagina again. This time he uses the vibrator to fuck me while he sucks on my clit. I claw at his shoulders, certain he'll have marks when we're done. When it gets so intense that my body starts squirming on the bed Will's free hand splays across my stomach and holds me in place. He keeps going and I feel my orgasm growing nearer.

This feels great, but I need to be filled again. I need to feel him thrusting into me with abandon. I want to be his undoing, as he is mine.

"Fuck me," I beg him.

Will releases my nub with a pop and grins devilishly at me. His mouth glistens with my arousal but his hand continues working the vibrator.

He slides it out and puts it into his mouth. Then he closes his lips and sucks my juices off of it. Will does all of this while maintaining eye contact with me. It's so hot I nearly orgasm at the sight of him alone.

He climbs my body with the vibrator in his mouth. When he's hovering above me, penis at the perfect height again I seize my chance. I wrap my legs around his middle, push his shoulders to the side and manage to flip us.

Will's eyes widen in surprise as I land on top of him. I can feel his penis below me and I wiggle my hips, drawing a moan from him. I stand up on my knees to align over his manhood and then slowly slide down his shaft.

Will removes the vibrator from his mouth and lets out a long, low, groan. "Fuck Nikki, just like that," he encourages as I ride him.

I close my eyes and tilt my head back. I lose myself to the feeling of him beneath me. He fills me to perfectly; it's unbearable. Then I feel the vibrator on my clit.

"Ohhh," I moan as he finds the perfect rhythm against my nub.

He pinches and bites me in all the right places as I bring us both closer to the edge.

Will grabs my hips and pulls me down harder against the vibrator. "Yes!" I cry out. "Oh gods, I'm so close, don't stop!"

With two more thrusts powered by his domineering grip on my waist, I climax, and my vision blurs to stars. I hear Will shout beneath me as his body convulses with his own orgasm.

I slow my pace on his cock, eventually stopping. Will removes the vibrator from my clit and I lay down on his chest. Will soothes his hand along my arms and legs as we come down from our high.

When my vision clears, I unsheathe his cock and lay down next to him on the bed.

We rest in silence for a few minutes. When I'm feeling grounded again I break the quiet. "Wow."

"Yeah," Will agrees.

"I really hate condoms," is my brilliant conversation opener.

Will moves his body to better look at me. "We didn't use one?"

"I know, I'm glad. That wouldn't have been nearly as good with one."

Will grins at me. "I've never heard a woman say that before."

I shrug in response.

"Wait!" His eyes widen and it looks like he's connecting the dots. "Is that why you had us both get tested? I thought it was for STI's?"

I take his hand in mine. "Yeah it was mainly for those, but also for better sex. That's why I'm on the pill too."

He chuckles. "If the trade off for sex like that is a little bit of blood, imagine how good it would be if you drained me dry."

I slap his chest and start to get off the bed. Will follows me and helps me clean off in the shower. He takes his soaping job very seriously and makes sure to lather every inch of my body. It's only fitting that I get to do the same in return.

When our cleaning is about to lead to round two I push him back against the shower wall.

I drop to my knees and take his penis in my hand. I don't think it stopped being hard for a second this morning. Will weaves his hands through my hair and encourages my mouth closer to his dick.

I open my lips and right as they're about to slide around his girth, I close them and give it a little kiss on the tip.

I rise to my feet and then kiss Will's lips. I exit the shower with a little pep in my step and towel off.

Will remains leaning against the tiled wall. He watches my every movement with hungry eyes. I don't hear the water to the shower turn off until I reenter our room and start getting dressed.

Once my bra and panties are securely in place I hear him pad up behind me. "You'll pay for that later," he promises huskily.

I pivot and see him standing there with a towel hanging around his waist. His shoulders are still damp and his abs are glistening in the soft morning light sneaking in behind the curtains.

I swallow, trying to remember why I stopped when we were in the bathroom.

"Promise?" I ask him. I meant for it to come out as a challenge, but when the words cross my lips they sound more like I'm begging.

Will stares at me and leisurely removes the towel from his body. He drops it to the floor next to him and gives me time to soak in his perfect naked physique. Without a word he turns and walks across the room to his suitcase and begins dressing.

He didn't have to do anything, and I'm already regretting not going for round two... or four.

"Are you sure you don't mind waiting in this line?" I nervously ask Will a few hours later.

He kisses my nose with a smile before replying. "Babe, you have no idea how adorable you are right now."

I beam up at him. "This is like, a once in a lifetime opportunity. How are you not more excited?"

Will chuckles at me. "Nikki, you realize we're the only people in this line that don't have children with them right?"

I quickly survey the people around us. Shit, he's right. I cross my arms and pop my hip. "That just means other adults are denying their true desires. Who in their right mind wouldn't want to do this?"

"You're on deck folks. Ready?" A voice from behind me announces.

I pivot and take a step forward.

My body is practically vibrating with excitement. *Is this really happening?*

Another employee narrates the encounter as Will gives one of them my phone to take pictures with. "Oh what a lovely couple. Entering mortal peril together. The gift that keeps giving."

I bounce on the balls of my feet and slowly approach the yellow safety line. We're standing in front of an iron fence covered in caution tape. Part of it has been clawed open by my favorite predator of all time. I know I need to turn around and smile for the camera. I can't yet. My eyes are glued to the mist wafting through the opening in the fence. I need a glimpse of her. I need to see Blue with my own eyes.

The racket of the amusement park around us fades to the background. I hear it, a thundering footstep. Then another. Through the fog I see the tip of her nose emerge. It's a beautiful grey I want to reach out and pet. Her lips are slightly parted showing off her carnivorous sharp teeth. I don't care. Blue can rip off my arm if that's what she wants for lunch.

Will's arm slides to the small of my back. "Babe, you gotta turn so they can get a picture."

I reluctantly take my eyes off her. I know it's a stupid move. *Jurassic Park* taught me better, but this velociraptor won't hurt me. Blue's my friend.

Will pulls me to his side but I don't have to pose for the photographer. My face has been stuck in a genuine smile since we got in the velociraptor encounter line. This is a dream come true.

"There we go." The employee comments once we're in a picture perfect position. "Blue." Her voice pitches to a level of concern. "Blue, best behavior."

I feel her nudge the top of my head. I jump, scared at first. Then I remember, this is how animals make friends. They need to get your scent.

"This may be her best behavior." The employee says with resignation.

I feel Blue tug on my ponytail.

I turn to look at her.

Razor sharp teeth bite down mere inches away from my face.

I scream.

"Get out of there folks. It's a low bar to clear. But all your limbs are intact, so we'll call it a win."

I thank the employee who was taking our photos and Will and I head out of the velociraptor encounter. We cross a walkway shaded by luscious jungle plants and pull up the pictures on my phone. Will looks over my shoulder as I scroll through them and mark my favorites.

His finger pauses my scrolling. "Oh send me that one babe. You're absolutely adorable in it."

I tap the screen and zoom in. It's a perfect shot of Blue roaring in the background as I duck away from her jaws. Will is standing there grinning without a care that there's a giant predator mere feet behind him.

I turn and slap his peck. "You didn't even react!"

Impossibly, his grin widens. I think his eyes might be sparkling as he looks at me too. "You know dinosaurs are extinct right?"

I scoff at his insult. "Don't you hurt Blue's feelings like that. It could really upset her. A lot of her friends didn't survive *Jurassic World*."

Will bends down and captures my lips with a kiss. I melt into him and wish there was somewhere private we could go again. This man's kisses are so delectable they're almost as fun as meeting Blue. Almost.

Will stands to his full height forcing our lips to separate.

I pout at him. "That's not fair. I can't reach your mouth when you're that tall."

His arm slings across my shoulders and we start walking the amusement park again. "How about a ride this time? Mummy sound good?"

I nod my head and Will steers us to our next destination.

We spend the rest of the day taking in the sights of Universal Studios, Hollywood. Will continues his habit of always touching me in one way or another. Either we're holding hands, or his arm is laced around me somehow. I find myself leaning into him throughout the day loving how steady he is beside me. I've never enjoyed spending a day with someone significant like this before. Just the two of us. No interruptions from the outside world. It doesn't matter how long the lines are because we spend the whole time talking. I learn about his childhood pets and how he struggled academically in school. He hears about the sports I played in high school and my hometown. No matter the conversation we're both interested in what the other is saying. By the end of the day my cheeks are sore from how much I've been smiling.

I stand on the escalator next to Will and I rest on him a little bit. My feet started feeling sore about half an hour ago. Will holds me up without effort, hands wrapped around my midsection.

He squeezes my hips. "Hey, better stand. I don't want you falling over when you try to get off the escalator."

I open my eyes, not realizing they'd closed, and prepare for the awkward step off of the moving stairs.

When we're both clear of the escalator Will takes my hand and leads me toward a view finder that looks over the San Fernando Valley. I bypass the periscope and stand directly behind the wrought iron fencing preventing us from falling to certain doom in the Lower Lot below us. I feel the heat of Will's body as he slides his hands across my stomach and hugs me from behind. He rests his chin on the top of my head. A small grin pulls at my cheek as I'm reminded how perfectly we fit together. We stand there taking in the view, content in each other's arms, for a few minutes.

Will lifts his head from the top of mine and twists to kiss me on the cheek. "Nikki, there's something I've been wanting to tell you."

I smile. "Hmmm, what's that?"

I feel his lungs expand against my back as he takes a deep inhale. He slowly pushes it out before answering. "Nikki, I love you."

Twenty-Six

A Tough Conversation

"TELL! ME! EVERYTHING!" TIPP squeals as soon as she sees me waiting for her in the quad on Monday morning. She texted me last night, demanding I get to campus early so she can hear all the details from my weekend with Will.

I tuck my loose hair behind my ear and wait for her to get closer. I'm not going to yell details of my sex life across campus. "There's not much to tell," I lie once she's within a normal level of conversation's earshot.

She plops down on the bench next to me. "Bitch, I know you're lying."

"How?" I ask incredulously.

"Your tell."

"What's my tell?"

Her lips make a straight line. "Yeah, I'm not gonna share that with you. Then I'd have to learn what your new sign would be. So, how was the sex?"

"Tipp!"

"Oh no, that bad?"

"You are the worst!" I push her lovingly.

Tipp cackles at me. An actual witch's cackle. "You know I'm the best, that's why we're best bitches babe!"

I loop my arm through hers. She's right, of course. "The sex was mind blowing. Literally. I orgasmed so hard I saw stars."

Her whole body shimmies in response to my description. Tipp demands more detail than I want to share in a public place, but if people are scarred from eavesdropping, it serves them right. After a recount of our sexploits in excruciating detail, Tipp is beaming in pride.

"Get it girl!" She commends.

I blush. "I'm never telling you about my sex life again."

"I give that goal a week tops," she corrects me. "Now that we've covered the important part of your weekend, how was all the rest?"

She's going to die in a fit of laughter at this, I know it. "Well, we had great sex, and his brother-in-law knows it."

Tipp's face recoils, her skinny neck grows a multitude of chins and she makes me think of Sid the sloth for a second. "You had a threesome with his brother-in-law?"

"No!" I shout at her. "But he does know what we both sound like in bed now."

Now her lip curls. "Why?"

I tell her how we had extra loud fun Saturday morning because Will thought the cars were gone. If I wasn't feeling uncomfortable revealing my most embarrassing sexual encounter to date I'd be laughing hysterically at all the facial expressions she's making during my tale.

I conclude, "He was sitting there, on his bed, dog in his lap, scrolling through his phone."

"No headphones?" Tipp asks, aghast.

"Not even the T.V. on quietly," I confirm solemnly.

"Why!" She shrieks. I think I see a few birds leave a tree nearby in response to how high a pitch she managed.

"I never plan on finding out." I quickly deter our conversation from more questions about Thomas' listening in on my morning sex with Will. "Other than that bit, it was truly a wonderful weekend. I got to know Will on a much deeper level, and I actually feel compatible with him, like, long term." I go into detail about Downtown Disney and wrap up with what we did at Universal.

I swallow back my nervousness about telling her the last detail of our weekend. I grimace before telling her the final part. "You know those escalators that you have to take to get to the top of the park? At the middle landing Will took me over to one of the outlook spots. We were standing there all wrapped up in each other and..." I trail off.

Tipp grows impatient with my hesitation. "And what? Don't drag it out like this bitch!"

I roll my neck before putting her out of her misery. "And, he said he loves me."

Tipp's eyes nearly bug out of her head. Then she clears her throat. "How long have you two been officially dating?"

I know the answer immediately, I did that math last night on the drive home. "The blind date was three months ago, but we've only been officially dating for one month."

She nods her head. "And what did you say in response?"

I wince. "Thank you?"

"Noooo!" Tipp makes the word three syllables long. "You didn't?"

I throw my hands up, "What else should I have said? I'm not going to lie to the guy and tell him what he wants to hear. There's no good answer to 'I love you,' if you're not there yet!"

"So what did he say, to what you said?"

"He turned me around and kissed me. He didn't look upset, but how could he not be?" I bury my head in my hands and mumble, "I fucked this up again, didn't I?"

"I wouldn't say that," Tipp reassures me. "Have all those romance novels you read taught you nothing?"

I look up at her, waiting to hear the rest of her argument.

"Rhysand loved Feyre first. Zade was clearly obsessed with Addie first. Hunt and Bryce? You know how adorable it is when the guy gets hit with the feelings first."

I chew that over. "There's one big problem with your theory."

"What's that?"

"Did you really just refer to a high fantasy series by the Queen?" I tick them off on my fingers as I list them. "Stalker-touch her and I'll send her your hands in a box, and the best fantasy world complete with the cutest animal companion from any novel *ever* as *romance novels*?" I bob my neck as I prove my point.

"What? They all end up with the girl they're crushing on from page two," she defends folding her arms across her chest.

I roll my eyes and look away from her, "There's too much wrong with this conversation for me to even start."

"Okay, I'll finish it. He loves you, you're eventually going to love him. Let time work it out. Stop worrying and enjoy the journey."

"Did you smoke a joint halfway through that?" I know her words are right, but Will is talking big emotions. It's one thing to daydream about having a cat or a dog with someone, it's so much more to say the L word.

"There's one more potential problem," I say. Tipp stands and we start walking to class.

Her posture straightens. "I'm feeling wise today, hit me." She sticks her hands out and makes a *come at me bro* movement with her fingers.

"I haven't told Will I'm leaving in a year. I've known it this whole time. Not telling him feels like I'm lying to him. He is so honest with me about his feelings and I'm hiding this huge truth from him." I've felt guilty over this since we went exclusive. I know I should have been honest in the car on the way to Anaheim. He's dating me right now, not committing to a life with me in another state.

Tipp states the obvious, "Sounds like you need to come clean."

I don't like this suggestion. "I thought you were feeling wise?"

"Just because you don't like what I have to say doesn't mean I'm wrong."

We finish the walk to class in silence. It's true, I don't like what she has to say, and I know she's right. I need to have a serious talk with Will.

"You're awfully quiet tonight Nik," Stefan points out once we've finished dinner Tuesday night before class.

He's right. I've been trying to figure out how to spill the beans to Will that I'm moving to Oregon in a year. I have no idea how he feels about leaving San Diego. If he's opposed to moving we might as well end this now before our feelings get too big.

I take hold of Will's hand and look at Stefan. "Yeah, um." I scratch my temple with my free hand. "Do you think I could meet you at class? I need to talk to Will about something."

Stefan objects to my idea. "You know he's going to tell me all about it anyway right?"

Will chimes in for me, "Come on man, go to class. If Nikki doesn't want me to tell you something I won't."

"Et tu, Brute?" Stefan accuses as he grabs his bag and leaves our table. I'll have to remember to thank him later.

I scoot back from Will so I can gauge his expressions. I prepare to break his heart. *Please don't let this be the end for us.*

"Nikki, you're worrying me. What's going on?"

His eyebrows are scrunched together again. He's so cute when he makes that face. I take both his hands in mine. "I haven't been telling you the whole truth," I start off horribly. Will's chin juts out a little further while he listens to my admission of guilt. "I'm moving to Oregon in a year."

Will shakes his head. He repeats what I've said skeptically. "Sorry, I thought I heard you say you were moving. That can't be it?"

"I'm not entirely sure where yet. Mom and I are going to Oregon this summer to figure out what campus we like best, but, yeah, I'm leaving next summer once I have my Associates."

I watch Will's chest rise and fall as he inhales deeply. He strokes his thumb over the back of my hand and I look up at his eyes scared of what I'll find there. His cheek is pulled to the side in a petite grin. His eyes are soft. His hands are warm, strong, and comforting; a feeling I've grown accustomed to in the last month. "That is a big deal," he replies. "But it's not the end of the world. You had me thinking you were ending things between us for a minute there."

The mere idea of that horrifies me. "Oh no! I would never. I just don't want to hide the truth from you. I'm moving, and if things are going well enough between us, well... I guess I want to see where this goes. But I also don't want us to waste time falling even harder for each other if you're not willing to move with me. "

"I honestly don't know how I feel about the idea of moving to Oregon. I'm guessing you're not looking for something long distance?"

I shake my head no.

"Okay, let me walk you to class." He stands and pulls me into an embrace. I hold on tight and inhale his scent. I don't know if this is the last time I'll feel safe in his arms. How has this behemoth of a man chiseled his way into my heart so effortlessly? The fear I'm experiencing currently is why I normally keep myself closed off emotionally. Fuck. I pray to Karma, *Please don't let this be the end of us!*

We walk to the science building in a tense silence. I hug Will one last time, hoping it won't actually be the last time. He places his hand gently on my cheek. I relish how warm and rough his skin feels against mine. I realize that while he might be trying to cup my cheek, he's holding half my face because of the sheer size of his hand. He leans down and kisses me so gently it feels like a feather brushing against my lips.

He pushes my head against his chest and he holds me again. I hear him say, "I need some time to think Nikki. Just looking at you makes me want to say I'll follow you anywhere. I need time. I know I love you. I have to analyze this from all angles before I blindly jump into the deep end, okay?"

I stiffly nod, still wrapped up in him.

His nose rests on the top of my head and he inhales deeply. It feels like he's trying to take in my scent before an inevitable goodbye. Then he kisses my hair. "Okay babe, you gotta get to class. I'm gonna take a few days to think this through like a logical person."

His joke makes me smile but I still don't pull away from his embrace.

"I appreciate you respecting my feelings and not leading me on. I'll call you when I've made up my mind." He moves his hands to my shoulders and holds me in place as he takes a step back.

My hands drop to my side. I don't want him to walk away. He could be walking out of my life forever right now.

I plaster a fake smile onto my face, "I'll talk to you in a few days then." I turn on my heel and trot down the stairs as the first tear crests down my cheek. I don't turn left to go to class. I go right and enter the bathroom. I hide in a stall until the tears stop flowing. Once my cheeks are blotted dry and my sniffles have subsided I exit the stall and look in the mirror. The only thing that will give me away is my bloodshot eyes. Let's hope Stefan understands body language enough not to ask me any questions.

Twenty-Seven

Brutal Honesty

I ADMIT IT. I'M moping. I'm not in love with Will yet. No chance. No way. However, I am in serious like with him. Going two days without talking to him sucks. I can't believe how quickly I eased into our weekly homework dates and nightly phone calls. He's not my sun, moon and stars or anything that dramatic, but he has become an integral part of my life.

I'm sitting in French, early as always, waiting for Tipp to arrive. I have my supplies on my desk, but I didn't bother getting The Goods for us today. My heart wasn't in it.

Suddenly, a green beverage is thrust into my face. I recoil from the startling visual onslaught. My eyes rapidly blink, trying to understand what is happening.

I hear Tipp laugh behind me, then she pulls the drink out from under my nose. It's a cup of my favorite: an iced matcha green tea latte with almond milk. I take it from her and do a test sip. It's the perfect combination of sweet nuttiness with a savory aftertaste. Combining those flavors with the vanilla almond milk our favorite coffee shop uses sends it over the edge. I sigh and my eyes close in delight as I take another sip. This is a beverage designed to be savored.

Tipp sits in her seat behind me and waits for me to broach the subject. It takes me less than a minute to turn around and spill all my feelings.

"I've fucked up right?" That was a horrible opener, but Tipp doesn't seize the moment to comment about my life choices. "I mean, I'm asking him to make a huge change to his future, but I'm not willing to negotiate about mine. That's what's fucked up."

"Do you know what his plans were beyond finishing his Associates?" Tipp asks.

Of course I know that. "He said he hadn't thought beyond this current goal. He still has a year left like me. I think Will was going to figure out his direction beyond that closer to the end of his degree."

"So, you're not uprooting some master plan."

I shrug. "Doesn't seem like it."

"He said he loves you, why didn't you say it back?"

"I'm not there yet," I defend. "I think I will be sometime, just not currently."

Tipp looks quizzical for a moment. "Can you handle a best friend moment of brutal, honest, truth?"

I twist my neck gently from side to side as I brace for her truth. "Yes."

She takes a sip of her drink and then in her serious voice asks me, "Is it fair to ask him to move to another state when you're not even brave enough to tell him how you truly feel?"

"What do you mean how I truly feel?" That's the only part of her comment that I don't agree with.

She levels me with a shit eating grin. "You miss him?"

"Yeah?" I don't like where she's headed with this line of inquiry.

"You tell him secrets that previously only I was privy to?"

"Maybe?" I begrudgingly utter.

Then she brings out the big hitter. "When you think about your future, is he there?"

"Shit."

This time Tipp moves her straw above the liquid in her cup to purposefully make that air sucking noise when she goes to take a drink. After an exaggerated "Ahhhh," Tipp smacks her lips and drives her point home. "You're in love with him. Now you know it."

"Double shit," I mumble as I turn away from her. I take a sip of my tea but the taste is less satisfactory. I have feelings for Will. They're the *"L Word"* level feelings. So much for making this decision before either of us let emotions get in the way.

Twenty-Eight

Falling Fast

WHEN I TOLD WILL I would give him time to process everything I didn't think forward to Tuesday. Does giving him space mean not meeting up with him and Stefan for dinner before class? I decide to err on the side of respecting him. I quickly get my lunner from the Griffin Center and head to the library instead of our usual spot.

When I get to Astronomy that night, Stefan is all smiles when he sees me. It's infectious and I appreciate that about him.

"Hey," Stefan calls across the classroom.

As I near our table he asks conspiratorially, "So, you had a fun weekend huh?" He even manages to wag his eyebrows at me.

Oh gods, does that mean he knows about *all* the things that happened? I feel my cheeks flush and I pinch my lips between my teeth. I don't want to accidentally tell him any details he doesn't already know.

I try to play it cool. "You know. It was nice." I shrug my shoulder hoping it adds a level of indifference to my remark.

Stefan must notice my discomfort. He puts his forearm on our table and leans toward me. Quietly he whispers, "Don't worry, Will didn't tell me any details. He's not like that."

I grin shyly at him. "Thanks."

Then the cocky Stefan that I've grown used to over the last few months rears his head. "He may not have told me anything, but the pep in that boy's step? Something tells me you both had a, shall we say, climactic weekend?"

My hand covers my face in embarrassment. I slide deeper into my chair hoping that the Earth will open up and swallow me whole.

Stefan continues, "But if you both had a wonderful weekend... Why weren't you at dinner with us tonight?"

"Reasons," I say under my breath.

Stefan pushes for more details. "Reasons I need to know about?"

I sigh. "I don't know if it's my place to tell you, considering Will didn't."

"He may have had some pep in his step, but he was also a little off. Did the weekend not go entirely well?"

"No!" I don't want him to worry like that. *Is it that bad if I tell Stefan?* Maybe it would be better if Will had someone to talk things through with anyway? "I just, okay. I told Will that I'm moving to Oregon next summer."

I sit down and Stefan remains quiet. I fidget with my hands while I wait for him to digest what I've said.

"You're both falling for each other hard. I can tell."

That's not the response I was expecting. "Yes?" I ask him.

"So what's the issue?"

"Umm, did you not hear the part about me moving to Oregon?" I reiterate.

"I heard that, but it's not like there's a lot tying Will down to San Diego."

I roll my eyes. "That's a ridiculous statement. He has all his friends and family here. That's basically his whole world."

Stefan catches my eye and his face turns sincere. "Not if you're becoming his whole world, Nik."

My eyes widen. I chuckle nervously. "No," I shake my head. "We're only dating."

"Isn't this a problem for a year from now, why are you stressing about it now?"

Part of my thumb nail suddenly needs all of my attention. I focus on it as I sheepishly tell Stefan. "I know it seems so far off. But what if we're perfect? What if everything is right and then he's unwilling to move? I've been hurt enough in the past, I don't want to hurt *myself* this time. I just..." I stare up at the ceiling hoping what I need to say will be written across it somewhere. "I'm a planner. I'll be looking into moving companies and apartments this year. I need to know if a small studio is a good size, or if I'll need a second room so Will can play on the computer while I'm sleeping. It's ridiculous to ask, but if he can't see himself moving then I can't keep pretending like there's anything beyond this year." I finish with a dejected sigh. He hasn't even said no yet, but I can feel parts of my heart breaking off and shattering on the floor around me at the possibility. If we were to spend another year falling for each other I might lose sight of my goals. If I like him this much after only a few months... I don't want to imagine what my feelings will be like a year from now. They could be strong enough to change my plans, I need to protect my future before that happens.

"Well, he's falling, fast. It looks like you might be too." Stefan challenges.

This can't be. "Well, Will's taking a few days to think things through. I don't want to have a long distance relationship, but I'm not staying down here. I also don't want to waste a year of our lives if he's not comfortable with moving. I want him to evaluate his options and make the most logical decision for his future."

"Makes sense," Stefan responds. Then he changes the subject. "Did you find the answer to number 27 on the final review document?"

I internally thank Stefan for moving on with our conversation. I pull out my study guide and show him where I found my answers. After a little double checking, Stefan adds on a detail I was missing.

As Mr. Fitzgibbons enters the classroom a few minutes later, he reminds everybody of the extra credit opportunity coming up at Balboa Park this weekend. I invited Will to join me on that. Hopefully he'll have a decision made soon or I'll be going to Balboa alone on Friday night.

Twenty-Nine

All In

"I CAN SEE IT." I tell the tomato slicer Wednesday morning as I'm opening the sandwich shop. We're alone, so I don't risk anyone thinking I'm batshit crazy right now. Just me and the slicers, working through my feelings and prepping for the day ahead. "We'll have a large house, five bedrooms, three bathrooms, two and a half kids. There will be plenty of pets, two dogs and two cats minimum. They need friends to play with when we're at work, after all. Maybe even a snake or two. I could get a corn snake to be my classroom pet and it can come home during breaks. We'll need at least an acre lot so that the pets and children have enough space to run around and get their energy out.

"Our kids will do extracurriculars that they like. I would love it if they enjoyed dance, but if baseball is their thing I guess I can learn to like it. Our summers will be spent back home at his parent's house or mine. Hopefully Will can get a job where he gets more than two weeks off a year, or where he can work remotely during the day and hang out with family at night if we're on vacation.

"Our house can have a library that doubles as the homework room. I know he likes video games so a spot for his computer of course. I think the most important aspect of our home will be an open concept living area. Mom and Nana are always in the kitchen during holidays, and I want a way that people who are cooking can interact with everyone else. So we'll definitely need a kitchen island too. I can see it, can't you?"

I didn't like what Tipp said about me falling for Will, but I needed to hear it. The visuals I have about our future are so vivid that I know she's right. I'm not only in like with Will, I'm in love with him. I can't tell him though. Not yet. Not after— I roll my neck and focus on the sensation of the knife between my fingers, how it's an extension of my hand, working to gut the bell peppers before I put them in the slicer.

When my mind is safely away from the last guy I said those words to I start daydreaming about Will again. If only he'd figure out his feelings, and tell me he's moving to Oregon with me in a year. Then, and only then, I'll tell him. I don't want me loving him back to change his mind.

I continue slicing the veggies for the morning shift. The rhythmic push and pull of metal on vegetables makes it incredibly easy for me to zone out. Before I know it, my shift comes to an end and it's time to change for class. I jog to my car to get my outfit and rush back into the store. In the bathroom, I check over my hair and make sure my messy bun is the perfect ratio of secured in place (by thousands of bobby pins) to looking effortless. At home I grabbed skinny jeans paired with Converse and an Alison Krauss and Union Station graphic T for today. It gives a vintage vibe, but I bought the shirt at one of their shows just a year or two ago.

As I leave the store, my eyes squint in the blinding light of the Southern California sun. I pop the trunk and throw my dirty work clothes into its dark recesses. I plop down in the driver's seat and put my key in the ignition. I twist. Nothing happens.

I twist the key again. She doesn't turn over.

Crap!

My hands grip the steering wheel at the proper ten and two places. *Think!* I rock back and forth, gently encouraging my brain to work.

"Tipp!" I shout to my empty vehicle. As I rummage around my purse, I justify my thinking to the car's stuffy interior. "She has a Jeep, maybe she'll have some cables and be able to give me a jump."

I unlock my screen and scroll to Tipp's name. I type out.

> Hey! Can you give me a jump at work? Car's dead.

Then I wait. I sit with the door ajar and watch people running their Wednesday morning errands and my mind wanders. How are so many people out shopping on a Wednesday morning? Do they have abnormal jobs? How many of them are students? Stay at home moms? How much money does your spouse need to make in order for one to afford to not work? Would I be able to find emotional fulfillment doing that? I don't think I could handle only talking to my children and random employees as I run errands. I may not be best friends with my coworkers, but I do enjoy getting to socialize with them, especially when they have puppy updates for me.

"Wait!" I shout to my car again. How had I not thought of the people working in the shop behind me? I head back into work. Luckily it's not packed with a lunch rush yet. Three of my coworkers are in the backroom when I swing the door open.

"Nikki, you're back?" my manager asks.

"Yeah, do any of you have jumper cables?" I ask the room at large.

Three heads shake no, in unison.

"Sorry Nikki," one of them says.

"No worries, I'll figure it out." I leave the store and rack my brain for more ideas. Tipp hasn't texted back, and I'm guessing she won't notice her phone before it's time for class. She either replies immediately, or it's hours before she responds. There's no in-between with that girl.

At least today's lesson was changed to drop by office hours so that Madame Krasse can glance over our final papers before we submit them in two weeks. That also means that Tipp and I weren't guaranteed to cross paths today, so she'll never know if I'm unable to get to campus.

My body slumps in my seat. I'm quickly running out of solutions for getting out of this parking lot. "Double shit," I sigh to the steering wheel.

I check my phone again to see if Tipp has responded. Nothing.

I flick the touchscreen of my phone to Nana's name. Then I dial. I have no idea if she even has cables, but at this point she'll probably pick some up at the store on her way to save me if she doesn't. The line rings out and I'm greeted by her voicemail message. I end the call before leaving one.

Tipp and Nana will both have notifications on their phones saying I've tried to reach them. At this rate, office hours with Madame Krasse are shot. I wilt in resignation, or because of this heat, not entirely sure which is worse.

There's a coffee shop down at the corner of the shopping center. I grab my bag from the passenger seat and lock up my car. In the shop I order a Chai and find a secluded seat. I pull out my never ending pile of homework and hunker down. If I can't make it to campus on time, I can at least make a dent in a few problems.

I set an alarm on my phone for two p.m. If no one has gotten back to me by then I'll officially feel desperate. English starts at three p.m. and Mr. Jedidah is a dick about attendance.

I can still hear his pretentious lecture from day one this term: "If you can't commit to showing up to your college classes you'll never make it in life." He has no leniency with absences and drops your entire grade half a letter, per absence. On top of that, if you're more than ten minutes late, he counts it as an absence!

I put my phone down and call on Hermione Granger to give me strength. I can compartmentalize enough to get homework done. If I have to book an Uber to get to class at two, then that's what I'll do. I sit up in my chair and firmly plant my feet on the ground. As my fingers slide across the smooth paper of my spiral notebook my brain focuses on its happy place. I zero in on my chicken scratch and the minutes drift by.

Suddenly the beep of my alarm blares, disturbing the coffee shop. I silence it and check my phone yet again. No responses from Tipp or Nana. Who doesn't check their phone for three hours?

I navigate to Google and type into the search: *How to ask for a jump start*. The first answer is a tow truck, but that doesn't help me, I'm trying not to spend a bunch of money. The second option is a friend or family member. Maybe if my friend or family member listened to their phones that would be a viable option.

I don't think my A in English can withstand losing 5% of my overall grade. I slam my phone onto the table in irritation. I startle the barista cleaning a table near me.

He looks at me with pinched brows. "Hey, you okay?"

My eyes widen and I speak with embarrassment, "I'm so sorry! I didn't mean to scare you."

He shakes it off. "No worries, but everything alright?"

I fling my hand into the air signaling a general irritation. "Not really. My car won't turn over and I can't find anyone with cables to give me a jump."

"Shoot, wish you'd said something fifteen minutes ago. One of our guys that just clocked off definitely would have had them."

I lean my elbows on the table and rub my forehead with my fists. "Do you think anyone else might have them?" I practically beg this poor barista.

"Let me check," he offers before walking over to his coworkers. I track his movements as he asks every employee in the shop. His hand motions to me in the corner and I can only imagine how pathetic I look stalking his conversations with the staff.

Once he's talked to every employee he looks at me dejected. He walks back to my spot. "Is there anyone you can call?"

I pick up my phone and check for any notifications. It's still blank. I explain, "I tried calling my bestie and my Nana, neither of them responded, and that was three hours ago."

The barista taps his chin as he thinks. "What about a friend that's not quite a bestie, or a boyfriend?"

"Mmmm," I groan. My face puckers as if I was tasting something sour. "Yeah, not sure if I have a boyfriend or not right now."

"Asking him for help with this might be how you find out?" he suggests. "Well, good luck, I gotta get back to work."

I internally wrestle. I told Will I'd give him time, but I don't see any other options. If he says no, I'll have to get an Uber and figure out my car issues after class.

It feels like the world morphs into slow motion. My finger takes an abnormal amount of time to click its way to Will's contact. When I hit dial the rings last forever. I don't think he'll pick up, he should be working right now. *Is that me hoping he won't pick up?*

"Hello?" Will's voice questions on the other end of the call.

Fuck, now I have to remember how words work! "Hey Will," I reply on a shaky exhale. "Look, I know I told you I'd give you all the time you need, but I'm beside myself right now."

"Shit Nikki, what do you need?" His voice is laced with worry.

I may have laid it on too thick. "Oh no, nothing too bad!" I quickly clarify. "My car won't start and I only have fifty seven minutes until my next class. I can't get ahold of anyone with cables. Is there any way that you magically have them and can come give me a jump?"

I hear him chuckle lightly. "Yeah, babe. You're lucky it was a slow day and they let me off early. You at work?"

"Yeah."

"I'll be there in ten." He clicks off the call and my brain starts stressing about an entirely new topic. I pack up my things in a daze. When I reenter the blinding light of the afternoon I barely squint. Did Will just call me babe? That has to mean something good right? Or was it a slip of the tongue?

I put my belongings in the passenger seat and lean against the hood as I wait for Will to show up. I want to be excited about his calling me babe, but I don't want to jump the gun either.

Will shows up right as the spot next to my car opens. My arms are crossed as he strolls up to me. Will is still wearing his mechanic outfit and has some grease smudged across his forehead. He reaches out his hands but pauses before taking hold of my hips. They fall sheepishly to his side and he says, "Well, let's get you up and running."

I give him my keys and watch the process unfold.

Will pops my hood with ease and locates the battery. He opens up a plastic box on my car and does the same to his. "It's a good thing I always have a roadside kit," he calls out as he's rummaging around our vehicles.

I watch enraptured with his ease around something I know nothing about. Will pulls out a black bag and unzips it. Then the cables come out. I don't know the first thing about fixing a car, but the way he handles those cables has my mouth salivating.

Will beckons me over to him. "I need you to hold these separate."

I nod.

"Whatever you do Nikki, don't let them touch," he warns seriously.

"Okay," I say breathlessly.

Will connects the other ends of the jumper cables to part of my car and then takes the red cable from me. He attaches it to his car followed by the black one.

Watching a man jump a car shouldn't be this hot but I think summer has come and I'm in the middle of my own personal heat wave. I'd fan myself if it wouldn't be a dead giveaway to how his skills are making me feel down under.

I'm leaning against the passenger side of his car, making sure no one walks between our vehicles to end up in a tangle of wires. Will turns on his car, circles behind the trunk, and then comes over to where I'm watching the show. He boxes me in by putting his hands on the roof of his car on either side of me. I look up at him with a deep smile on my face.

"Well Nikki, if this works, it's your battery. If not, I'll give you a ride to class and we'll figure it out after that." He kisses the tip of my nose gently and turns around. He crouches down into my Beetle and tries the ignition.

It turns over!

He looks up from my driver's seat to see me jumping up and down clapping my hands like I just watched a Cirque du Soleil show.

This makes Will smile in turn. He wipes his hands down his pants and finally touches me. His grip lands on my hips and he weaves his thumbs through my belt loops. Will pulls me off his car and I have to brace my fall by slamming my hands against his chest. Before I've had time to center myself, his lips are on mine and he's kissing me deeply.

I melt into his strong body. My arms crawl their way up his chest and end up looped around his neck of their own accord.

Will breaks the kiss too soon for my liking and pushes me back to an arm's length away. His voice sounds gravelly. "Three days is too long to go without getting to do that."

I bite my lower lip and wait for him to proceed.

He strokes his thumbs across the top of my jeans. "I know you need to get to class, but I also think you should know I'm all in."

"Are—" I begin but he's not done.

"There are details we need to discuss but right now isn't the time. I just want you to know that I'm all in and we'll figure out the rest, somehow, someway." He squeezes me one more time before he walks to the front of our cars and starts undoing the jumper cables.

I want to say something, but the thoughts racing through my mind feel inadequate. I smile as I watch him. This gentle giant of a man who is apparently all in now.

He packs up the cables and tosses them carelessly into his trunk. Finally my mind remembers how to function. "Thanks, Will," I say as I take his cheek in my hand. I brush my fingers across his stubble and smile up at him.

"You're welcome babe, but you gotta go. You know Jedidiah is a killer with his attendance rules," Will reminds me. He suffered through Mr. Jedidiah's rules last term so he's well versed with the unrealistic expectations set upon us.

I fidget with my hands, not wanting to leave Will's presence when it feels like I can take a full breath for the first time in days. I barter with him, "Only if you agree to me coming over to do homework tonight."

Will's face splits into a grin that spreads from ear to ear. "It's a date," he says before kissing me. Then he lightly swats my ass to get me moving.

I get into my car, close the door, and roll down the window. Will leans through the opening to give me one last kiss but pauses halfway across the distance. "Looks like we found the culprit," he declares as he reaches his arm past me and turns off one of my backseat lights.

"That'll do it," I agree.

"I'll see you in a few hours. Now go. You've barely got enough time to make it across town. Don't let Jedidiah's unyielding rules win."

I manage to sneak into class with two minutes to spare. A stupid smirk is on my face the entire lesson. I may have physically been in my seat, but I didn't hear a single word our professor said. Will's all in; that's what matters.

By the time class ends, Tipp has called me two times and has sent me seven messages. I text her letting her know that while she was no help, Will is back to being my knight in shining armor. This of course triggers another round of calls and texts.

I tuck my phone into my pocket and laugh into the fresh air of campus. She's not getting an update until I know all the details.

I don't think Will and I will be getting much studying done tonight, but I bring my bookbag up to his sister's condo to keep up pretenses. I jog up the stairs and knock on the door before trying the knob. It swings open and I enter.

"Hello?" I call out to the seemingly empty living space.

"I'm in my room," Will's voice calls out.

I walk down the hall and open the door. I'm greeted by Will's abs on display. He's pulling on a shirt and I lean on the doorframe watching the show unfold before me.

"You're doing that wrong," I tease him.

He grabs his towel off the bed and pulls his hair through it, "How so?"

"Your shirt is supposed to be coming off when I get here, not going on." I step into his room and give him a hug. Will takes my head in his hand and angles me perfectly for his mouth. He pulls me snug against his body and kisses me passionately. His tongue strokes my lips asking for entrance and I open gladly for him.

"Not when I'm home, you don't!" Meghan's voice interrupts us.

I break our kiss, startled, and my cheeks turn crimson. I bury my head in Will's chest and leave him to deal with his sister.

"Good thing you're going out tonight then isn't it?" His icy words send a warning to his sister.

"What if I changed my mind?" She challenges him.

Will tucks his fist below my chin and beckons me to look up at him. As he stares into my eyes he informs his sister, "Then you'll be wanting some ear plugs Meghan, because my plans tonight involve you not being around."

I shiver in response to his lust filled gaze. I bite my lip, anticipating what he has planned for tonight.

"Gross!" Meghan shouts behind me. "The things I never want to know about my baby brother!"

Will breaks our gaze and continues torturing his sister. "Might want to send me a text when you're on your way home, make sure we don't scar you for life."

"Oh my God!" Meghan wails. She closes Will's bedroom door behind her. We hear her shuffling throughout the living room before the front door snaps shut as well. Will holds me tightly in his arms until we hear her car leave from the carport beneath Will's room.

"What about Thomas?"

Will backs up to his bed and pulls me down on top of him, "He's working a night shift, already confirmed it."

My devil horns pop up as I move to straddle Will. "Good."

He guides my hips with his hands and I lower to kiss him. Our lips reconnect like long lost friends. Will kisses me soft and sensually and I don't like it. I abruptly sit up and rest my hands on his pecks. "You're not going to go soft and," I air quote, *'Make love,'* are you?"

Without warning Will grabs my waist and flips me beneath him. One of his powerful legs ends up between mine and he grabs both my wrists in a single strong grip. He growls at me, "No Nikki. We're going to fuck. After the emotions you put me through the last three days we've got some angry sex to work through."

I know that should intimidate me, but I also know he would never do anything against my consent. My lids lower and I stare up at my mountain of a man. I lick my lips and whimper the one word he's been waiting for, "Yes."

Thirty

Logical Love

WILL'S HEADLIGHTS ROLL DOWN the driveway at seven on the dot Friday night. I head out my private exit and lock it behind me. Nana has company and I don't want to interrupt whatever they're up to as I depart.

When I make it out front, Will is stepping out of his car. My eyes drink in every inch of him. He's wearing Converse, straight legged dark wash jeans, an olive green shirt, and his blond locks are brushed back into a natural wavy mess. I thought Wednesday night's angry fuck fest would be enough to sate me for a while. However, seeing him dressed up, and going on a nerdy date with me? Well it's a good thing Nana is home or I don't think we'd be leaving the house tonight.

Will saunters to where I've stopped mid stride on the pathway leading out to the driveway. When he reaches out and brushes some hair behind my ear I snap out of my trance and realize he knows exactly what was distracting me from rational thoughts.

"Right on time," I greet him.

He graces me with a smile. "Well, I know how quickly you can turn into a ball of stress if you're running late."

I blush and disagree, "I'm not a ball of stress."

"Maybe right now you're not," Will counters with a wicked grin.

I cross my arms at him, pretending to feel affronted.

Will holds my gaze and huffs a laugh. "Fine, you're the most easy going person I've ever met. Is that better?"

My brows lower on my forehead and my lips pout at him. "No! Because we clearly know you're lying saying that!"

He takes a step closer to me and I have to crane my neck to keep glaring him down. "Nikki, you may stress rather easily, but I think that's adorable." He leans down and kisses me.

That's not fair; his kisses always disarm me. Will doesn't deepen the kiss. Instead, he takes my bottom lip between his teeth and gently sucks on it. Thank the gods that Nana's house has enough trees and shrubs lining it that I know she and her guests can't see us. I push off of Will's chest before he gets a second chance to bite me. Only when there's a slight distance between us do I feel like I can think clearly again.

Will grins, knowing exactly what he's done to me. I look down to his crotch and smirk back. We're both willing to fight dirty tonight, but my Astronomy extra credit assignment won't accept horniness as a viable excuse.

My teeth are making a meal out of my lower lip thinking of all the things I'd rather do with Will than Astronomy.

He takes an exaggerated breath and steers us in a responsible direction. Slowly, he holds out his arm for me to take and leads us to the car. "Ready?"

I realize I have no idea what we're about to do. "I'm not sure," I answer honestly as I gracefully sit down in his car.

Will snaps the door shut and I shamelessly watch his ass as he walks around the vehicle. Maybe someday I'll get the chance to take a good bite of it. Will opens his door and slides in. "So what exactly did you invite me to do tonight?" He asks while buckling up and putting the car in reverse.

I duck my head and squint as I nervously scratch my temple. Then I admit, "I don't exactly know."

He stops at the end of the drive and stares at me momentarily. When he's safely pulled onto the street he continues, "Guess we're both in for a surprise then."

I put my hand in his lap. His jeans feel soft and well worn under my fingertips. "Thanks for being my adventure buddy."

Will weaves his large calloused fingers through mine. "Anytime Nikki." He kisses the back of my hand.

The drive to Balboa passes uneventfully. With the numerous study sessions we've had this term, I've grown comfortable passing time without conversation in Will's presence. After he merges onto the freeway I turn on the radio and we listen to the country hits the D.J. has chosen for tonight.

When we enter the Balboa Park parking lot it's almost barren. Will pulls into a spot near the pathway leading to the science museum.

"I've never seen the lot this empty before," I remark as I get out of the car and loop my arm through Will's.

He smiles at me and kisses my hair. "Guess it's more popular in the daytime. Do you know where we need to go?"

I take the lead. "I think I remember Mr. Fitzgibbons saying if we walk toward the science building you'll run into the event first."

Will follows at my pace. The sun is below the horizon now but our surroundings still glow with an orange tint. The trees have exaggerated shadows and birds are calling their final songs of the day. We walk in opposition to most of the traffic filtering out of the park. We round the back of the dinosaur exhibit building and I lead us to the right.

The path opens up to a large fountain. A few kids are laughing and screaming as they run too close to the water and get drenched in the process. Will and I watch them as we round the spectacle. On the far side of the fountain, I see people gathered and a few telescopes are in the process of being set up.

I point it out to Will. "I'm guessing that's where we need to be."

He nods. "It would make sense."

We close the distance quickly and stand on the outskirts of the crowd. After a few minutes of us observing and listening in on conversations, an older man notices us. "This must be your first time!" he greets.

I smile at his naturally jovial disposition. "Yes Sir. I'm here for extra credit in one of my college classes."

He claps his hands together, "One of Fitzy's students then?"

"Uh yeah," I giggle. "But I don't think he'd want us calling him Fitzy."

"Nonsense," the boisterous older man says. "If you mention it in your paper he'll give you even more points."

I make a mental note to write my professor's nickname in somehow.

"Okay kids, you'll want to hang out for about half an hour. When it's a quarter after, the fountain will shut down and the park lights will turn off. We ask that you please don't get your phones out because their light can interfere with others looking through the telescopes."

Will and I listen to his directions and nod along with the specifics.

"All our telescopes will be focused on a different phenomenon tonight so you can hop from one to the next. The owner of the telescope should be standing nearby to explain what you're looking at. Ask them any questions you've got."

He pauses and I ask, "Anything else we need to know about tonight?"

His eyes crinkle as his cheeks revel a delighted smile, "Absolutely, I haven't gotten to the best part!"

Will speaks up, "And what would that be Sir?"

The older gentleman puts a hand on my shoulder, and his other hand on Will's shoulder. He looks at both of us in turn and bestows his wisdom. "The most important thing about tonight is that you have fun and maybe learn a little bit while doing it." He squeezes our shoulders, gives us a final grin, and turns to a new group of people. I hear him begin his spiel as Will and I rotate to take in the position of all the telescopes.

I spy a bench about twenty feet removed from the crowd and guide Will toward it. We sit down and he drapes his arm around my shoulders. "I forgot to tell you something earlier," he breathes into my hair.

I lean my head against his shoulder. "What's that?"

His finger grazes down my arm in lazy circles as he says, "You look stunning tonight."

I grin at him. I did put some effort into my appearance tonight. It's a coincidence our outfits complement each other so nicely. I'm wearing black slip-ons because I wasn't sure how far we'd need to walk tonight. I paired them with my newfound obsession: skinny jeans cuffed at the ankle. To top off the look I have a burgundy tank top with a glittery black skull in the center of it. I knew tonight would probably get chilly so I grabbed my fake leather jacket on the way out. My I.D. and other essentials are zipped into various jacket pockets so that I don't have to bother with a purse.

"Thanks," I reply to Will. "You look nice tonight, too."

He squeezes me gently in response. Then he asks, "What would you like to do while we wait for the main event to begin?"

My hand finds its way to his thigh and I rest it there, savoring his warmth and silent strength. "I rather like this, honestly. Would you be okay with people watching for a while?"

Will kisses my temple. "Of course."

We sit there and enjoy the scene unfolding around us. You can tell who has been a regular for weeks on end by how they greet one another. A lot of the people with telescopes are finished setting up and are congregating in the middle of the group. At this distance I can't decipher what they're saying but the group looks at ease as if this is a natural part of their Friday routines.

Slowly the people gathered start to disperse and return to their individual telescopes. I spy one that is empty with a gentleman standing alone waiting for someone to wander up.

"Ready?" I ask Will.

As I stand he slides his arm down my back and gives my ass a slight squeeze. I jump a little bit and swat at him in response. Will grabs my hand from midair and pulls me down to give him a kiss. Only then does he rise and follow me to the telescope and its corresponding human.

We stroll from telescope to telescope being told about everything we're seeing. Will and I take turns looking at the astrological phenomena and conversing with the various scientists surrounding us. By the time we make it through half of the viewing stations we've seen Mars, the Moon, the Gemini cluster, the Auriga constellation and a few others I've never heard of before. We also learn that Venus is incredibly bright this month.

I know I should be focusing on the science surrounding us, but Will is proving equally fascinating to observe. A few times when I glance in his direction, I've caught him staring at me. Every time, it brings a flush to my cheeks that I'm glad he can't see in the dim night-lighting. What's cuter yet is how interested he is in all the astronomy observations. He's asking the scientists more questions than I am.

When we get to the halfway point I ask him, "Did you agree to go on this date because I asked you, or because you were secretly excited to look at outer space through a bunch of telescopes?"

He returns my question with a timid smile. "Can my answer be both?"

I squeeze our joined hands in reassurance. He's barely let go of me the whole night, even when I'm looking through the viewfinders. "Of course it can."

We walk to the next telescope and the owner tells us it's focused on Mars.

"Oh, I thought we saw Mars already over there?" pointing to one of the first spots we stopped.

The sweet elderly lady smiles at me patiently. "Dear, we have two telescopes focused on various things tonight. If you've already seen through those," she points to the half we've already stopped at, "Then you've seen everything for tonight." She finishes with a smile. "If you want to take a second look you're welcome to hang around, of course."

Will and I look at one another. He puts his arm around my shoulders and replies, "Thank you so much." Then he guides me out of the way of people waiting to engage with her.

"Want to go for a walk?" I ask him hopefully. I don't want tonight to end. It's felt so natural to hang out with Will doing something low key. Apparently we're both nerds. I didn't know he was a bigger astronomy nerd than me, but that's not difficult to achieve. I do prefer my books over outer space.

He takes his arm from my shoulder and laces our fingers. We walk further into the park side by side. I've always enjoyed this historical place. The architecture is unlike anything being created these days. There's detail and craftsmanship in every nook and cranny.

We continue ambling through the main stretch of the park. I mentally overlay the crowded daytime visual with the sparse open pathways before us. There are crickets chirping in the shadows and I hear rustling of leaves in the slight breeze filtering through. We're surrounded by large arching buildings on both sides. I see other couples in the alcoves talking in hushed tones. Will and I keep walking through the park until we reach Suicide Bridge.

"Do you know the name of this bridge?" I ask him.

He points to a sign. "Yeah babe, it's the Cabrillo Bridge."

I pause our walking and prop a hip against the cemented walkway. Will stops as well and looks out at the view of Downtown San Diego. We watch a plane fly by, preparing for landing, before I explain, "It's nickname is Suicide Bridge."

I can tell I've surprised Will because his eyebrows shoot to the middle of his forehead.

"The bridge has a rather tragic history. It was built in 1915. In those first fifty years the First World War happened, the stock market crashed, World War II happened, along with the Korean Conflict and the Vietnam War. With San Diego being a military town families were torn apart either from the depression or from war." I point to the ground below the bridge. "Currently it's a freeway, but back in the thirties there was a man made lagoon there instead. Some people actually survived the jump back when there was water at the bottom."

Will looks at me still shocked by the turn of my conversation. "What a romantic conversation, Nikki," he responds sarcastically.

"Well, I don't find this bridge romantic in general knowing its backstory. Over fifty people have chosen to end their lives where we're standing."

He shakes his head at me and starts walking back the way we came. Once we've cleared the edge of the bridge he asks, "Why do you know all that?"

I shrug. "Nana told me one day."

"Do you and Nana regularly talk about such morbid topics?"

"Not always, but Mom and I watch a lot of serial killer shows together," I reply flatly. I find them fascinating.

"Why?" Will exclaims, too loudly for the peaceful night.

I mull that over and purse my lips into a thin line. "I honestly don't know. Now that you're asking me to think about it though, I think it's because I'm less likely to be a victim like the women before me if I know how to act better."

"And walking alone with a man in the middle of the night at an abandoned park with acres and acres of secluded wilderness is one of the wise things these shows taught you?" He's teasing me now, but he has no idea how much I've thought this through.

"Will, I'm a woman."

"No?" He draws out the single-syllable word.

"Which means I've thought this through. You have yet to make me think you'll hurt me. Nana and Tipp know where I am and who I'm with, so if you are guilty at least they'll catch you and lock you up." I pause to breathe. "Furthermore, we may be in a seemingly deserted place, but we've never actually been alone. There have been other people walking past us in the night at regular intervals. We've never walked so far away from the telescope group that they wouldn't be able to hear me scream if needed. We won't be walking down to the aerospace museum, or through the tree paths because that is asking for something to happen. You might think we're alone, but we're not."

Will stops in his tracks and regards me. His brows are pulled in and his lips are slightly parted. I can see the wheels of what I've said working in his mind. He reaches and grips both my hands in his. "You've actually thought about this before? How to not be a victim?"

I nod my head. "You have no idea how much mental energy goes into being a woman in our society."

His eyes go wide and his brow puckers. "I'm beginning to think how incredibly right you are babe. I'm sorry you have to put that much work into going on a nighttime stroll with me." He takes a step forward and engulfs me in a huge hug. I bury my face into his warm chest and inhale deeply. He smells of woods and citrus again. I think it's growing to be my new favorite scent.

"There's something else I haven't owned up to yet," my words are mumbled due to his tight embrace.

"What's that?" He asks the top of my head.

"You would put yourself between an attacker and me. So I'd have enough time to run to safety while you're getting stabbed, defending me."

He takes a second to process what I've said then loosens his hold and takes a step back. Will's stare is accusatory. "You'd leave me as bait?"

I cross my arms. "It's not leaving you as bait if you willingly jump in front of an attacker to save me." I wave my arm in the air to emphasize my point. "And I'd bring back help. Promise to apply pressure, not rip the knife out, yadda, yadda."

"Gee, thanks." Will deadpans.

I smile ruefully at him and perch on my tippy toes. "It's the least I could do," I say as I kiss him.

He quickly forgives my well thought out plan of allowing him to get stabbed and tucks me under his arm again. We continue wandering through the park, stopping in front of the lily pond to watch nature unfold before our eyes.

The sun has fully set by now, but I still see sporadic ripples spreading across the pond. The crickets are louder here and I pray they don't make their locations known to me. I don't want to tell Will about my irrational fear of them just yet. Learning that I watch serial killer shows to better prepare for an attack is bad enough; we don't need to add my traumatic past with crickets to this evening's agenda.

The water laps up against the shore and trickles under the bridge we're stopped on, guiding my thoughts back to reality. Will's hand is laced with mine, warm under my icy fingers. I wrap my free hand around his arm, trying to absorb his warmth. Will notices and unzips his jacket. He holds it open and invites me to hug him. When I'm wrapped around him, he closes either side of his jacket around me and holds me there.

We stand there, surrounded by Balboa Park's majestic nighttime beauty. This might be the closest I'll ever get to being serenaded by Scuttle and Flounder in real life. The pond trickles. There are croaking frogs in the distance. The tree's leaves are rustling in the consistent light breeze filtering through the park. I stand there embraced by the man I'm in love with and decide: it's time he knows.

I lean my head back so I can see Will's eyes. He looks down at me and I swear I see a twinkle in his smile. Before I can say anything, Will kisses me. His arms keep me close. I feel my core temperature rising as his tongue brushes my lips. We lose sense of reality in one another's arms and enjoy the setting of our date.

When we part, Will is the first to speak. "I meant it when I said I'm all in, Nikki. I love you, I'll always be here for you. No matter what." He smiles down at me and finishes. "Let's move to Oregon next year."

My breath hitches. I wasn't expecting him to be so agreeable. I beam at him as he continues.

"Let's move vertically across the country and go on a new adventure together. We'll find an apartment, go to school, and finish our degrees. I know I'll love every step of the way as long as I'm by your side."

His words have me feeling as light as a cloud. How is he this perfect?

He wraps up, "Besides, in a few years, once we have our degrees, we will move back home, anyway."

He looks down at me with adoration in his eyes and kisses me again.

It feels like everything is working out perfectly. I'm with the man of my dreams. He wants to move to Oregon with me. I know that wherever the future takes us our love will endure. Whether it seems logical or not.

Author's Note

Thank you to anyone who took a chance and read my debut novel! Logical Love began in 2023 when I had an undiagnosed, invisible, chronic illness. The creation of this love story gave me something to look forward to on the darkest of days. I hope Nikki and Will brought a smile to your face as they figured out their shit. Writing these characters was a labor of love. Nikki and Will may be ready to move to Oregon now, but there are plenty of hurdles in their future. Check out the next part of their love adventure in *Finding Forever*, coming July 2024.

To anyone out there dreaming of becoming an author. Do it. One day, one page, one word at a time. I took this insane dream I had and forced it to become a reality. Very little was easy. A lot of people told me I was crazy. I wanted to give up a thousand times but found a reason to keep going a thousand and one. Holy, fucking, shit... I did it, and so can you.

Acknowledgements

There are so many people who deserve acknowledgment for making this book happen. In no particular order:

To the woman who nurtured this book into existence. I don't know how many hours you spent laboring over commas, learning about the role of an editor, and not feeding me bullshit when I begged you to tell me everything would be okay. You helped this book blossom and inspired some amazing plot details. You shunned me when I wrote a fade-to-black scene. Grace, I will never be able to say thank you enough.

JJ, Hannah, Wendy, and Sarah, thank you for not batting an eye when I texted you: *Any ideas for a feminine sounding, Harry Potter based, dildo name? It's for my book not a recreational toy hahaha.* More importantly, thank you for responding with genuine ideas. I love how you all demanded I tell you what I chose for my final decision. Thus, Belladix was created.

Erica and Nancy, thank you for being such sweet and supportive teaching partners when I would go on a tangent about my novel. I know we were supposed to be lesson planning. I'm sorry!

To everyone else I work with who looked at my cover art when I shoved it in your face, helped me pick side character names, and were my cheerleaders when I needed it. You're all amazing people and

I'm so lucky to get to work with you. Kirsten, Jackie, and Haley, you were stuck listening to my insecurities the most. Thanks for repeatedly bitch slapping me with your kind words of encouragement.

Kodie and Jordan for creating Books, Gowns, and Crowns. If I hadn't attended Chapter 1 who knows if I'd ever had that divine moment of clarity when I decided I wanted to be on the author's side of that experience.

All my Beta readers and your amazing feedback. Every single one of you found a different detail that needed my attention. A million thanks to you all: Nancy, Cara, Olivia, Summer, Shannon, Kendall, Wendy, Mom, and Nana.

The person behind the legend of Stefan. When I told you that your character was a pompous, posturing, socialite, your eyes literally lit up. I'm so glad we became lab partners in community college and that you had a friend who looks just like you. Kevin, thanks for hooking me up with your bestie.

To my family, Mom, Dad, Nana, and Ian, you have all been huddled in my corner this entire time. From Ian saying he'd read my book, even though he doesn't read romance, to Dad offering to take a look at my grammar, you've been so supportive. Nana, I tried to do your love origin story justice. Mom, I can't list all the ways you've supported me without writing a second novel. I love you all so much.

Most importantly, thank you, Mike. You are my inspiration for Will. Thank you for not getting mad when I hit snooze on my four a.m. alarm fifteen times because I didn't want to get up yet. Thank you for remembering to feed me on days when I disappeared to write in my library. Thank you for helping me figure out if a position was even possible, teaching me how to use chopsticks again, and giving me a second chance all those years ago. You are my better half. And babe, can you fill my water, please?

About the Author

Kate Pelczar is from a small town in Southern California, but now she lives in rural, central, Oregon. By day she is an elementary school teacher, by "night" she writes as much as she can. When she's not teaching or writing, Kate enjoys reading fantasy and romance novels, playing board games with her husband, and cuddling their fur babies. To find the latest news about upcoming books you can follow her on TikTok @katepelczar or Instagram @kate_pelczar.

Made in the USA
Middletown, DE
01 April 2024

52279531R10201